The Debt

The Debt

TYLER KING

New York Boston

Forever Yours
Hachette Book Group
1290 Avenue of the Americas
New York, NY 10104
forever-romance.com
twitter.com/foreverromance

First published as an ebook and as a print on demand: May 2016

Forever Yours is an imprint of Grand Central Publishing.
The Forever Yours name and logo are trademarks of Hachette Book Group, Inc.

ISBN 978-1-4555-9523-5

For Hadley

To my husband, my best friend
Now it's your turn

To you
You have excellent taste

And for me
Good job, me

Acknowledgments

I must first thank my husband, who didn't bat an eye when I quit bringing home a paycheck and told him I wanted to sit at home all day to write. Thank you. And thank you to my parents, who never said a degree in creative writing would get me nowhere. Thank you to my chorus teachers, drama teachers, English professors, and all those who encourage young people to embrace the arts. Thank you. To Heather, who held out her hand to help an aspiring author who had no clue where to start. To my agent, Kimberly Brower, for her faith in me and her infinite patience. To Dana, my editor. We were always meant to be. Thank you. To Colleen Hoover and Sylvia Day. Can we be friends? Call me. Finally, to the reason this book came to be: my readers. Thank you to Hadley, Bee, Stace, Annie, Jamie, Kennedy, Mariah, Vagabond, Sally, Mina, Packy, Cristina, Teresa, Sarah, Ivy, Shannon, Sabrina, Silvia, Flyr, Kat, Betsy, Lea, Kelli, KM, Noël, Gordana, and the rest of the underground.

Prologue

Session 3

Our conversations always began the same way. This woman was only interested in the worst parts of me. The ugly. Shame and contrition and all the ways I'd found to abuse myself since…

"Why are you here?"

These rooms made me anxious. The claustrophobia of one woman's undivided attention. She still smelled like the walk across campus: damp denim and wet grass in the tread of her shoes. She watched my knee bounce. Watched me drive the serrated edge of a plastic knife into the cast wrapped around my right hand. Her fingers tapped across the screen of her iPad to the rhythm of my tongue piercing flicking between my teeth. And she waited patiently for an answer. A still, quiet patience that only irritated me further. She was a fucking wax statue of perfect fucking patience.

"Why are you here?"

"Because I fractured a man's jaw." And broke my hand for the trouble.

"Why are you here?"

"It wasn't my choice."

"But why are you here, Josh?"

Because eighteen years ago a woman I only remember by the back of her head left me on a public bus. No matter the answer I gave, it wasn't good enough. Not humiliating enough. She wasn't interested in my remorse. I had none. This woman wanted to cut me open and watch me writhe on the floor.

"Why are you here?"

"Are you going to start every conversation with the same question?" The end of the knife snapped off inside my cast. Goddammit.

"Josh…"

"Asked and answered."

She wanted to sigh. I could see it in her eyes. The boredom in this room was contagious.

"A violent outburst put you in that chair, but I want to know how you got here." She set her iPad aside and crossed her legs, entwining her fingers in her lap. "What is it like?"

"What?"

"The panic attacks. How do they feel?"

I closed my eyes, flexing my wrist against the severed shard of the knife. "Like waking up with your hands tied behind your back and a plastic bag cinched over your head. It feels like dying in terror."

"Let's start there…"

Chapter 1

I stood in the shower with the lights off and my forehead pressed to the tiles. My palm lay flat, fingertips gripping the thin grout trench for support. Scalding spray beat against my back, but it could not chase away the frigid, crackling sting of ice pumping through my veins. I held my semi-flaccid dick in my hand, trembling as my lungs ached to push past the boulder lodged in my throat. My body caved in on itself, shrinking. Gravity squeezed me. It pressed and it pushed until the weight was so much, the pain so great, I collapsed to the bottom of the tub, naked and shivering. The room spun forward and back, end over end. I grit my teeth, clenched my fists. Static filled my head and numbed my face. The sick, black poison of nausea seeped its way into my gut. Bubbling. Boiling. I heaved and clenched, vomiting acid and whiskey, leaving me a huddled clump of shaking agony in a soup of sweat and putrid bile swirling around the drain at my feet.

The water ran cold before I could move again. A silent sob

cracked through my chest. Coughing, I choked on the air filling my lungs. Exhaustion was a relief.

When the panic attack subsided, I reached for the soap and rubbed it between both hands, then lathered and rinsed my body from face to feet. I hated it. Hated touching my skin with wrinkled fingers while my nerves were still raw.

Withered, I planted my hands on the tiles and climbed up the wall to stand on trembling legs. My muscles were mud. Wobbling out of the shower, I reached for a towel.

In my room, a naked woman lay asleep in my bed. I dropped the towel on the floor and slipped under the covers.

But sleep wouldn't come.

Hours later, just after 8:00 a.m., I was still awake when the woman next to me stretched and reached for her phone on my nightstand. Propped up against my headboard, I watched the silhouette of a leggy blonde dressing at the foot of my bed. She shoved her tits into a push-up bra and wiggled her way into a tight black dress.

"It was fun," she said. "See you around, MacKay."

"Later."

She tiptoed away with her shoes in her hand and closed the door behind her. I knew I shouldn't have brought Kate home, but at the time I didn't have the clarity of mind to do otherwise. Women had always been transient in my life. This one was no different.

I pried myself from the covers, then crossed the room and stood at the floor-length mirror beside my dresser to inspect the new ink peeking around the right side of my rib cage. The skin there was still tender and swollen, a result of six hours under the needles to continue the design that decorated my back. Bear was an artist with an implement of pain.

My eyes fell to the framed photo lying facedown on my dresser: a younger me in a tux, standing onstage with my adoptive parents beside a piano before my first sold-out concert. It was one of the happiest days of my life, and I couldn't bear to look at it.

I was skinnier then, and lanky. Hadn't yet grown into my body. Next to my pale, freckled parents, I stood out like one of those exotic adopted children of yuppie celebrity parents. Dark skin. Black hair. Green eyes. People told me I was "interesting" to look at, to gawk at. So little by little I covered all the pretty bare flesh in tattoos.

The first piece I ever had done was of a raven with its wings spread wide across my chest. The tips of each broken wing nailed down. I was seventeen then. After my first sitting, I came to understand why people said tattoos were addictive. I suppose I became a glutton for pain, because when Bear's wife offered to put a hole in my lip, I let her stick a needle through my face. For shits and giggles. At twenty-one, I had two full sleeves. My dad only asked that I keep the modifications within reason. I was a bit fuzzy on that definition.

From the top dresser drawer, I grabbed a tube of antibacterial ointment and applied two fingers' worth to the new tattoo. My stomach growled. It was empty and angry from last night. So I sifted through the field of laundry-pile bunkers scattered around my bedroom until I found a black shirt and dark jeans on the passable side of clean.

When I hit the landing at the bottom of the stairs, I felt a pair of knowing brown eyes watching me from the living room. Nothing good ever came from the morning-after ritual. Even so, I couldn't help but glance at my roommate curled up on the leather couch with her laptop open and earbuds hidden under her long dark hair. She held seven fingers over her head. Hadley averted her gaze back to the computer screen rather than look for my reaction. Like she didn't give a fuck.

"Don't you have anything better to do than wait for the walk of shame?"

"Don't you have an appointment to get your dick swabbed for STDs?"

"Fuck off."

"Get bent."

And so everything was par for the course on a Sunday morning. I held out my middle finger as I turned toward the kitchen. *That was fun. Let's do it again next week, shall we?* I had yet to decipher her scoring system. Asking for clarification would only validate her participation in my sex life.

Neither of us enjoyed living together. My parents' house in the middle of nowhere was too big for two people and not big enough for the both of us. Since my dad left to take a job in New York during our freshman year of college, every day was a special kind of torture. But Hadley needed me. And as much as I couldn't stand being near her, I wouldn't abandon her again.

Besides, that girl could cook. I walked into the kitchen and pulled the tinfoil off the food Hadley had left for me on the stove. After I poured myself a glass of orange juice and prepared my plate, I took a seat at the granite breakfast bar that framed the gourmet kitchen. Her scrambled eggs, bacon, and cinnamon toast were reason enough to get up in the morning.

Hadley wasn't so bad. I knew I could be a surly, inconsiderate bastard. Our spats weren't entirely her fault. For the most part, we were resigned to grin and bear it for the next two years until graduation. Hadley was set on moving to Boston for her master's degree. I was going to New York the second I fulfilled my promise to my dad and had my bachelor's in hand. No one was under the misconception that this arrangement would last forever.

"You're an asshole." Hadley walked in to lean back against the counter beside the stove. She wore my black Tool sweatshirt with the sleeves rolled up and the hem brushing her legs just at the apex of her thighs. And those tiny black shorts that made my dick twitch every time she bent over. Those fucking shorts.

Reaching toward me, she swiped a piece of toast off my plate, never mind the three pieces still sitting on the platter. She did that all the time, and it drove me up the wall. Since she was the one doing all the cooking, I'd given up trying to break her of the habit and teach her to keep her thieving fingers to herself.

Rather than answer, I shrugged one shoulder and shoveled another forkful into my mouth.

"Stephanie Slater has sent me three text messages asking me to ask you to call her." Her dark eyes looked past me or at the floor, anywhere but my face. "Do your own dirty work. I clean up after you enough as it is."

"You know how much I dislike confrontation."

"This is a new low, even for you. If you screw your friend's sister, you could at least take her calls."

"I'll keep that in mind."

"And stop fucking the crazy ones. She's giving off a stalker vibe."

"Anything else?"

"If Scott shows up with a hatchet, I'm not covering for you." One corner of her lips turned up in a wicked smirk.

I gave her a wink. Hadley laughed, rolled her eyes, and sauntered off with my last piece of bacon.

I never went out of my way to piss Hadley off, but I rarely exerted too much effort to stay on her good side, either. That ship had sailed, hit an iceberg, taken on water, snapped in half, and dragged all souls aboard down with it a long time ago.

Half the time I wanted to throttle that girl. The other half I wanted to wrap her in blankets and swear undying allegiance if she'd smile again. I cherished the rare moments when Hadley was relaxed, laughing, and more like her old self. I had a debt to Hadley that I'd spend the rest of my life repaying. I owed her my head on a platter. And if ever given the chance, I'd take a bullet for her.

* * *

After breakfast, Hadley sat on her bed with a sketchbook on her lap. The shard of charcoal between her fingers rubbed across the page, making a soft scratching sound in the otherwise silent space. I enjoyed watching her work. The expression of intense concentration she wore. Bobbing her head to the music playing through her earbuds.

I sat on the edge of the bed. Hadley flipped her sketchpad when I tried to steal a peek. Reaching over, I tugged one of her earbuds out. The sound of Fiona Apple's voice sprang from the tiny speaker.

"I've got to take the Les Paul to the shop. You want to come along?"

"How bad is it?"

"The neck is loose. It sounds like shit. Vaughn will have to strip it down and reset it."

"What an asshole."

Not Vaughn. The asshole was the drunken bastard at my show

last week who jumped onstage to give us his best Slash impression. He grabbed my Gibson Les Paul, so I decked him and tossed the guy to the floor, but he managed to take my guitar to the ground with him.

"We can run by campus to pick up our textbooks and hit the grocery store on the way back."

"You're going to class this semester?" She arched a sassy eyebrow.

"I go when it's necessary."

"Right. What could an institution of higher learning possibly teach the prolific Josh MacKay?"

"I'm still waiting to find out."

Hadley rolled her eyes and swatted me with the back of her sketchpad. "Swing us by the art supply store and you've got a deal."

Really, Hadley never asked much of me.

"Sure. You need me to wait outside first?" I got off the bed and shoved my hands in my back pockets.

"Nope." She stood to put her sketchpad away in her nightstand. Hadley tied her hair up in a ponytail and wrapped the wires of her earbuds around her neck. "I'm good."

She proceeded mechanically toward her bedroom windows that looked out on the woods behind the house. In the same order, always the exact routine, Hadley unlatched and latched the locks five times, clicking back and forth. Her hand lingered for a few seconds. Fingers squeezed and twitched to repeat the action. Then she took a breath and spun around to continue throughout the house.

To every window and door, I followed behind as Hadley performed her ritual. I never rushed her, was never impatient about her process. I'd done this to her. It was my job to assure her later, when she teetered on the edge of an anxiety attack, that she hadn't missed a single point of entry.

She had done well today, and I smiled at her when we made it to the alarm keypad in the foyer in less than four minutes. I felt like an arrogant shit for trying to offer her my approval, but Hadley seemed to take some level of pride on the days when we didn't make two or three trips mid-ritual back to the second floor to start all over again.

She keyed in the code three times, disarmed the alarm three times, and didn't hesitate to take a step back when she was ready for me to finish up. Definitely a good day.

At the front door, Hadley locked up and only jiggled the handle for seventeen seconds before she sighed and plastered on a calm expression. I held open the passenger door to my black '65 Mustang, watching as Hadley got in and brought up the security app on her phone to check again that the system was armed.

In the car, she sat with fists clenched and knuckles white as the engine groaned and came to life. One finger pried its way free to tap the stereo to cue Black Keys at an earsplitting decibel. Her attention was aimed straight ahead at the tree-lined dirt driveway that spanned a hundred yards out to the two-lane road.

When the stone-faced house was no longer visible behind us through the thick surrounding forest and my front tires crunched over the last of the uneven dirt and gravel to the flat pavement, I hit the clutch and slammed the stick shift. Hadley rolled down her window as we exceeded the posted speed limit toward the highway. She liked it when I drove fast, so I was more than happy to oblige.

Chapter 2

The downward spiral into this spectacular status of stagnant awful between Punky and I began four years ago. It was the best night of my life, until it wasn't.

* * *

Junior year of high school, the football team had just won the homecoming game. In our tiny town, people gave a whole lot of fucks about such things. It was a daylong circus of pep rallies, parades, and bonfires that culminated in underage drinking and shooting off sparkly small explosives. That night, there had to be nearly a hundred people crammed in every room and pouring out on the lawn of Nick Watson's house. Almost as many cars parked two and three wide and clogging the cul-de-sac all the way out of the neighborhood.

On the back patio, I shot darts with my friends Corey and Trey while fireworks crackled overhead and half-naked jocks chased cheerleaders with water guns filled with eight-dollar tequila.

Stephanie Slater hovered around us, tossing back her weight in smuggled vodka. When she offered me a body shot out of her cleavage, I told her I had to take a piss.

I worked my way into the living room, then past the kitchen. The music got louder the farther I passed through the meat grinder of sweaty bodies. Dozens of incoherent conversations fought to be heard over the bass rattling the floral-print walls. When I found Nick pressing Hadley up against a door, his hands on her, I lost my fucking mind.

My fist cracked bone before I made the conscious decision to hit him. One punch, and I opened up a tap in the center of his face. It poured two thin streams of blood down the lumps of Nick's lips and over the fall of his chin to drip down his shirt.

"Josh! What the hell? He's bleeding!" Hadley yanked on my arm, the only thing that kept me from landing a second blow.

"Keep your fucking hands off her, you son of a bitch. I swear I'll break your fucking jaw if you ever—"

Corey and Trey grabbed me, one of them wrapping their arm around my neck. "Back off, man. Let's go. Leave it."

"Try me, asshole." I struggled against the arms restraining me, reaching for the kid somewhere under the blood-soaked napkins stuck to his face.

"Shut it, Josh! It's done. We're leaving." Corey pushed me toward the front door.

He outweighed me by about thirty pounds, so I didn't have much of a choice. Once outside, he kept his arm around my neck until we hit the curb by my car.

"Can I let you go, or am I going to have to tackle you to the ground?"

"I'm fine. Get off me."

"Say it nicely."

"Damn it, Corey. I'm fine. Okay?"

He released me, smiling like an idiot. "That was badass. You dropped him with one punch."

"Are you kidding me?" Hadley shoved at my chest, shoulders high and tight around her neck. "What do you think his parents are going to say when they find out? Shit, Josh. What about your parents?"

"What? You'd rather I leave you in there to get groped by that date rapist?"

"You're being ridiculous."

"He touched you! He grabbed you. I won't put up with that."

"And I could have taken care of it myself! You didn't have to hit him."

I shrugged. "It felt good."

The guys laughed. Hadley whipped around, eyes sharp and fierce. "Boys are so stupid. Seriously. You're all animals."

"Aww, come on, Punky. You can't stay mad at me." I wrapped my arms around her waist, pulling her into a hug. "I was just trying to protect you. Me man. Me take care of little girl."

"Shut up, stupidhead." She pressed her cheek to my chest and hugged me tighter.

"Come on. This party blows. You ready to head home?"

"Sure."

By the time we got to Hadley's house, I had been forgiven for going all caveman on her. I parked in Hadley's usual spot in the driveway. Her car was in the shop again. Though she had an inheritance from her birth parents, she refused to spend the money to get a new vehicle that didn't leak oil and stall going uphill.

Hadley's godfather, Tom, was a truck driver. He worked odd hours hauling up and down the state. When he couldn't be home at night, Hadley used to stay at my house when we were little. Since we'd gotten older, I'd go to sleep on the couch at her place. It made Tom feel better that Hadley wasn't left alone all the time, and I had an excuse to see her at night.

"You're staying, right?" Hadley flopped down on the couch and turned on the TV.

It was only 11:00, still early for a Friday night.

"Yeah." I went to the DVD shelf and scanned through her collection. We'd seen almost every one of these at least three times. "Funny, scary, explosions, or sappy chick crap?"

"Um…something Stephen King, but not *It*. Anything but that one."

Hadley had been terrified of clowns ever since Tom made her watch the movie when she was ten. Not a great parenting move, but it wasn't like he knew any better. Growing pains. I pulled *The Shining* off the shelf. Last time we'd watched this was during a wicked storm. Just to pass the time, I'd chased Hadley around the house with my best Jack impression.

After making popcorn and pouring a couple of sodas, Hadley and I settled on the couch. I pulled the throw blanket off the back cushions and tossed it at her. She swatted it down before it landed over her face.

"I'm not cold."

"That's for hiding under."

"Whatever. You're still afraid of *Cujo*, so don't start with me."

"What? It's not weird at all that you're scared of Drew Barrymore. *Firestarter* is a scary movie, and *Never Been Kissed* is terrifying."

"Shut up." Hadley shoved at my face.

Well, I couldn't let that stand. I pinned her arms to her sides and dragged her over my lap. She landed with her back against the arm of the couch, her legs draped over my thighs.

"Behave, Punky."

"Shh. The movie's starting."

I took the blanket, draped it over her legs and mine, and settled back to watch.

Throughout the film, Hadley jumped at every scare. She had most of the blanket up to her nose with her fingers gripping the edge for dear life. The more she squirmed, the more my dick noticed how not-terrible it felt to have her legs writhing in my lap. When Scatman Crothers took an ax to the chest, Hadley jumped again, grabbing my arm and burying her face in my shoulder.

"You're so predictable." I wrapped my arm around her back and pulled her closer. "You know it's coming, but you still get scared anyway."

"It's the anticipation. I can't stand the waiting. It makes me nervous."

"Chicken."

She smacked my chest. Again with the hitting.

"Really, you never learn." I grabbed both her wrists and pinned them to her sides. "Be good. There are consequences for bad little girls who can't keep their hands to themselves."

Her lips twisted into a dangerous smirk. "You don't scare me."

"Wrong move, Punky. Never tease a man who knows where all your ticklish places are."

Hadley writhed and struggled to get away, laughing and threatening me with all manner of bodily harm as I tormented her.

"I swear. Josh. You are. So dead!"

"Say you're sorry." I didn't let up, following as she fell backward on the couch, my fingers playing against her ribs and stomach. "Just say you're sorry, and I'll stop."

"Never!"

I saw stars. Hadley kneed me right in fucking balls. I groaned and released her, grabbing my battered manhood.

"Shit, Punky. Fuck."

"Oh no. I'm sorry. Crap. I didn't mean to." Her words came out as the staccato breaths of laughter with a big, delighted smile. Evil ball crusher. "I'm sorry. Really."

Rolling over, I was pinned between Hadley and the back of the couch. "Stop laughing."

"I can't help it."

She tried to turn toward me, and it made me flinch. I was justifiably dick-shy now. That only made her laugh harder.

"What can I do?"

Nothing, you vile woman. Or kiss it and make it better. But I wasn't stupid enough to say that out loud. "Nothing."

"Aww." Hadley ran her hand through my hair and down the side of my face. "I didn't mean it. It was an accident. I'm sorry."

"It's fine." After a minute or so, I caught my breath. Rather than move, I just closed my eyes and wrapped my arm around Hadley's back. "You suck, you know that?"

"Bad Hadley."

"Very bad Punky." I tightened my grip around her back and tugged her closer. "You should make it up to me."

I had no idea what she might do. But when Hadley's soft, tender lips pressed to mine, I knew what I wanted. I kissed her back. Our first. No hesitation. Not even a second of apprehension. I took her bottom lip between mine and kissed her like she deserved, purposefully and with complete devotion. Hadley threw her leg over my hip and dug her fingers into my hair as she rolled over to straddle me. My hands found her hips and latched on, holding her on top of me as if I wouldn't continue to breathe if she pulled away now.

Hadley wasn't timid. She held me down like a woman on a mission, kissing me cross-eyed. Since I didn't know where I was allowed to touch her, I just kept my hands locked to her hips and let her have her happy way with me. Sporting a hard-on that was determined to dig right through my jeans to get into hers, I tried to think about baseball or Corey in a bikini, but nothing was enough to quiet the fuck-fantastic feeling of Hadley on top of me.

"You can touch me," she whispered against my lips. Hadley ground herself against my cock.

I was so fucking done for.

"It's okay," she encouraged.

I worked my hands up her ribs and hesitated a moment, just to make sure and give her time to say stop or slap me. I'd never felt a girl up before, so I gave up trying to concentrate on kissing and let Hadley do as she pleased while I focused all my attention on feeling the pliable weight of her tits in my palms. As I brushed my thumbs over her nipples through her bra, Hadley moaned and pressed down on my dick. Fucking hell.

"Let's go upstairs," she whispered.

Because I wasn't a complete tool and I had a pulse and pocket full of wood, I did as the lady commanded.

Hadley and I lost our virginities that night. We were awkward and clumsy and had no fucking clue what we were doing, but it was perfect. She was perfect. I'd always loved her. That night, I fell in love with her.

But even Hadley couldn't stop the panic attack that followed. As I climaxed, my body was gripped with tension, not relief. Horrifying memories flooded my mind. A cold tremor shot down my spine. I wasn't in Hadley's bed anymore; my head was trapped in the musty master bedroom of our old foster home.

I ran like hell, leaving Hadley naked and crying, screaming after me as I slammed the front door shut.

* * *

For a few brief moments, I'd experienced perfection. Making love to Hadley was the single greatest experience of my young life. Better than performing at Lincoln Center or the first time I picked up a guitar in Vaughn's shop. What followed in the aftermath of that night in high school was the worst week of my life.

A perfect storm of heartbreak and tragedy washed my foundation out from under me. The levee collapsed, the seawall was breached, and the once sturdy ground beneath my feet became a quicksand that pulled me into a debilitating darkness.

I had spent most of my childhood in therapy. By seventeen, I had thought I was doing well. My psychiatrist had not informed me, however, that my first consensual sexual experience would completely fuck with my head.

Chapter 3

Session 4

"She became a bad memory," I said, shoving a chopstick into the cast around my broken hand to dislodge the severed end of the plastic knife. "A living reminder of everything I wanted to forget."

"Why?" she asked, her head tilted to the side. Something about that posture felt condescending.

"Seriously?"

"Because Hadley was there when it happened?"

Was this woman being purposefully obtuse? Like the real mission of our time together was to watch me unravel. Provoke me to madness. See the moment when the switch flipped and I lost all ability to function on a rational level.

"Damn it!" The chopstick splintered inside my cast, and I now had a burgeoning collection of broken utensils stuck in there.

"Josh?"

"What? For fuck's sake, what?"

"Hadley."

I breathed out a gust of air as my chest constricted. "I was five years old when it started. Living in my third foster home. That's where I first met Hadley. And every night after *he* finished with me, I went to the room she shared with two other girls and cried on the floor beside her bed."

"Did she know?"

"That our foster guardian was molesting me?" My tongue piercing flicked between my teeth. My clenched fists turned white in my lap. "She understood as much as a five-year-old can."

"She became someone you trusted. Someone who made you feel safe."

"Hadley helped me survive that place. We were only there for a few months. A year at most before her godfather adopted her. But that foster home felt like a fucking nightmare that wouldn't end. She was the reason I finally got out of there. It was because of her that the MacKays came to adopt me."

"Simon and Carmen."

"Yes. As far as I'm concerned, they are my real parents. They took me in, gave me everything I have. Hadley made that happen."

"But after the panic attack..."

"I couldn't stand to look her in the eye. I looked at her, and I saw *him*. I thought about being with her and knew that meant forever reliving those nightmares of what that man did to me. No girl wants a guy who can't finish without turning into a paralyzed little shit shaking on the floor."

My life was like a web attached to Hadley on all sides. From the moment we landed in foster care together, we became inextricably linked. I couldn't escape her. I wasn't sure I wanted to, despite what she represented.

And I could have lived with all of that—the girl I loved within sight but always just out of reach—if I hadn't so thoroughly shattered Hadley. Because whatever happened that night after I peeled out of her driveway, she suffered so much worse.

For that, I didn't deserve her.

Chapter 4

By the time Hadley and I got back to the house from running our errands, my bandmates were already tuning up for rehearsal in my garage. We had a weekly gig at a college bar in the city. Nothing spectacular, but it gave us a hobby and a little extra money. For me, it was an excuse to keep writing music.

Corey played a double paradiddle at his drum kit while I pulled a couple broken strings from my guitar. He had no great musical aspirations beyond dive bars and the occasional street festival. Though he was proficient enough, Corey's first concern was attracting the attention of women who fawned over musicians.

"Where the fuck is Scott?" I had energy to burn and there were changes to the set list that we needed to practice. There was just one problem: We were short one rhythm guitarist.

"He had a date." Corey laid his sticks on his tom and cracked his knuckles.

Scott had always been a bit of a flake, but lately he'd been a stranger. Skipping rehearsals, never answering his phone. He would show up ten minutes before a gig, looking hungover and like he hadn't slept in days.

"I thought he broke up with Tori," I said, pulling a broken E string off my guitar.

"He did." Corey leaned back against the wall behind his kit, thick arms bent behind his head. "I think he's out with that chick from Saturday night."

"Getting his dick wet is not a good excuse."

"Speaking of which..." Trey, our bassist and resident buzzkill, walked in from the house and sat on a road case. "I heard what happened with Stephanie."

In our collective of misfits, Trey was an oddity. Two happily married parents. Never arrested or institutionalized. No addictions or personality disorders. Had we not become friends, I would have hated the prick.

"Spare me the lecture. I got enough of it from Hadley."

"What the hell were you thinking? You can't fuck Scott's sister and then hide from her."

"Hey, she came on to me."

"Doesn't mean you have to pull your dick out for every girl who flirts with you."

"The way things are going, Josh might have to leave the country. Or marry her." Corey eyed me with a stupid grin. "Stephanie's been posting photos of you from our shows on Instagram."

"She keeps calling Hadley. Someone sent me half a dozen tit pics since last week."

"Maybe it says something about your lifestyle that you aren't sure who," Trey said.

"What does that mean?"

"I don't mind if you want to throw a groupie my way."

"Piss off, Corey." I rubbed my hands through my hair, tired of the subject. "She'll get bored and move on eventually."

"I get it." Corey barely contained a laugh. He was built like a linebacker but gossiped like a pubescent girl. "She's been after your dick since high school. But she's straight-up psycho. You know she keyed Clint Holmes's car at prom in eleventh grade because he took Lisa Libby instead of her, right?"

"Clint was an asshole."

"Senior year Michael Falk found his cat dead in the driveway after he broke up with her."

"You don't know it was her. Could have been a raccoon or something."

"Sure." He stood, placing the covers on his drumheads. "But it makes you wonder."

"This is why I don't date."

* * *

There was a time I could fill a concert hall, one kid at piano performing to an audience of thousands of well-dressed patrons. Something about a child in a tailored tuxedo created a spectacle. They called me a prodigy, an oddity worth paying for. To me, playing was fun and composing was easy. The music was all in my head; all I had to do was write it down.

Standing onstage Saturday night, I sang to a couple hundred inebriated college students at the Nest. And Scott, my inept rhythm guitarist, was doing his best to ruin it.

I was going to kill him, or perhaps maim him a little. Nothing would please me more than to wrap a steel guitar string around his neck and tighten my grip until the life left his eyes. I'd strip Scott of his guitar—he'd clearly forgotten how to play the instrument and therefore had no further use for it—to demonstrate my best Babe Ruth impression, pointing to the audio booth before taking a swing at his head. The crack would be satisfying, as would the *thud* when the decapitated former member of my band collapsed to the floor.

By the end of the first song, it had become apparent that his body had been possessed by some unholy creature bent on destroying music as we knew it. Scott was out of tune and falling behind on the rhythm. He kept his eyes on his fingers, like it was taking all his concentration to suck this badly. I was so fucking done with his punk ass.

When the set was over, I walked right the fuck off.

Kicking through the flimsy door to the greenroom, I set down my Les Paul and picked up the first thing my eyes landed on. Scott's guitar case went flying across the room to put a nice dent in the graffiti-covered wall. The greenroom was just a dingy little space with a bathroom attached. There were two disgusting brown couches and a counter with a mirror that spanned the distance from one wall to the other. Not fancy digs, but it matched the motif of the college dive bar where our band, Mad Electro, played on Saturday nights.

I knew better than to put my fist through the wall. Breaking my hand was not something I longed to do again. Although shattering the mirror that reflected my impotent rage would have been satisfying, I reined myself in and tamped down the urge. Two hundred hours of anger management supposedly had done me well. Whatever. I was still angry. But now I threw inanimate objects like a girl rather than throwing a punch. Progress.

Scott's guitar case lay open on the floor. Inside, a tiny plastic bag caught my attention. Unless Scott was hiding some broken bones, he had no business carrying around eighty milligrams of oxycodone.

Noise spilled in through the door behind me. In the mirror, I stared at the guy too chicken shit to look me in the eye.

"You're a fucking twat."

"What the hell is your problem?" Scott collapsed onto the couch by the door. He propped his foot up on the stack of milk crates that made a coffee table. Sweat-matted hair clung to his sickly pale face.

"You sounded like shit out there."

"So I had a bad night. Get off my back." The middle and forefinger of his right hand bled on his lips while he chewed at his nails. Gnawing, spitting the jagged shards on the dirty green carpet.

"Maybe if you fucking showed up for rehearsal—"

"Did you see my stick nail that guy in the face? I'm like, duck!" Trey and Corey barged into the room.

"Here we go." Scott kicked at the milk crates, scattering them across the floor. "Another one of Josh's righteous tantrums. No one is ever fucking good enough."

"Whoa, simmer down," Corey said, a massive presence in the center of the toppled mess of blue crates. "What's the damage?"

"Him." Scott jumped up from the couch. "I'm tired of this asshole always running his mouth like he's Mozart." He came at me, stopping only when Corey held him back. "You're a fucking has-been, Josh. You washed out. You're nobody."

"You're out. Get your shit and go."

"Fuck you." He backed off and looked to Trey standing silently against the door. Scott wasn't going to find any sympathy there. "I'm not the problem."

"You're an addict."

The accusation hung in silence. Seething, breathing heavy, Scott stared at the bag of pills as I held it up.

"You don't know what you're talking about."

"Fine. Then flush them."

Corey turned to Scott. "Dude, what's going on?"

"Nothing." He shoved Corey away. "He's full of shit."

"Do it." Trey came forward, trapping Scott between us. "Flush them."

"To prove what? I'm not—"

"Then I'll do it."

I went into the bathroom and kicked up the lid to the toilet. Before I could get the bag open, Scott was on my back. He reached for the pills, his bloody fingers slipping down my arms. Corey tried to pull him off, the three of us crammed into the tiny room, elbows knocking into walls, feet slipping on the exposed cement floor. I was shoved sideways at the sink and dropped the bag. Scott dove for it but was yanked back, Corey with his neck in a choke.

"This is your one chance to ask for help," I said, and dumped the pills in the toilet.

Corey dragged Scott away from me.

"All will be forgiven. Check yourself into rehab or fuck off. Those are your choices."

"Fuck you, Josh."

Corey let him go. Scott grabbed his guitar case and left, slamming the door behind him.

* * *

The trio that comprised Mad Electro was silent as we packed up our gear. No more needed to be said on the topic of Scott, and so the matter was closed. We could worry about the consequences later. I doubted he'd admit he needed help, and for that he had my pity.

Back inside the bar, the guys went to join Hadley at our usual table while I found the bar's owner, Nate. His office was more like a large closet with a single desk and chair. No room for visitors to sit among the file cabinets and boxes of flyers stacked along the walls. He sat hunched over his desk with piles of money in neat rows.

Nate was a skinny middle-aged man who looked like he might have been a meth head at one point in his life. His eyes were too sunken and large in his head. His skin was tight and papery. But he always paid us in cash and invited us back week after week. I didn't need to know his life story.

"Josh, hi." Nate nodded as he wrapped a rubber band around one stack of cash and slid it into a white envelope. "Just in time. Here's your take for tonight."

I folded the cash and stuffed it in my pocket. We did pretty well here, taking a cut of the door and liquor from ten to midnight from the eighteen-and-over crowd. The Nest was always slammed on Saturdays, and I suspected the bartenders were lax on checking IDs.

"I caught a few minutes of your set." Nate lit up a cigarette and kept counting bills. "A little rough."

"We sounded like shit. Scott is out. We'll be better next weekend."

"What's he doing for work?"

"Washing dishes at a sports bar, I think." Though I didn't see how that mattered. "Why?"

"I could always use another bar-back."

"Right."

Scott would probably poison me the first chance he got.

Nate glanced up. He eyed me for a moment. With nothing left to say, I thanked him and left him to it.

Making my way through the bar, I pushed and slithered past the bodies in the crowded space. It was standing room only, save for a set of reserved tables in the back separated from the floor by two steps to the raised platform and a wooden railing.

Trey and Corey were alone.

"Where's Hadley?"

"She was talking to a guy," Trey said.

"A guy?" That wasn't helpful.

"They went to the bar." Corey pushed a chair at me. "Sit down and relax. She'll be back."

Hadley was capable of taking care of herself. She didn't need a babysitter looking over her shoulder. Nevertheless, running off with some random guy wasn't her style. Of course, it was only under the pretense of wanting a drink that I headed for the bar. Not because I was checking up on her.

A group of teetering coeds took their drinks from Troy, the bartender, making an opening for me to slip in. Troy spotted me. After he passed off a few drinks and swiped a customer's card, he pulled down a bottle of Scotch. Two fingers neat was passed my way. The band drank for free when we played. A nice perk.

"You see Hadley?"

Troy wiped his hands on a bar towel, then slung it over his shoulder as he looked around. "She was with a guy a second ago. Don't know him."

I swallowed a mouthful of whiskey. Searching the horde pulsing to the canned music pumped out over the sound system, I couldn't spot Hadley.

Someone tapped me on the shoulder. I made it a quarter turn before I took a sucker punch to the face. My drink shattered on the floor. I stumbled, thrown off balance by the force of the blow. Pain flared across my cheek and blurred my vision. Noise overwhelmed me for a moment as the crowd reacted. Scott came at me again, pushing us into a wall of people. I barreled into him, shoving my shoulder into his gut to knock him against the bar. He was trapped beneath me with nowhere to run. Blind rage propelled my fist against his jaw, his nose. His skin turned wet, his face soft and muddy.

By the time Corey had me in a headlock and blood dripped from my hand, Hadley was screaming at me. Whatever. Scott started it. And I never did get to finish my Scotch. But I found Punky.

Chapter 5

The next morning, Hadley sat on the couch watching cartoons, six fingers held over her head.

I wasn't in the mood for our usual spat. "What's with the score?"

"This"—she extended her fingers toward me—"is for the shiner. It's a nice piece of work."

The black eye hurt like hell, though most of the swelling had gone down overnight.

"Is higher better or worse?" Just to be clear. Not that I was amused.

"Better for me," she said. "Worse for you."

"Wonderful."

"Get a move on, sunshine," Corey taunted from the kitchen. He sat hunched over the breakfast bar with Trey.

"What are they doing here?"

"We're going to the beach," she said.

Hadley slid her sketchbook off her lap. She wore a pair of cutoff jeans and a baggy cropped white T-shirt. Underneath, I saw the outline of her blue bikini top. Goddamn.

"And if you want breakfast, you better hurry. The guys have been in there for a while."

Perfect. I didn't finish one drink last night, my band was short a member, and now I'd have to fight for my meal. Fucking brilliant. Didn't I at least get dibs in my own home?

"You're invited," Hadley called after me as I headed for the kitchen.

I had assumed as much, but her comment said that perhaps that assumption was premature.

Sure enough, I'd barely been saved scraps from breakfast.

"Thanks for cleaning me out, assholes." I grabbed the last piece of toast off Corey's plate and the bowl of fruit salad that sat in front of Trey.

At least they knew better than to sit in my spot. Certain customs had to be observed for the sake of my sanity. I'd sat on the same damn stool since I was eight.

"She made us wait for an hour." Corey showed not one bit of remorse. "It was either start without you or wake you up."

Trey slathered his toast with strawberry jam. My jam. "Just make something else."

I grumbled a "fuck you" and polished off the two strawberries and three pieces of cantaloupe I'd been left to consume.

Granted, Hadley and I were weird about food, but for good reason. In the foster home where we'd met, there were three other kids ranging in age from nine to thirteen. We had to throw elbows at the table for our rations, and even those were small. Some days we wouldn't have breakfast at all. Now that Hadley and I didn't have to worry about money or someone else stealing our food out from under us, I bought too much and she cooked too much. Anyway, I sucked at cooking. The best I could do was a bowl of cereal. She'd conditioned me. It wasn't my fault my stomach had certain expectations.

"Stop sulking." Hadley's voice whispered into my ear from behind me. "Like I'd let you starve." She came around the counter and opened the oven, pulling out a plate covered in tinfoil.

"What's this for?"

"Eating," Punky answered with a condescending eye roll. Snarky thing. She pulled the tinfoil off to reveal an omelet with bacon and a biscuit. "Hurry up. We're leaving in twenty minutes."

* * *

We arrived at high tide just as the clouds on the horizon began to turn an angry shade of gray. A stiff breeze blew in from offshore. Foam licked at the tidal line. A storm was moving in, electrifying the atmosphere—my favorite kind of weather.

Waxing my board, I watched the white blip of a sailboat on the water make its way south. A sharp whistle caught my attention as a group of guys made their way toward us.

"Andre, hey!"

Hadley jogged past me, shoving my shoulder like I was rude for taking up space, and right into the waiting arms of the shirtless guy who offered her a huge smile. He picked her up. Damn near squeezed the life out of her.

I hated him on the spot. Hated that he could touch her. That he made her smile more brightly than I'd seen in a long time. Most of all, I hated that he'd weaseled his way into her life without my notice. Who the fuck was this dickhead?

"Glad you made it," Hadley said.

And that just drove the knife deeper.

I couldn't remember the last time she'd looked happy to see me. Well, I could, but I preferred not to think about it.

"Of course." The guy was about my height, maybe six-three, and built like an athlete.

"Josh, you remember Andre." Hadley stood between us, looking at me to say something.

"I do?"

"It's been a long time. Good to see you." He stepped forward and held out his hand.

Well, fuck. Now I was the asshole if I didn't play nice, and Hadley's sharp expression made it clear she'd make my life hell if I didn't accept. Steeling myself to the taste of my pride going down my throat, I took his hand and shook it. He squeezed hard, and I squeezed harder.

"Okay, girls. You're both pretty," Corey taunted. "Go find a tree if you're going to start a pissing contest."

I dropped his hand. Hadley went through the introductions, but I tuned it all out as I stepped into my wet suit and pulled the tight neoprene up the length of my body. I should have stayed in bed.

Grabbing my board, I headed for the water. My toes barely touched wet sand. Hadley wouldn't let me off that easily.

"Hey," she called, running to catch up with me. "What's your problem?"

"You could have mentioned we'd have company. For that matter, what's with you picking up a whole pack at a bar?"

"Really? Fuck you, Josh. You drag random skanks home, but I can't hang out with my friends?"

"Are they skanks because they're fucking me, or is that just a blanket insult?"

"Take your pick."

"Then who the fuck is he?"

"That's Andre Evans, jackass."

"And?" Was I supposed to be impressed?

"His dad used to have those big Fourth of July parties every year. I was friends with him in middle school. He saw me at the Nest and we started talking."

I vaguely remembered the name, but the Andre Evans I had known was a short, pudgy kid with an overbite. Years ago, he'd gone to live with his mother in Georgia or Alabama, something like that.

"You coming, Josh?" Corey and Trey jogged past us, tossing down their boards to paddle out.

"Sorry. The name doesn't click." I tucked my board under my shoulder and walked away, leaving her there.

"You're such as ass!"

Couldn't argue with that.

* * *

"I know a guy." Corey straddled his board beside me, drifting beyond the breakers as the swells rolled beneath us. "I could bring him by next week to jam. You know, feel him out as a replacement for Scott."

"Sure." My attention was fixed on the shore.

Hadley had her shirt off, skin glowing against the fabric of her dark jean shorts and sapphire bikini top. It had been a while since we'd been to the beach or had any other occasion that made it acceptable for her to wear so little clothing. I hadn't seen so much of her in a long time.

"He's played with a few local bands, mostly alternative and punk, and he's got decent chops."

"Great."

Hadley played football with Andre and his friends. Of course they kept throwing the ball to her, an excuse to grab at her. Motherfuckers.

"But he's only got one arm, so he strums with his toes."

"That's cool."

My fists clenched the sides of the board as Andre wrapped his arms around Hadley from behind and hauled her off her feet. I could hear her laughter from the shore. It had been years since she'd let me hug her.

"Fucking hell, Josh. Take the creeper meter down a notch." Corey splashed a bear claw full of water at me.

Fucking child.

"Damn it, Corey." I wiped the salt out of my eyes, snarling at his stupid grin. "Grow up."

"Says the guy who left his balls in Hadley's purse."

"What the fuck is that supposed to mean?"

"Really? You've been seething over Andre for the last hour," Trey said. Cocky bastard. "Surfing requires you to chase a wave."

"So it doesn't bother you? If they were manhandling your girl, it wouldn't piss you off?"

"Ah, he said it!" Corey smacked another handful of water at me.

"Goddammit," I growled. "Quit doing that. Said what?"

"You called Hadley your girl," he said, curling his fingers into air quotes. "Not 'the' girl. 'Your' girl."

"So what? I'm not arguing semantics. I've known her since we were practically in diapers. She lives in my house."

"Give him a break," Trey said. "He means that Hadley is like family. You know, a sister."

"Punky is sure as fuck not my sister."

"Then go piss a circle around her if you want to claim your territory. Or, I don't know, ask her out like a normal person. Shit or get off the pot."

"First of all, fuck you. And if you keep it up, I'm tossing your bass off my roof."

I wasn't blind, and I wasn't dead. Hadley was gorgeous, funny when she wanted to be, a total pain in my ass, snarky, smart, talented. Yes, I knew she was a keeper. But I'd lost her already. There was no retracing my steps down that road.

"Josh, for some stupid reason, we actually give a fuck about you," Trey said. He had a way of making a kind sentiment sound like an insult. "If you don't hurry up and figure out a way to fix this thing with you and Hadley, you are going to regret it for the rest of your life. No one gets over a girl like that."

"It's been four years. She hasn't run off yet." Corey's fatal flaw was his total faith in people. "Don't you think that means something?"

"I'm not listening to this." Chin to the board, I paddled after a wave and didn't stop until lightning chased us out of the water.

* * *

Later that night as Hadley went through her ritual to lock up the house, she barely said a word to me. I took her silent treatment as punishment, an art she had perfected over the years. It was all the more tormenting because there was no shortage of questions I wanted answered about Andre and her intentions with him, but both of us knew I wasn't about to ask them aloud.

In the living room, Hadley opened the sliding glass door to the back patio and shut it tight. She flicked the lock closed, open, closed; four times in all. I turned toward the front door, but she hesitated. Hadley stood still, her finger stuck to the lock.

Open, closed.

Open, closed.

Her fingers twitched. Hadley held her breath. I wanted to do...something. Say something that might, I don't know, help. But I'd learned that lesson. Interfering only led to arguments and the nearest object within her reach flying at my head.

Her hands balled in fists, she huffed a breath through her nose. The rest of the routine wrapped up quickly after that as I went around turning off lights while she set the alarm and locked dead bolts, but I noted her frustration when Hadley slammed her bedroom door shut without letting me say good night.

I wasn't sure if it was my shit attitude that had affected her. Maybe I was an asshole for assuming I had anything to do with it. Fact was, I never had a fucking clue what was going on in her head, but I'd give anything to still have the right to ask.

Chapter 6

Session 5

"A lot changed for both of you after your first intimate experience with Hadley," she said.

Her eyes scanned the iPad in her lap, then up to my fingers drumming on my notebook. That sound drove her nuts, which was why I kept doing it.

"For you it was the panic attack," she said. "What happened after you left her house that night?"

"I almost didn't make it home in one piece. Between the shaking and dark spots clouding my vision, I lost control of my car and wiped out in a ditch, inches from wrapping my car around a tree." Convulsing, I had thrown myself from the driver's seat and collapsed in the mud. Vomit splashed around my hands and knees, soaking into my clothes. There was no voice to my screams as I had fought the vivid memory of that man—his hands on me, even the smell of him coating my skin.

No panic attack since has matched the same level of severity as the first, but that was like talking about the difference between being mauled by a bear or a tiger. Did it really fucking matter? The outcome was the same—an unrecognizable heap of human meat in the dirt.

"When I finally dragged my ass home that night, I stood in the shower until the water ran cold, then crawled into bed to stare at the ceiling until the sun came up."

"When did you find out about what happened to Hadley?"

"The next morning. Hadley's godfather, Tom, called my dad. He'd gotten home to find Hadley asleep in their attic. She'd hidden there after hearing glass shatter downstairs. She swore someone had broken into the house, that she'd heard voices and footsteps. So she'd stayed in the attic all night, terrified."

Tom had called the police to take an incident report, but it was more for Hadley's peace of mind than anything. There was no sign of forced entry. Nothing stolen. All the police came up with were a couple of broken beer bottles outside her bedroom window. Rowdy neighbors had partied too hard. Maybe some kids passing through the neighborhood had thrown the bottles at the house. Case closed.

But not for her. Hadley never again slept a full night in that house.

"It got to the point where Hadley couldn't stay at Tom's anymore. She'd have nightmares and jump at the slightest sound. Too many mornings he would find her hiding in the attic. We had a spare bedroom at my house, so my dad invited her to stay with us as often as she liked. By senior year of high school, she was living with us full-time."

"And you were okay with this?"

"What could I do? It was my fault. I'd left her there alone. If I had been there..."

"But your relationship didn't improve," she said. "Even after your mother—"

"Don't." My ears stung with a sharp, shrill ringing. All the blood was sucked from my extremities. I wasn't ready to talk about her. I hadn't been for four years.

Just once, she took pity on me. "You had the opportunity to get away from Hadley. To, as you said, move to New York with your father and try to escape the memory she represented for you. But you didn't."

"I couldn't. She was being stubborn. A couple weeks before high school graduation, she turned down her acceptance to Emerson and said she wasn't moving to Boston. Hadley wouldn't admit it, but I knew she was too afraid to face living in a new city with a strange roommate. She was terrified. So I declined my acceptance to Columbia and talked her into enrolling with me close to home. She was going to college if I had to drag her to classes myself. I didn't want that night, what I did, to ruin her life."

So I stayed behind while Hadley continued to live in my house, and we existed under an excruciating agreement to never speak of that night again.

"What about your friends? Corey and Trey. From what you've told me, it sounds like they wanted to help."

"They don't know."

"About that night?"

"About our foster home. They don't know what happened to me. I don't want them to know. As far as they're aware, I'm just an asshole who slept with his best friend and then ditched her."

"Why haven't you told them?" she asked.

"Would you want people to know? That kind of information

changes the way people see you, how they look at you. Suddenly you're not the same person anymore. Now you're..."

"What?"

Dirty. Weak. Damaged. "Different."

"Is it difficult for you to trust people? Even the ones closest to you?"

"Who are we talking about?"

"Tell me about Corey," she said. "Why is he your friend?"

I rubbed my hands over my face. For fuck's sake. "I don't know. I guess he's fun to be around. Corey's one of the few people I know who is never in a bad mood. It's almost impossible to wipe the smile off his face. I mean, he's a fucking child, but he seems to enjoy himself, so who am I to shit in his cereal, right?"

"That must be nice." Her tone took on that taunting inflection. The one she used to lead me around by the nose. "To go through life with such optimism. To feel so unburdened."

"Sure. Ignorance is bliss, or whatever."

"And Trey? What special quality does he possess?"

"He's a fucking snowflake. What do you want me to say? Trey's probably the least complicated person I know. Dull, but happy. You'd love him; he's freakishly well adjusted. Born with a perfect understanding of the universe and his place in it. So of course he finds constant fault in every other thing I do."

She contemplated me for a moment that stretched on until I began to fidget in my seat, tapping at a rhythm with the barbell against my teeth.

"What?" I said.

"We tend to make friends with people who possess personality traits we covet. Just something to consider."

Chapter 7

Monday morning I began my junior year of college sitting in the dean's office. The space reflected a man who wanted to appear interesting. Laminate bookshelves held paperbacks with uncreased spines. A layer of dust bordered leather-bound classical volumes. His desk was a playground of tabletop art meant to represent the exotic places he'd been and people he'd met. I'd pay him a hundred dollars if he could show me just one that didn't have "Made in China" stamped on the bottom.

"Sorry I kept you waiting, Mr. MacKay." Dean Alcott walked in and took a seat behind his desk. "How was your summer?"

"Fine."

"Thank you for stopping by. I wanted to mention—"

"I have a class—"

"We're holding a seminar next week, featuring distinguished faculty and a few invited guests. There will be a panel discussion, and I'd like to invite you to participate, add your thoughts to the conversation."

"On what?"

"Contemporary classical music." He smiled, folding his hands on the desk. "Something you are uniquely qualified to speak on."

The man had a serious hard-on for me. Well, for my name and reputation. To Dean Alcott, an old man who dressed how he thought Harvard professors looked in the fifties—bow ties and sweater vests under wool or tweed jackets—I was just the accumulated sum of my CV.

But that wasn't me anymore.

"Not interested." My fists flexed in my lap. "I told you this."

"You've experienced a level of success that other students here will only dream of. What you've given up—"

"I sat in this office. With you and my undergraduate advisor freshman year. I was very clear."

"I hoped I could convince you to reconsider. Just think about it."

"I'm not interested in returning to the piano. I have no inclination to write contemporary classical anymore, and I've nothing else to say on the topic."

Somewhere in his misguided imagination, he believed I'd spontaneously wake up one morning and declare that my muse had returned and I'd composed a new concerto. He probably yanked it to fantasies of the speeches I would give professing my love for my alma mater and the reawakening I'd experienced while in its hallowed halls.

"A talent like yours—"

"Is mine to waste. We done?" I grabbed my bag and walked out, rushing to my first class of the morning.

* * *

What was it about me that made people think I had a mind that wanted changing? Every semester was the same ordeal with Dean Alcott. Since I first sat in his office two years ago seeking late acceptance to the university, he'd made it his mission to convert me. He considered it a great tragedy that the former child prodigy had walked away from touring as a concert pianist four years ago. The real tragedy was losing my muse and my motivation in the same horrible month.

It wasn't as if I had stopped playing out of spite. I wasn't so high on myself that I needed men like the dean to beg in order to shore up the foundation of my ego. I loved playing. It was my passion. If I could physically tolerate putting my fingers to the keys, I'd do nothing else. Scott was right; I had washed out, because the thought of even looking at my mother's piano...

Damn it.

I took a deep breath and shut my eyes. My stomach rolled with grief and nausea. The ache in my chest was as pronounced as ever. My fingers curled into fists in my lap.

Sitting in the lecture hall of my music theory class, I sank into my seat at the back of the room, begging my body to calm the fuck down. My knee bounced. The barbell in my tongue flicked between my teeth. It clicked against the hard enamel like an anxious metronome. As the professor elaborated on the PowerPoint presentation projected behind him, the room deflated, closing in. My vision became a warped, blurry bubble of bleeding colors. I tried to think of anything else, but the memory insisted:

Three days of avoiding Hadley after the night I'd run out on her four years ago were consumed with rehearsing for my upcoming show. While I was hiding in the music room, my adoptive mother,

Carmen, came to sit next to me at the piano bench. For a while, she just listened to me play. I adored the way she smiled and hummed along while my fingers danced over the keys. In those moments, I knew she was proud of me.

"That's a beautiful song. Will you play it this weekend?"

"No." I transitioned the second movement into a new composition I'd been tinkering with. "That's Hadley's song. I don't play it for the public."

My mom set her right hand to the keys beside me, improvising as I continued to play. "She called again this afternoon. She's come to see you twice this week while you've locked yourself in here."

"I can't...You don't understand—"

"You're right, Josh. I can't possibly understand. And neither can Hadley. But she loves you. She wants to be there for you. I know she'll forgive whatever you think is unforgivable."

"It isn't about forgiveness." I'd been at the keys for hours, but it was the topic that had me exhausted. As if Hadley wasn't on my mind every moment. "I'm broken. I'm not capable of… She should just move on."

"Could you? Just move on from your best friend?"

"No." Hadley was it for me. She always had been. "But if I wait it out long enough, she'll learn to hate me. It'll be better that way."

For two more hours, my mom sat with me as I gave up rehearsing and just let my mind wander while the two of us improvised together. It was sort of a pastime of ours. My mom would start a verse and then I'd come in next to her, and on and on.

She would never abandon the cause of pulling me out of my depression and masochism, but Carmen knew when to push and when to retreat. Hadley had always been my creative muse, and her song was the first I'd ever composed on the piano, but Carmen was my motivation in music.

My mother died of a brain aneurysm that afternoon during *Rachmaninoff's Third*, collapsed across my lap with blood trickling out of her nose, while her pained, vacant eyes stared up at me.

The lecture hall was empty when I opened my eyes from the memory and took a deep breath. I gathered my stuff and got the hell out of there.

* * *

On the third floor of the student union, I found a quiet place to sit in an overstuffed chair by the window that looked out on the brick-paved courtyard. The wide walkways were cluttered with frightened-looking freshmen navigating the folding-table market of student clubs and thinly veiled cults smiling under Greek banners.

Tuning out the noise and chatter of those around me in the study lounge, I dug into my pocket and pulled out my phone. My father picked up on the second ring.

"Josh, hello."

"Hi, Dad."

"You're up early."

True. I wasn't usually functional before 11:00 a.m.

"Hadley likes early classes. I worked around her schedule this semester."

"That was diplomatic of you."

"Yeah, well...How's your day going?"

"Oh, you know. The same. No one is ever happy to see me when I walk into a room."

My adoptive father was psychiatrist at a hospital in Manhattan. Dr. Simon MacKay had briefly entertained the hope that I might find an interest in medicine but supported me when my aptitude for music became apparent.

Simon took the job in New York after my initial acceptance to Columbia. The two of us were all we had left after Carmen died. We needed each other. Then Hadley needed me more, so I stayed behind while Simon tried to get on with his life. Whatever that meant.

He was still talking. Somewhere in the middle, I realized I'd not been paying attention. I was content to listen to his voice rather than the words.

"Josh?"

I leaned back and fixed my attention to the woven patterns in the upholstered chair. "I'm here. Sorry."

"I spoke to Hadley last night."

Her weekly informal therapy session. As if I wasn't supposed to understand the coded language there. Sunday nights I knew to make myself scarce on the other side of the house so I didn't hear Hadley's voice traveling through the walls as she talked about her level of anxiety during the week and told my father what an insufferable jackass his son was on any given day.

"You brought a woman home."

Fuck. "I had too much to drink and uh…" Fuck. Fuck. "Well, Hadley didn't want to leave the bar yet…So, yeah. It's not like I make it a habit. Why, did Hadley say something?"

"I wouldn't tell you if she did," he reminded me.

I was his son, but Hadley had been his patient before Simon and I ever met.

"I ask out of concern for you. Are you sexually active?"

"Dad—"

"If something's changed..."

"Yes, I'm having sex. No, nothing's changed." I blew a breath through my nose, pinching the bridge between my fingers. "Can we not do this right now?"

"Talk to me, son."

"I was thinking about Mom. And about playing. Figured I'd call."

"I'm glad you did."

It'd been four years since Carmen died, and still I was rendered nearly immobile when my mind slipped to her memory.

My throat was dry when I tried to speak again. "I was sitting in class. Had an episode. No one seemed to notice, I think. But by the time it passed, I was the only one left in the room."

"What do you think brought it on this time?"

There wasn't a good answer that was any different than the others. "I miss her."

"Of course you do. I promise that it will get easier in time. But not allowing yourself to feel the grief and deal with it will only prolong the healing process. Don't deny yourself her memory."

I felt my eyes begin to sting. My fingers went a little numb. "I have to go. Class."

"I love you, Josh. I'm here. Anytime."

"I know. Love you." I hung up the phone and escaped toward the stairs before I had another public meltdown.

* * *

When a child's first memory is abandonment, he tends to latch on tightly to those who show him affection. Losing Carmen four years ago was just one loss too many, and I didn't know how to deal.

That first memory—I was maybe three at the time—was of a woman sitting on a public bus next to me. She told me to stay in my seat, that she'd be right back. I saw her squeeze down the aisle toward the door, get off the bus, and that was it. I never saw her again. When the last passenger boarded for that stop, the bus driver closed the door and pulled away from the curb. I must have ridden along the route for hours until the end of the driver's shift when he spotted me sitting toward the back. Next stop was the police station. From there, it was a series of foster homes.

Hadley Mitchell saved my life. I'd gravitated toward her the first day she showed up in my third foster home when we were five years old. To this day, I don't know what drew me to her.

Her parents had been killed in some kind of accident. She had no surviving family. But the day Tom Hughes showed up to rescue her from that living hell—the state had finally gotten its shit together and tracked down her godfather—was both the best and worst day of my life to that point. She was getting out, but it meant I was alone again. While nothing Hadley could have done in that home would have saved me, having her there when it was over was better than suffering alone.

I didn't understand until many years later, but it was Hadley who freed me from the foster system and the daily hell I'd endured. For a week straight after going home with Tom, Hadley pitched fits, had nightmares, and ran away. When Tom exhausted his parental knowledge on how to deal with the situation, he took Hadley to see a psychiatrist named Dr. Simon MacKay. After a few sessions, Simon learned the truth. That this little girl had left behind her only friend, a boy in pain who needed help. So that was it. Simon and Carmen put in a call to start my adoption proceedings and put my tormentor in prison.

Hadley had needed me once. Instead of being her savior and repaying that outstanding debt, I failed her. It only sickened me further that, despite all of this, Hadley still showed me compassion. She still lived in my house because she felt safer with me sleeping next door than she did in her own home.

If that didn't just twist the knife.

* * *

After my last class of the day, I went to meet Hadley. Through the narrow window in the lecture hall's door, I saw her sitting alone in the back of the room. Her head was bent over her sketchpad, her long cascade of dark hair concealing her profile.

I checked my phone and noticed I'd missed a text message from Scott.

I want my money from the last gig.

Fat chance. He'd pissed all over any goodwill I had for him. Besides, I'd already split his share with Corey and Trey. So I sent what I thought was an appropriate reply.

Tough shit.

A loud *pop* caught my attention. Leaning against the opposite wall, a chick stood popping a sheet of bubble wrap hanging out of her purse. She looked like half a Kardashian escaped from a Judas Priest concert: layers of black fashionably distressed clothing and metal studs. Her long black hair hung over her shoulder, one side of her head shaved down to stubble.

She stared at me, though I couldn't place her. Not exactly the kind of girl I would forget.

"You look deep in thought," she said, pinching tiny plastic bubbles between her fingers.

"Do I know you?"

"I'm Asha."

"And?"

"And I need a ride to your place."

"That's forward. Don't even offer to buy me dinner first."

"Sorry, you're not my type." Her red lips curved into a sarcastic smile. "You're pretty and all, but I don't do the whole tattoos and piercings thing."

"You sure?" I would have pegged her for exactly that type. She was attractive, and maybe in another life...

Asha leaned her weight on one foot and studied my arms. "I find it all too distracting. You"—she came closer and twirled her finger in my face—"are too high maintenance. I don't have that kind of time on my hands."

"I'm confused."

She was fucking with me. Had to be.

"I'm Asha. You're giving me a ride."

"That's the part I'm having trouble with."

The door to Hadley's class swung open, people pouring into the hall. Asha pushed her way into the stampede.

"Late much?" She snagged Hadley by the wrist to tug her over. "I met Josh already. We're old friends now. Ready to go?"

Hadley dug her sunglasses out of her messenger bag and slid them on top of her head. "You don't mind, Josh?"

"No. But, uh, how is she getting home?"

Making another trip into the city and back today was out of the question.

"I'll catch a ride with Trey." Asha put her arm around Hadley and turned on her heel to head down the hallway. "You coming or what?"

Well, damn. That was something.

Chapter 8

"Fuck it!" Corey shouted as he crashed into the greenroom. He was always half deaf after our shows. "We don't need a fourth guy. We killed it tonight."

We'd auditioned two replacements for Scott but found no one we could all agree on.

"There's still that guy from my econ class." Trey took a swig of water and wiped a towel over his face. "And, uh, What's-his-face."

"I want to keep looking." I collapsed on the scratchy brown couch and stretched my arms along the back. "It's only been a couple weeks."

"I'm getting used to splitting the cash three ways," Corey said. "It's a nice bump in my income."

Asha, looking like the unholy love child of Skrillex and an Iron Maiden album cover, pranced her happy ass inside and straight to Trey's lap. "You guys just missed an entertaining aftershow."

"Thanks for knocking," I said.

"Nasty." She recoiled when Trey wrapped his sweaty arms around her waist. "You're all gross."

Those two as a couple was difficult to get my head around. He was a buttoned-up take-home-to-daddy type. Asha was...something else.

Corey sank onto the couch beside me. "What happened?"

"One of your groupies got tossed out," Asha announced, wiping her lipstick from Trey's cheek. "Some blond chick Hadley was talking to earlier. She was arguing with some guy and threw a drink at him. Bouncer tried to break it up and the guy slugged him. They both got dragged to the door."

"What does that have to do with us?" I asked.

"She kept shouting that they couldn't kick her out because she was with the band. I think her name was Stacey?"

"Stephanie?" Trey shot me an accusing look.

"Yep, that's it."

Wonderful. Somehow this would become my fault. Like my dick was responsible for the future indiscretions of everyone it came into contact with.

"On that note..." Corey stood up and pulled a fresh shirt out of his bag. "I'm buying the first round."

"Oh, Corey, there's someone I want you to meet." Asha hopped up, briefly scowling at Corey's post-show stench. "She's just your type. But I'm warning you now—she hates your music. So, maybe skip over that part of the conversation. And put on some deodorant."

"Does she have a nice rack?"

Asha smacked his arm, tilting her head back to glare at him. "You're a pig. I have a class with her, so don't embarrass me."

"You're impossible to embarrass," I said.

"True. But still. At least don't hump her leg. And try to make eye contact, okay?"

"Do I do that?" Corey looked between me and Trey. "I've never humped a girl's leg in a bar, right? I've clubbed a few over the head and dragged them back to my hut, but I'm not a canine."

"I regret this already," Asha groaned as she tugged him out. "I don't know why I bother."

* * *

By the time I got our pay from Nate, Hadley was at the bar in the middle of Andre and his friends. Since I had no interest in playing the fifth wheel to Trey and Asha trying to engineer a love connection between Corey and the girl of the week, I hung out at the end of the bar with a glass of Jameson. I was maybe a half hour into tracing patterns in the wood grain of the sticky bar top, half my attention on Hadley laughing among the din of conversation, when Kate slid in beside me.

"You look like shit," she said, waving down the bartender. "Want another?"

I glanced down at my untouched drink, then back to the empty spot where Hadley no longer stood. Fuck it. I swallowed the mouthful of whiskey and nodded at Troy to pour me a second with Kate's gin and tonic.

"You sounded good tonight." Kate turned her back to the bar, pulling the little black straw toward her lips to sip her drink and make sure I watched her do it.

"You don't care."

"No, I don't."

Kate wasn't here for the music. Blond hair tied up in a messy bun. Oversized cropped T-shirt hanging just right over her tits. I took a moment to appreciate how the light created a fuzzy outline along the legs of her tight leather pants. Fifteen minutes later, I appreciated the way the material stuck to her pale ass as I peeled the leather to her thighs and bent her over the sink in the greenroom.

Staring at myself in the mirror, my mind was on anything but sex. In my head, I composed a melody that had plagued me recently.

With both hands gripping the sink, Kate was demanding. Harder. Faster. More. I composed the bridge, hearing the chords clearly as she reached her orgasm.

I tried to get there. Grabbing her hips, I slammed into her. Harder. Faster. More. But I couldn't come. My body wanted it. Every muscle begged for release. When she braced her hand against my leg to tell me to slow down, I gave up and faked it before I slipped out of her and quickly tossed the condom.

I was fucking pathetic.

* * *

That night, like most nights, I dreamt of Hadley.

* * *

I couldn't get enough of her lips. There was an entire naked landscape of Punky beneath me, but all I wanted to do was feel her mouth on mine. She tasted like sugar and salt, soda and popcorn.

Lying in her bed, I was wrapped in the scent of her hair, her skin. It soaked into every part of me.

And she laughed at me.

"What?" I looked down into her eyes, Hadley's face barely visible in the darkness.

"I can't help it. You're funny."

"Why? Am I not—"

"No." She wove her fingers through my hair, tugging my face closer to hers. "You're a good kisser. Are you ready?"

"Are you?"

She nodded with a cute, nervous smile and bit her lip. My dick twitched every time she did that, and this time Hadley noticed, giggling at me.

"You have to stop doing that. You're killing my ego."

"Sorry," she said, sucking her lips together to hold back a laugh.

Balancing my weight on one forearm beside her pillow, I reached between us and held my dick in my right hand, adjusting my position to find her entrance. Her breath caught when I slid the head of my cock through her slit. I froze there, thrilled and terrified about what came next.

"Go ahead," she said, spreading her legs and placing her hands around my back to urge me forward.

Slowly, I pushed inside her, deliberate and excruciating. I was scared to hurt her and afraid I might buckle under the pressure to restrain myself. She cringed, tensing. My forehead dropped to hers.

"I'm okay. Keep going. Gently."

Inch by inch.

"Still okay?"

"Mmm-hmm."

Inch by inch.

"I'm—"

Hadley looked into my eyes. It was the sweetest, most vulnerable expression I'd ever seen, and it broke my fucking heart. It seemed barbaric that I had to cause her pain to love her.

"I'm ready." Her fingers flexed against my back. "Do it."

I pushed past her barrier and stilled inside her. She clenched around me, squeezing my cock as she adjusted to the pain. Neither of us could take a breath. My arms shook to hold my body in place.

Then Punky let out a long exhale and smiled, bright and mischievous. "That part sucked."

All the tension drained from my muscles as I kissed her forehead. "Sorry?"

"Yeah. Gah, you should be. That thing's dangerous."

"You want to keep going, or should I pack up my toys and go home?"

"Well, we're already here, so..."

The bliss was short-lived. It was always at that moment that my conscious mind tried to take control of the dream. I knew where this was going, but no matter how hard I fought for a different outcome, the result was the same.

My hips jerked. Sweat slid down my spine. Moving inside her, every muscle clenched for release.

"Hadley," I panted, "I'm gonna come."

My fingers went numb and a cold shiver crept up my legs. I came on her stomach because what the fuck, I didn't know what I was doing and we didn't have a condom. The relief of climax turned to a sick, black feeling that squeezed my stomach. My chest caved in. No air could reach my lungs. Everywhere my naked skin was exposed felt like acid bubbling on the flesh.

I saw him kneeling over me. Smelled the musty carpet of the foster home. The moment he opened his eyes and looked down at what he'd done, as if it only then occurred to him that he was a monster.

* * *

I woke from the nightmare in a puddle of sweat, the bedsheets tangled around my feet. There wasn't enough air in the room. I gasped, choking on my own spit, seizing with panic. My right hand firmly gripped my semi-erect cock. On my abdomen, a stream of semen.

Falling out of bed, I scrambled in the dark to my bathroom. With the door shut behind me, I crawled in total darkness to the toilet and poured out my stomach, heaving with violent convulsions. Everything hurt. Even the air from the vent above me was too much stimulation against my flesh. The disgusted, unnerving feeling persisted in agitating every inch of me.

When there was nothing left to throw up, I stumbled into the bathtub and let the spray from the showerhead drown me until the shaking stopped.

During a panic attack, I always had an absolute certainty that I was going to die. I mean, in that moment, with my lungs caving in like two wrinkled, expended balloons, the only thing real was his rough hands on my bare skin and the thought that I was going to die on my bathroom floor with my dick in my hand and semen between my fingers.

Every single time.

Nothing helped. There was no cure that packed the memories of that man away and locked the box. I just kept hoping that if I tried, maybe one day I'd fight my way past it. That surely there had to arrive a day when I could have sex with a woman and come without faking it or shriveling up in a ball. The alternative was too devastating to consider.

Chapter 9

The next morning, I woke to a loud *thwack* as something hard smacked me on the forehead. Sunlight bled through my clenched eyelids.

"Get up, jerkoff."

I knew that voice. I loathed that voice. Another *thwack*, this one to the bridge of my nose. I groaned, swatting at the air to no avail. Evil hag.

"Get." *Thwack*. "Up." *Thwack*.

"Fucking hell, Asha. Lay off me. And get the fuck out of my room." I pulled a pillow over my face. I was naked under the sheets. Unless she wanted a show, she needed to leave.

"No."

Goddammit! That little wench smacked my nuts through the blanket with what now definitely felt like a rolled magazine.

"Shit," I hissed, and clutched my junk as I rolled over. "What is wrong with you?"

"We need to talk. Now." The bed dipped as she sat on the edge.

"What time is it? Why are you here?"

"Morning, asshat. Hadley and I are going out. Honestly, Josh, I thought she was exaggerating."

That got my attention. I tossed the pillow aside and rubbed the sleep from my eyes. There was Asha, glaring daggers. I put the pillow over my lap.

"Hadley? What did she say?"

"Oh, now you're interested? This needs to stop." She waved the rolled magazine over me. "First, it's gross. Second, it's gross! Third, I can't believe you'd do that to her."

"Hey. You're way out of your depth here. This is my house and my room. Feel free to fuck off. I don't need your approval."

"You two have a twisted relationship. I see you looking at her like a sad puppy half the time. The other half you're just blatantly staring at her ass like you're going to drop to your knees and take a bite out of it. And here's the real kicker: She's looking at you, too, asshole. While you're up there singing, Hadley is eye-fucking you like she might burst a blood vessel." She stopped, staring at me as if I'd missed my cue. "Shall I go on, or are you getting a clear picture?"

"You're full of shit."

"No, Josh. I'm just the only person who cares enough to tell you the truth but not enough to worry about pissing you off. So, suck on that." She smacked me on the nose again to emphasize her point and then sauntered toward the door.

"Why do you care?"

"Maybe I'm a sucker for a lost cause. Don't make a fool of me, Josh. I can be an ally. If you can get your shit together."

"I don't want your advice."

"No, you don't." Asha took a hard look at me. I got the impression she found me lacking on a fundamental level. That shit pissed me off. "But you should take it. Step one: try keeping it in your pants. You're this close"—she held her fingers an inch apart—"to losing her." With that, Asha walked out of my room and slammed the door behind her.

What the fuck just happened?

* * *

There was no trace of breakfast waiting for me downstairs. Not even a discarded meal in the trash can or a note saying, "Fend for yourself, dickhead." Nothing. Just a too-big and empty house. I didn't much care for that feeling. Even though I'd heard the girls leave after I'd gotten out of the shower, I still stopped at the bottom of the stairs and glanced at the living room—not expecting Hadley to be there with her fingers up, but still sort of hoping she would be.

Fine. Whatever. This was better. Hadley was out having fun with a girlfriend, doing girly shit, and I could be lazy on a Sunday morning in peace. Perfect.

Except that the house was too big and too quiet. And Punky hated girly shit. And I hadn't bothered to buy cereal the last time we'd gone shopping.

On an empty stomach, I went to the garage. I picked up my acoustic guitar and attempted to play the bits and pieces of the song that had been swirling around in my head, but it was complete garbage, nothing like the melody that had so easily composed itself last night.

Rachmaninoff's *Piano Concerto No. 3*, partially tattooed to wind around my right forearm, stared back at me as I strummed.

I used to wake up at the crack of dawn like every morning was Christmas. I'd run down the stairs, push open the heavy soundproof door to the music room, and spend hours fiddling with Carmen's piano. At first it was just noise. One morning, my mother came in and sat quietly amused as I played total nonsense. But it wasn't nonsense to her. Something in the notes struck her. We sat at the piano all morning and well into the afternoon as she attempted to teach me a simple series of notes.

I had learned to play "Chopsticks" on the piano in three days. The usual melodies and nursery rhymes were within my repertoire in three months. I could reproduce nearly any song I heard by ear in the first year under Carmen's instruction. It escalated and grew until I won state competitions against students twice my age. Juilliard invited me. Harvard, Carnegie Hall, Lincoln Center. And it all went by so fast.

The first song I'd ever composed was a birthday present for Hadley. My mom had suggested that I write her a song—something thoughtful, personal, and unique. Give her a gift that only I could. Carmen was great like that.

I played the song at Hadley's tenth birthday party after we'd finished eating cake and her other friends had left with their parents. Hadley cried when I finished the song. I was terrified as I searched her eyes and those of my parents. I thought I'd upset her. I thought she hated it. For a few seconds, I seriously considered running. But Hadley insisted they were happy tears. That concept made not a damn lick of sense. She laughed, hugged me, and said she loved it. She used to make me play it for her constantly while she hung around during my rehearsals. Well, she didn't make me. I'd have played her anything so long as she looked at me like I was hot shit.

At some point in my reminiscing, I'd stopped strumming. My fingers had the neck of my acoustic guitar in a death grip. The imprint of the strings was red in my palm as I pried my hand free and set the instrument down.

Three hours later, Asha's words still plagued me—not that I had a reason to put an ounce of faith in the tiny devil.

To prove that I wasn't completely uncivilized, I spent a few hours whittling down my laundry pile. That task didn't require any actual work past starting the machine and switching out loads, so I kept up the cleaning mode as I went over the rest of the house. It was too damn big.

Sometime between trying to figure out how to empty the vacuum bin and throwing the fucking thing across the room when I finally pried it loose, I realized that I was agitated, cranky. I had a temper tantrum over a fucking vacuum. Everything was out of sorts, and it made me antsy.

Fuck this shit.

* * *

I met up with Corey and Trey at a pub downtown, where they were finishing a game of pool. I got a beer and a round for the guys, taking a stool at the table in the corner.

On a Sunday afternoon, only a few old guys occupied the bar, chain-smoking while watching soccer on the tiny TV on the wall. The pleather cushions on the stools were all ripped and held together with duct tape. The felt on the tables was scuffed, and there wasn't a straight cue stick in the building.

Trey scratched and sent his stripe in the pocket. "You're bad luck," he told me as he grabbed his beer from the table. "I was up three shots on Corey before you showed up."

"That's a matter of perspective. Corey's not complaining."

"Yeah. Come over here and rub my ball for luck," Corey said as he picked the cue ball out of the pocket and held it up. "Trey owes me a new drum head if I win."

I winked at Corey over the rim of my beer bottle. "Bring 'em over here, handsome."

He laughed, then missed his wide-open shot entirely. "Fuck."

"My bad. I didn't mean to get you all hot and bothered."

"Don't tease me."

Corey plopped down on the stool across from me and chugged almost half the beer in one huge gulp. It was like his thick neck was just one big drain straight to his stomach.

Trey got up to take his turn. "Have you heard from Scott lately?"

"Texted me demanding a cut from his last gig. I told him to fuck off. Why?"

Trey made his shot easily and proceeded to sink one after another while Corey hung his head.

"Came asking me about it. I told him it was up to you."

"Thanks."

"That's the deal: You handle the money, Corey does promotion, and I take care of the gear." He chalked his cue, circling the table to line up his next shot.

"And what was Scott's role?"

"Nothing. He missed that day of rehearsal."

The cue ball cracked off a stripe to knock it into the corner pocket.

"You guys are so tough on him." Corey swigged his beer. "He just needs a little help."

"Hey, how'd it go with the blonde? Grace, right?" I asked him. "The one Asha pushed on you."

Trey sank the eight ball with a decisive *thunk*, winning the game. "She hates him."

"Already? Doesn't it usually take at least four hours for a chick to decide you're a pervert?"

"Nah," Corey said, huge grin on his face. "Not that long. I think I'm in love," he barked through a laugh.

"You lost me."

Corey was the best kind of friend, but he had the emotional maturity of a dachshund.

"She's the future ex-Mrs. Clark. Legs for days. Round ass. Great tits. Fuck, I got a stiffy just looking at her lips. Really fuckable lips."

"That makes no sense."

"She'll come around. And it would be the perfect relationship. Since everything I say pisses her off, we just won't talk."

"Great plan. Let me know how that goes."

"She asked Asha about coming to the show next week." Trey took a seat at the table. "Either Grace is a closeted rock groupie or a glutton for punishment."

Corey spun his bottle cap on the sticky wood tabletop. "I'll spank her if that's what she's into."

"Speaking of Asha. I woke up naked with her this morning. You need to do a better job of putting your toys away at night."

Trey flipped me off and then chucked his empty beer bottle in the trash can behind the pool table. "That girl does what she wants. I'm just along for the ride."

I respected that about him. Trey wasn't the jealous type. I couldn't remember him ever getting into it over a girlfriend before, or ever having a bad breakup. He'd tell the girl that it was over, and by the end of the talk, she'd thank him for his honesty and all that shit.

"At any rate, I'd consider it a favor if my personal life was not a topic of conversation with you two," I told him. "She busted into my room, smacked me around with a magazine, and crossed too far over my not-your-damn-business line."

"You know," Corey said, "some guys pay for that kind of kink."

"Neat."

Her diatribe had been running laps around my head all day. I couldn't seem to concentrate on anything without her irritating voice talking over my thoughts. I also couldn't get over the fact that Hadley had talked to her about the girls I hooked up with.

"Trust me," Trey said, "I know what to do with a beautiful woman, and it doesn't include talking about you."

"So..." I eyed my beer. Nothing left but the bubbles of backwash around the beveled bottom. "She swept Hadley out of the house first thing this morning."

"Fuck yeah," Corey barked as he slammed his fist on the table, shaking our bottles. "Pay up!"

Trey narrowed his eyes at me as he dug a ten-dollar bill out of his pocket and slapped it down in front of Corey. "Just so you know, Josh, I was on your side. You let me down."

"The fuck is that about?" I caught the bill before Corey could pull it away. "You're betting on me?"

"Betting against you." He tugged the bill out from under my hand.

"Start talking."

Why was I suddenly so fucking interesting?

"I bet Trey that you couldn't go twenty minutes without asking about Hadley."

Corey looked so proud of himself. I wanted to knock that stupid smirk off his face.

"You didn't make it ten."

"We have plans on Sundays. We have, you know, shit to do. We have a routine."

"*You* have a routine," Trey said. Semantics. "And Hadley just goes along with it. Didn't you ever stop to think that maybe Hadley misses having other friends? I like you, but sometimes you're shitty company."

Of course I'd thought about it. I knew it wasn't Punky's preference that her entire social calendar included school, hanging around the house with my sorry ass, and going to gigs with the band. But everything changed after the night I left her alone.

Chapter 10

Four years ago…

Our first day back in school after my mom's funeral, I felt the eyes on me all morning. Thinly concealed whispers behind my back. Sideways glances. Sitting at my desk in English, I gritted my teeth and clenched my fists. Hadley sat beside me, an unfortunate result of our assigned seats. Eyes planted in the book in front of me, I toyed with a pencil between my fingers, afraid to glance in her direction.

"Herot is not just a setting, right?" At the front of the room, Mrs. Barnett tried to ply intelligent responses from the class on the major symbols in *Beowulf*. "It represents what?" She looked at the vacant stares of the class and then turned to write in tall blue letters across the whiteboard. "Civilization. And..."

She got no response. Behind me, girls snickered. From the corner of my eye, I saw Christina looking toward Hadley. Whispers turned to murmurs behind Mrs. Barnett's back.

"The achievements of Hrothgar," the teacher said, continuing to write on the board. "How is the hall described? Someone?"

Christina tapped me on the arm and nodded at Hadley. Reluctant, I looked over. Everyone looked. Hadley was shaking, trembling, her arms folded over the back of her bowed head to hide her face. Her knee bounced to an erratic rhythm.

"Hadley?" Mrs. Barnett approached her, walking through the row of desks. "Are you okay?"

"Back up, she's gonna puke!" someone shouted.

I jumped out of my seat and knelt beside Hadley, trying to pry her arm free so I could see her face. "Hey, Punky. What's wrong?"

Her skin was freezing. She tensed at my touch, recoiling from me.

Shit.

"What's wrong with her?"

Ignoring the teacher and room full of gawkers, I slung both of our backpacks over my shoulder. She fought me as I tried to pull her from her seat. She made her body rigid, face covered. I wrapped one arm under her knees, the other behind her back. Cradling Hadley in my arms, I ran out of the class and away from the laughter.

After I took her home to Tom, I drove around for hours before walking into Bear's shop for my first tattoo: the raven Hadley had drawn for me that always sat in my back pocket. I wanted to feel the pain, if only to have something to concentrate on, so I sat under Bear's gun and bled.

Every ounce of ink carved into my skin had a meaning. Only posers and dipshits got tattoos for the fuck of it or picked a doodle out of a book. The raven with two broken wings nailed to my shoulders represented the only thing I'd ever been afraid of.

He had a raven tattooed on his back.

Chapter 11

After I got home from the bar, I checked my phone to see if Hadley might have left a message. At least to tell me if she would be home for dinner. Instead, I had a text from Tom asking if I wanted to meet up at the range this week.

When the decision had been made that Hadley and I would live here while we went to college, Tom had asked me to come by the house one morning. I was informed, not asked, that I would take a gun safety course, apply for my permit, and keep a pistol locked in my nightstand. Last year, Tom conveniently left a hunting rifle in the hall closet behind a stack of boxes.

Hadley hated guns. She didn't trust them. I sort of understood that. Nothing good ever happened when you needed to use one. But it made Tom feel better to know I could handle myself.

Downstairs, the front door shut. I still smelled like stale beer and smoke from the bar, so I stripped out of my shirt. As I came out of my room, Hadley passed by with two shopping bags in her hands.

"Hey. Have fun?"

"Yeah." Her eyes paused on the new image on my rib cage. "It healed well. Looks good."

"You're a good artist."

Hadley had drawn the sketch for everything inked into my skin.

She kept walking to her room where she dropped the bags on the floor next to her bed. I followed her in and leaned against the dresser. Hadley tossed a look over her shoulder but didn't kick me out while she slipped her shoes off and emptied her pockets on her nightstand.

"What did you do today?" I asked.

"You smell like the bar." Hadley turned around. Her sassy eyebrow was up.

"Just shot some pool with the guys for a couple hours. After I cleaned the house."

"You cleaned?"

She picked up her bags and dumped them out. A couple of vintage band shirts fell out, along with more art supplies—she had some kind of fetish that wouldn't be sated no matter how many times she fed it—and a couple of vinyl records. Those caught my attention.

"I had a productive morning," I told her, sitting on the other side of the bed to look over one of the records. Some band I'd never heard of, which was impressive. I wondered if this was Asha's influence. "So I rewarded myself."

"I'm impressed."

"You're mocking me."

"I am."

"Fine. So what kind of trouble did you girls get into all day?"

"Pretty scandalous stuff." Punky yanked the tags off the shirts and folded each to place them in her dresser. "We checked out the new work at the gallery, got lunch, looked around at few shops, bought some music..."

She trailed off as she turned around to find me lying on my side while scanning the album jacket. I looked up, thinking that I'd given her the impression that I wasn't listening. My brain could multitask.

"Bought some music..."

"And that's it." She came to sit on the edge of the bed and yanked the record from my fingers. "Nothing exciting, but it was fun. Asha's cool."

Again her eyes raked over my bare abdomen. I didn't mind her looking. If I had the sort of artistic talent that Hadley possessed, I'd probably stare at my work all day, too. One day, when her canvas was old and flabby, she'd be on my case for fucking up her designs.

"Tell me about them." I nodded at the album in her hand. It looked folksy.

Punky ducked her eyes as she flipped the album over. "Never heard of them. I...uh...kinda picked these out because I liked the sleeves."

I sat up, snatching the record from her fingers. "Come on. Let's see if they're half as good as their cover art."

The only record player was in my room.

"Now?"

"You got better plans?"

* * *

I owed Asha a present, something loud, shiny, and expensive. I'd have that fucker wrapped with a big black bow and a marching band to deliver it at her front door.

Despite how irritating and nosy that chick could be, Asha was my lucky charm. Whatever voodoo magic she'd worked on Hadley, it had definitely played in my favor. Punky came home in a good mood, which continued while we lay on my bed and listened to what had to be the world's worst Kentucky bluegrass band to ever press vinyl. It was bad—really fucking painfully bad—but Hadley laughed all the way through the lyrics and even did imitations with a pretty poor country accent.

"No!" She shot across the bed and grabbed my arm as I got up to change the record. "I want to listen to it again. I liked that last song."

I gave her a look, at which she collapsed back on the bed and laughed.

"Okay, *like* is a strong word. But it was sort of catchy."

"Not a chance." I pulled the record off the turntable and shoved it back in the sleeve. "This shit sucks. And you're not allowed to do accents anymore. Stick to drawing pretty pictures."

Punky launched a pillow at me.

"So violent. Give me the other one. We'll try that."

It had gotten dark outside. Thick gray clouds moved in over the tree line in the backyard. I'd always liked thunderstorms at night—the colors, the sounds, the electricity that made my hair stand up straight on my arms, and the smell of the rain getting closer. I'd been in Clearwater once when a hurricane changed course and pounded us for two days. I'd watched from the balcony of our hotel room as it moved closer to shore. That was by far my favorite kind of weather, right before all hell broke loose.

"What is it?" she asked.

"Nothing. Storm's coming."

"Then start it already, Mr. Music Snob."

I narrowed my eyes at her, setting the needle to the record before climbing back on the bed. I sprawled out on my back and closed my eyes to just listen. We lay sideways across the mattress, Hadley on her stomach while she flipped through the booklet that went with the record.

For five tracks, we listened to the tragic tones of the blues album. This one was good—heartbreaking and enviably great, actually. The guitars made me feel like a complete hack. I let my mind wander inside the melodies, all but ignoring the lyrics. It was so elegant and simple to the ear but complicated to produce. Like good classical piano, the result of so much intricacy was to make it sound effortless. These guys were fucking geniuses. Well, Hadley was never getting this record back.

A flash of white light filled my room. A deafening crack shook the house. We both flinched; my breath stuck as a lump in my throat for the second it took to recognize the storm had arrived. Hadley let out a fit of relieved laughter.

"Storm's here," she said.

To punctuate her statement, another and impossibly closer burst of white lit up my room, followed by the shattering thunder. The music stopped. Hadley and I were left in complete darkness.

"Maybe it will come back on," she said.

Not likely. We lived in the middle of fuck-all nowhere. The power lines were old and fickle. The slightest tremble in the weather and we'd be without power for hours—days if heavy winds downed trees across the two-lane road or too much rain caused flooding that made repairs more time-consuming.

"I've got a flashlight." I sat up and reached into my nightstand, grabbing the torch that sat next to the lockbox for the Beretta.

I set the flashlight on the nightstand and let it reflect off the wall. It was enough to fill the room, and with that, I noticed her fingers worrying the hem of her jeans.

"Give it a second," I said. "The generator will kick on."

Without fail, I checked the generator outside the garage on the first of every month to make sure it was fueled. During a storm freshman year, we lost power for two days, which meant the house was without the security system for just as long. We got by just fine at Tom's house, but Hadley didn't sleep at all. She was agitated and anxious all night as Tom and I stayed up to watch movies with her as a means of distraction. Following that episode, I made the investment in a generator. It was enough to power the security alarm and floodlights on each corner of the exterior, plus connect the fridge and A/C.

Just as it was supposed to, three beeps sounded from downstairs, indicating that the keypad in the foyer had reset itself.

"See? No worries."

Hadley looked up and nodded. She was doing her best to fake it. "Thank you. For remembering."

"It's my job."

Hadley was in the unenviable position to sort of need me. The least I could do was take my responsibilities seriously.

"Right." She looked out the window being pelted by rain.

"We should probably go ahead and lock up."

It was too early to contemplate sleeping, but the sooner we got it over with, the sooner she'd relax.

"Yeah."

Her mood had deteriorated. For the last hour, everything had been as close to perfect as I could hope for. I didn't want to let this little hiccup ruin her evening, but I didn't know what to do about it.

I held the flashlight as Hadley led the way to her room. She stopped in her bathroom to light a candle and set it in front of the mirror. Enough to brighten her bedroom while the door was open.

In precise order, Hadley performed her ritual through her room and then downstairs. I gave her a bit of space while I found candles to light and leave burning in the kitchen and living room. The orange glow bounced off the windows and shiny appliances, filling the open floor plan with soft light.

After setting the alarm, Hadley stood looking out the front windows.

"All good?" I asked.

"Yep. So...I guess I'll get ready for bed."

"I downloaded some new music on my laptop. We could go back upstairs and listen to that."

I'd missed Punky's company. We hadn't sat and listened to music together in a long time. I wanted to get that feeling back.

"Or a movie," I offered. "I have a few on my hard drive, but we could pick a DVD if you want."

"Yeah, okay."

Hadley's expression perked up, so I assumed I'd done something right.

"I want to change clothes and stuff. You pick something," she said, "and I'll be there in a minute."

I handed Hadley the flashlight to find her way up the stairs and went into the living room to look through the DVDs. Best to err on the side of levity, so I picked out a few comedies to choose from.

I grabbed one of the candles from the coffee table, made sure that the others downstairs wouldn't ruin any surfaces or burn down the house, and then went back to my room.

Hadley's door was closed, so I set the candle down and quickly pulled off my jeans to put on a more comfortable pair of lounge pants. I sat back against the headboard and waited for the laptop to boot up. Punky appeared at the threshold of my bedroom wearing my sweatshirt, which hung midway down her slender thighs. She looked adorable.

"What?" Hadley pulled her long hair out of the neck of the sweatshirt and came toward the bed.

I shrugged. "Come take a look at your options."

"You were supposed to pick."

"You know how bad I am at following instructions. I narrowed the field. Lady's choice."

"That one." She pointed at one of the DVDs laid out on the nightstand.

I liked that about Punky. She was decisive. And she had great fucking taste in movies.

"I haven't watched *Four Rooms* in years." I popped it out of the case and slid the DVD into my laptop.

Hadley crawled up on the bed next to me. She rearranged the pillows behind her until she was comfortable while I set the laptop down between our legs and turned the volume up as loud as it would go.

"Homecoming, freshman year of high school," Hadley said, pointing out the last time we'd watched this movie together. "I didn't want to get dressed up—"

"And you were mortified at the idea of dancing—"

"So you rented a limo, picked me up at Tom's in a tux, and brought us back here."

"I'll take Tarantino over high school rites of passage any day. But you did dance."

"And you've been sworn to secrecy about that," Punky reminded me with a potent glare.

I'd taken requests at the piano at her insistence. To fit the occasion, I'd opted out of my classical repertoire in favor of Billy Joel and Elton John. Punky could get down to some "Uptown Girl" as long as no one else was watching.

"On my honor as a gentleman, your secret is safe with me."

"Fuck off and start the movie, MacKay."

Through the opening credits, Hadley adjusted her position against the headboard and messed with the pillows behind her.

"Can you see okay?" I tilted the screen in her direction.

She shifted again, closer to my side.

Oh, fuck it. It wouldn't be the first time Hadley had punched me in the nuts. *Man up, MacKay.*

"Come here." I put my arm over the back of her pillows and slid her until she was leaning against my shoulder. "There. Better?"

For the viewing vantage point. That was all.

"Yeah," Hadley answered as she dropped her head against my chest. "Better."

* * *

Her fingers dug into my shoulder and nails lightly scratched down my back. I groaned, thrusting deeper. So fucking tight, her body clenched around my cock, pulling me inside. With my weight leaning on my forearms on either side of her head, my tongue laved at one pink nipple. She whimpered, arching her back to push her tits in my face. I bit down, tugging the erect tip between my teeth.

"Fuck, Josh."

I moved one hand between us as I sat back on my heels, dragging her hips up with me to slide deeper, feeling her stretch around me. She moaned an almost painful sound. Watching her, I played with her clit. Her entire body convulsed as my thumb pressed harder.

Around my hips, her thighs trembled. She sucked her bottom lip between her teeth and bit down. I watched, fascinated with the sight of my dick disappearing inside her. It felt too good. So tight. So warm. I grabbed on to both of her hips, thrusting up and embedding myself deeply as she climaxed. I spilled inside her a moment later, my orgasm clenching every muscle.

I couldn't hold myself upright anymore and collapsed on top of her. Her fingers slid up and down my spine as I kissed along her collarbone and up the side of her neck, nipping at her warm flesh along the way.

"I love you, Punky."

"I like you pretty well, too."

I raised my head to glare at Hadley. She wore a cocky smirk. Narrowing my eyes, I thrust inside her.

"'Like'?"

"Like a lot," she said with a playful smile.

Bad Hadley.

"Bend over, naughty girl. I'm going to fuck you till you love me."

I woke up hard, sweating, with my hand fisted around my cock. I'd known it was a dream even while the fantasy played out in my sleep, but that didn't lessen the disappointment when my eyes finally opened to confirm that I was alone. It was rare that I had a dream about Hadley that didn't end in a panic attack. When I did, it was all the more damaging. Wishful thinking only made reality suck that much worse.

I blamed Asha for putting ideas in my head. Fucking irritating little monster.

Or maybe it was having Hadley curled up in my bed a few hours earlier, her head resting on my shoulder through a second movie, that motivated my subconscious. I was a fucking tool, because I'd been half hard under the blanket while watching *Who Framed Roger Rabbit*. I couldn't help the fact that my dick responded with interest when he knew Punky was in range. Having her warm body tucked under my arm elicited certain natural responses.

Frustrated, I threw back the blankets. My phone read 3:00 a.m. There were three text alerts from Corey. Since none of them were a plea for bail money, I ignored him. Might as well take a shower and rub this one out, or I'd never get to sleep.

Out of habit, I flicked the light switch in my bathroom, which reminded me that the power was out. Right. Brilliant.

Hadley screamed.

My blood went cold.

I ran to her room and collided with the door, damn near pulling the handle off when it refused to open.

"Hadley! Are you okay?"

The door cracked open and I shoved it aside, almost clipping her in the process.

"What's wrong?" I demanded.

She wouldn't look at me. I grabbed her face between both hands, urging her eyes to meet mine.

"What happened? I heard you scream."

"It was nothing," she whispered. Her pulse throbbed against my fingers splayed along her neck. "I...Nothing. It's stupid. I'm sorry I woke you up."

"Stop it with that shit. What happened?"

"I woke up and heard something at the window. It startled me. That's all. I'm fine."

Tapping. Scratching. Beneath the sound of rain, a tree limb battering her window. I cursed under my breath and let my lungs inhale. She stepped out of my grasp.

"You scared the shit out of me," I admitted. Both hands ran through my hair and scrubbed at the back of my neck. "You're sure you're all right?"

"Fine."

"Okay." I made no move to turn around and go back to my room. I just couldn't make myself move. "I...uh...Fuck. Give me a second."

Leaning against her dresser, I forced a few deep breaths to go in and out. It wasn't lost on me that I might have been more terrified than she was. My hands trembled with the adrenaline still running through my body. I'd been ready to murder someone with my bare hands. Now what?

"I'm sorry," she muttered. "I—"

"You know what I'm thinking about now?"

Hadley didn't say a word. Right, that was a poor way to open.

"The time you dislocated your shoulder when you were nine. I saw you disappear down the hill on your bike, and then you screamed louder than I'd ever heard in my life. I think I almost shit myself."

"I still say that tree came out of nowhere. It jumped out in front of me."

"So I ran down there, expecting to find you flattened by a car or something, and you're lying at the base of the tree—a good ten feet from the road, by the way—laughing your ass off with tears running down your face."

"Yeah, I don't know. I was surprised as hell to be alive? No idea, because it hurt like a bitch. But you carried me all the way up the hill to Tom's house. I'm surprised he didn't melt my bike down after that."

"But he did have you suited up like a hockey player before he let you ride it again. You were so cute in that bright pink helmet," I teased, pushing her hair off her face. It took a second for me to realize how I'd touched her, and then I just felt awkward and self-conscious.

Dipshit.

"I should...um..." Hadley trailed off and looked to her windows.

The wind howled outside, rain battering the glass and that damn tree limb clawing at the window like a bony talon.

"I'll take care of it. Corey will probably have a chainsaw I can borrow. It won't take anything at all. We should trim all the limbs back from the house anyway."

"Yeah. Okay."

She still didn't sound quite right, and I got the impression she wasn't entirely calm.

"Come on." I grabbed her pillow off the bed and put my arm over her shoulder as I led her to my room.

"What are we doing?"

"You won't sleep at all in there tonight. The stupid tree is going to keep you up as long as the storm continues. You're sleeping here." I tossed her pillow on my bed and pulled back the blankets. "Hop in. I'll take the futon."

It wasn't great, but my futon sofa wasn't awful to sleep on in a pinch.

"Josh—"

"I'm not going to sleep if you don't. Spare me the argument and just get in. Unless you'd rather we both camp in the living room."

Because I wanted to be close by if she had an anxiety attack.

"Gee, when you put it that way."

That was better. Sarcasm meant she was calmer.

"Don't get lippy. In," I ordered, pointing at the bed.

Punky huffed. I was sure she tried glaring at me, but the effect was lost in the dark. She did, however, follow my command. She could go right on and consider herself tamed for the night.

"Good." I tucked the blankets around her, realized that was a fucking creepy thing to do, and went to the futon against the opposite wall.

"Josh?"

"Hmm?"

"You don't...um...You don't have to sleep over there."

My dick stood at attention, now quite interested. I really fucking hoped she couldn't see me pointing at her like a goddamn weathervane.

"I don't want to kick you out of your own bed. Just...just shut up, don't argue with me, and get in."

"Since you asked so nicely."

In truth, I was teetering somewhere in the middle of dumbly standing still and taking a sprinting leap right at her. Not at all calm or collected, I walked around the other side of my bed and slipped in beside Hadley. Fucking goddamn torture. If I got up to rub one out now, she'd definitely notice. How was I supposed to sleep with blue balls?

Hey, Hadley, would you mind rolling over and wiggling that little ass against my cock? I've still got this raging hard-on from dreaming about fucking you senseless.

Just. Peachy.

Chapter 12

In the morning I found Hadley sitting at the kitchen counter with a white bakery box.

"Hey," I greeted her as I took a peek inside. "You got up early."

"I ran out and grabbed breakfast for us since the power is still out." Her voice was chipper, light. She smiled at me. "Dig in."

Best not to question my good fortune and just sit down, shut up, and enjoy the moment. If I was honest with myself, I was feeling chipper, too. But I was rarely so forthright within my own mind. I picked out a maple doughnut and shoved half of it in my mouth before I said something stupid to piss her off.

There wasn't a doughnut in the world big enough to fill the silence between us.

"Hey, umm—"

"I wanted—"

"Go ahead," I told her.

Hadley turned on her stool, propping one elbow on the counter. "Thank you. Not just for letting me share your room...but for keeping me company and whatever. And if you tell anyone I freaked out over a tree, I'll smother you in your sleep."

"No need to make threats."

Hadley reached over and picked off a piece of my doughnut. I glared at her irritating habit, but she just shrugged and popped the piece between her lips with a cocky smirk.

"It was fun."

Punky raised an eyebrow, which had me backpedaling.

"Movie night," I corrected. "We haven't done that in a while. And it was a hell of a lot better than staring at the ceiling by myself."

"That's high praise," she said. "I'm more entertaining than doing nothing at all. Unless that's code for watching porn?"

"Fuck. You're right. I could have been watching porn. Now I feel cheated."

Hadley slapped my arm.

"Keep those weapons to yourself, girly. I've got your pillow hostage in my room. Behave, or I'll defile it in all manner of unsavory ways."

"That's a low blow. Not nice." With an unapologetic smirk, Hadley stole the last bit of my doughnut and popped the huge piece in her mouth, chewing in a big, satisfied motion while wiping the icing from her fingers and licking her lip.

Goddamn. Why had I ever tried to break her of that habit?

"Did you sleep well?" I asked.

"Uh-huh."

Was that code for "I spent the whole night trying not to get groped" or "I've never slept so well in my life, and I'm never going back to my own bed"? How was I supposed to interpret the two most vague syllables in the English language? For that matter, why was I putting so much thought into the answer at all?

Because a certain wicked fairy stepsister stuck a bug in my ear that was slowly burrowing into my frontal lobe, digesting gray matter, and coiling around my brain stem.

Fucking Asha.

* * *

As a rule, I tried to avoid participating in discussion during my lecture courses. This one was an elective for songwriters that explored the correlation between popular literature and contemporary music. I'd skimmed the reading, grasped enough to sort of follow along, but I was only half listening. The majority of my attention, as I sat near the back of the room, was dedicated to my notebook. A melody I couldn't pin down existed on the edge of my consciousness, bobbing on the tide just within sight, though it often disappeared over the horizon. It was teasing me, taunting my ability to isolate and transcribe it in any useful way. That shit pissed me off.

Songwriting and composing, no matter the instrument or style, had always come naturally to me. I was that irritating sort of person who just shat lyrics and melodies like effortless sentences. At least I had been until this particular tune. I scribbled bars of music. After a few minutes, I reviewed my work and determined it looked nothing like the composition I heard through the distortion in my head, like a garbled radio transmission. I just couldn't hone in on the frequency to clear the noise.

"Mr. MacKay, care to offer an opinion?"

I exhaled a disgruntled breath, not bothering to offer my eyes to the front of the room.

"Or are we distracting you from something more important?"

Dr. Richardson was a pretentious asshole. He dressed like Steve Jobs, with rimless glasses, a short gray crew cut, and that I-think-I'm-still-twenty-five stubble around his chin. A fortysomething never-was stuck lecturing elective courses while granted one entry-level classical composition course. I was—or had been at one time—everything he would never accomplish.

He hated me, and I was fine with that.

"I do have a thought," I answered. "Do you think the planet is getting lighter or heavier? I mean, a few years ago there were only six billion people on Earth; now there's more than seven. But the planet is a closed system, right? We can't create more matter, only transform it. So all the burning forests and cremated people and rotting whale carcasses on the ocean floor become something else. We're all made of stardust and whatnot. So it doesn't matter how many people are born; they're just made up of other stuff that used to be. So that sort of cancels itself out. But I think the planet is actually getting lighter."

"I'm not sure how that—"

"Follow me here. Thanks to space travel, we've poked a hole in the closed system of our planet. Every year we shoot all sorts of stuff into space, much of which never returns. So that trims a few tons. Then there's atmospheric escape of gasses. Hydrogen and helium heating up and traveling out into space. I think I read that somewhere. Like ninety-something tons of gas leaving our atmosphere every year. So the Earth must be getting lighter."

"Mr. MacKay—"

"I know what you're going to say: 'What about meteorites and random space debris falling to Earth?' Well, apparently that's only like fifty-something tons a year. So you eat a hamburger and run over a squirrel on your way home, and that becomes a baby in Cambodia. But with all the stuff we send into space and the gas we produce, I'm going with lighter. Either way, kind of blows the mind, huh?"

"And how do your less than cogent points apply to the resurgence of activism in popular music during the Bush administration?" Dr. Richardson asked.

"They don't. You didn't ask for a relevant opinion, only that I give one."

The room shifted in his direction, waiting to see if he'd stoop to my level. Instead, he fired a shot across my bow.

"Friday evening. There will be a mandatory seminar for all Composition and Performance majors. The department chair has invited a special guest lecturer who will talk about the landscape of modern classical music and the evolving genre. There will be a talkback followed by a special performance. Pianist Alexei Annikov will perform a selection from his current international tour, including compositions from Igor Stravinsky."

Fuck me running. I suddenly felt an infectious disease coming on. Perhaps I could catch pneumonia by Friday.

"Oh, and, MacKay?" The satisfied smile was plain in his voice. "Your distinguished presence has been requested by the dean. He is hosting a reception following the event. I'm sure you look forward to catching up with your old friend."

Brilliant. What were the odds that a new Cold War could break out in the next five days? How hard would it be to get a certain Russian put on a no-fly list?

Alexei Annikov was the Stravinsky to my Schoenberg. I had no great respect for his musical ability. He had the finesse of an untrained chimp—saying otherwise would be an insult to trained chimps everywhere—and as much creativity as a paint-by-numbers illustration. Worse, he was a self-righteous prick who propped himself up on the fame of his grandfather, a national treasure of the Russian cultural sphere who by thirty-two had composed two instant ballet classics that still toured the world to sold-out crowds and rave reviews.

We'd met several times during my years on the circuit. When I began touring Europe, Alexei would bust a nut to find a rag willing to quote him in an article where he could wax philosophical about how Americans did not have the cultural competency for classical music. Turnip-eating dipshit.

* * *

Again I stood waiting outside of Hadley's last class as her professor presided over a PowerPoint presentation while his students waited to be released. He was already four minutes over. I had a mind to walk in there and spring Punky from her loquacious instructor but figured she'd yell at me for being impatient.

"Hey." Asha, dressed up like she'd just come from a funeral for My Chemical Romance, loped up the hall and peeked inside the little window in the door to Hadley's class. "Waiting for Hadley?"

"Obviously."

"What's with you?" Asha stood with her hands on her belted and studded hips, her feet in first position.

I wondered if she'd been forced into ballet as a child, having since rebelled against the stringent regimen but still unable to break from certain natural habits so ingrained in her consciousness. My head was full of useless shit. Anyway, my mind was wandering. I didn't understand the question, so I shrugged and looked back through the window.

"Granted, you're usually a surly shit, but I detect a particular bug has crawled up your ass."

"Why? Is it crowding your living quarters in my rectum?"

"See? This right here"—she waved her judgmental fingers over me—"is why you two don't communicate."

"Who two? Hadley? We communicate." Sometimes. When we felt like it. And why the hell did I have to justify myself to her?

"Right." Asha picked at the black nail polish on her thumb. "I heard you two spent the night together."

I wouldn't give Asha the satisfaction. Frankly, her fascination with my life was beyond obnoxious. Whatever kind of diplomatic mission she was on, she'd struck my last fucking nerve today.

"Look, I know you think you married into the family or some shit, but dating Trey doesn't buy you the right to leech off me and interfere in my life. Get a fucking hobby."

"Josh—"

"Tell Hadley I'll meet her at the car," I said, leaving her behind.

I took the long way back to the parking lot, circling the commons a couple times to cool off.

My outburst had more to do with misplaced anger than anything. Asha didn't deserve it, but she was the nearest target, so she took the brunt of the force. I had sort of always been this way. The older I got, the more vicious my temper. It wasn't a good look on me, but today it seemed I'd hit my limit of keeping the pressure contained. I was bleeding anger, bubbling over. Something had to give.

"Josh!"

I turned to see Scott rushing toward me from across the lawn. Just in the time I'd seen him last, he must have lost ten pounds. Shadows framed his face. His wrinkled T-shirt and dirty jeans dangled off his skeletal frame. He really didn't want to pick another fight with me today.

"I don't owe you—"

"Stay the fuck away from my sister," he said, damn near standing on my toes. His breath stunk of tooth decay.

"I haven't—"

"Uh-uh," he said, shoving my shoulder. "I know you were with her, and I saw what you did."

"Hey, I don't know what—"

"Stephanie still has bruises on—"

"Hold on." I pushed him away. "I had sex with her, weeks ago, but I didn't—"

"You're lucky you're still breathing." He poked a needle-sharp finger at my chest, eyes red and wild.

"Have you even talked to her about it?" Stephanie was clingy, but I didn't believe she'd accuse me of hurting her. Given Scott's current state, it was more likely he'd conflated the whole thing in his head. Then I thought about the night she'd gotten kicked out of the bar for arguing with her date. "I'm not the only guy she's been with lately."

"Fuck you. What would you do if someone did that to Hadley, huh?"

"Listen, asshole." Rage turned my skin numb. That hot rush of adrenaline. I'd have laid his ass out if not for the certainty that this time he'd press charges. "I don't know what she told you, but I didn't hurt Stephanie. I don't beat up on women. You threaten Hadley, I will end your fucking life."

Scott looked around, seeing that we'd drawn an audience of gawkers waiting with their phones out and ready to capture a brawl.

"Next time I see you..." He stalked off, his threat an open possibility.

* * *

Asha sat barefoot on the trunk of my car when I got to the parking lot, her knee-high black boots on the pavement.

"Where's Punky?"

Asha looked up from her phone. "Who?"

"Hadley." Who the fuck else?

"Why do you call her that?" Asha tucked her phone into her pocket and held out her hand. "A little help."

I bent and picked up her boots. "Where is she?"

Asha slid her foot inside and tightened the laces up to her knee. "Went to meet Andre. She was going to text you, but I told her I'd pass the word along."

"Fine. How's she getting home?"

"Said she'd catch a ride with him."

"Then what are you still doing here?"

"And miss the chance at an hour alone together?" She hopped down from the trunk and smiled with a look of sadistic intent. "Nope. You and I are going to get some quality time."

* * *

Asha's idea of quality time felt more like waterboarding. As I drove, words kept coming out of her mouth as if she'd forgotten how to close it.

"I don't get you," she said. "I mean you and Corey make sense. And Trey and Corey, I can kind of see. But how did you and Trey become friends. You're so..."

"I could say the same about you."

"We have more in common than you think. You two are so similar in ways. You're both serious. But he's quiet, reserved. You're just cranky."

"Why don't you just ask him?"

"I could, but then what would we have to talk about? Unless you want to tell me all about how you ended up in bed with Hadley last night."

Fucking hell. Anything to shut her up.

"In ninth grade we were both the new kids. I was homeschooled until then. He had just moved to the area. We shared a couple classes and kept getting paired up for projects, science labs, that kind of thing. We got used to each other. Then he said he played bass, so we formed a band with Corey and Scott."

I didn't recall a day when either of us had made the decision to become friends. I didn't hate Trey on the spot, and throughout the year of classes and partner assignments he hadn't given me a reason to. Spending time together, seeing each other every day and occasionally after school, became a habit. Actually, it was probably Punky's doing that Trey got absorbed into our collective. I didn't know how to make friends, so she started inviting him out with us and made the connection for me.

"Why do you have so many tattoos?" she asked. "Do you have any other things pierced?"

"Because," I grunted. "And yes."

"Where?"

"None of your business."

"Why not? Why get the ink and the hardware if not for people to look at it?"

"It isn't for attention."

I hated that assumption. Just because some asshole got a dumbass tribal band around his bicep or a naïve girl was convinced that those Chinese letters said "Happy" or "Dragonfly" rather than "Stupid American," it didn't mean that my tattoos were intended for public consumption.

"It's for me. Period."

"Why?"

"That's a long story." I ran one hand through my hair, my tongue piercing flicking between my teeth.

The laws of physics were finite things that I could not bend by will to make the distance home any shorter.

"I've got time," she said.

"Yeah. I'm trying to do something about that." I hit the clutch and shifted, hitting eighty-five. I kept my eyes out for highway patrol.

"You know, you might just like me if you didn't try so hard not to."

I expelled air through my nose, resting my head back against the seat. Her curiosity wasn't invasive. I suppose it fell into the category of getting to know someone. One way or another, I was stuck with this chick for a while. Hadley and Asha had hit it off, and Trey wasn't tired of her yet. Maybe the tiny terror had earned a little reciprocation.

"My body is my own, so I made myself over to fit my own desire, not for anyone else."

"To take ownership," she said.

"Yes."

"Because someone took that away from you once."

"More than once."

"I understand."

"No." My hands tightened on the wheel, twisting. "I don't think you can."

"But you're sort of like Guy Pearce in *Memento*. He got tattoos to remember. Like the one on your arm." She nodded at the concerto wrapping around my right forearm. "That one is for your mom."

"Okay. That's enough sharing."

For a while, Asha seemed satisfied. I, on the other hand, was edgy as the long drive seemed to drag out the closer we got to my house. Eventually, my passenger exhausted her supply of polite silence.

"Andre seems nice," she said.

Punkyfucker.

Shit. All I could see was his hands on her practically naked body at the beach. The way he manhandled her. The way she laughed and squirmed. Me sitting yards away on the water watching it happen. If that son of a bitch fucked her, I'd break his neck. First, I had to try not to drive off a cliff on the way home.

"Wow," she said. "That was something."

"What was?"

"If looks could decapitate..."

I turned up the volume on the stereo and silenced Tim Burton's nightmare sitting next to me.

It wasn't that I begrudged Hadley finding someone else. Maybe Andre was good for her. She deserved to be happy. I just couldn't help my jealousy. There was a big part of me that wanted to keep her locked up in our house, all to myself, if only to protect her from other assholes like me. More often than not, that instinct got me in trouble.

Freshman year of college, I'd taken that jealousy and ridden right over a cliff.

Chapter 13

Two years ago...

Following rehearsal with the band one night, I followed Corey and Trey inside from the garage. Trey headed for the living room while Corey started foraging in the kitchen.

"You guys hungry?" I grabbed a bottle of water, glancing between the two rooms from the foyer at the foot of the stairs. "We could order a pizza."

"Two pizzas," Corey said with his head in the refrigerator. "Large."

Trey propped his feet up on the coffee table and turned on the TV. "Is Hadley home yet?"

"I think so." I wiped my face with my shirt, pulling it off when I got a good whiff of myself. "I'm going to clean up and see if she's upstairs."

"Three pizzas," Corey said. He took out a Tupperware of Punky's lasagna from last night and popped it in the microwave.

It was an appetizer where he was concerned.

In my bathroom, I splashed some water on my face and hair, grabbing the washcloth to wipe down my chest and neck. I heard voices coming from the other side of the wall, Hadley's room, and figured she was watching TV. Out of habit, I knocked on the wall.

"We're ordering pizza," I shouted.

When we were kids, Hadley would often spend the night at my house when Tom was on the road. After we bargained to stay up just one hour, thirty minutes, and then ten minutes longer, my parents would shove us in our rooms and order us to bed. For hours following the designated bedtime, Punky and I would sit on either side of the wall between our rooms and talk. I'd play music for her, we'd play Battleship, and sometimes we'd fall asleep on the floor with our ears pressed to the drywall.

For that reason, I knew she'd heard me when I shouted to get her attention. I could still hear voices. She was either ignoring me or maybe had her earbuds in.

Her door was closed, but I didn't bother knocking. I learned a valuable lesson that night. And so did the Punkyfucker I found naked on top of the girl I'd fucked once and run out on.

"Josh!"

"Who's—" He didn't get to finish that sentence.

Hadley shoved him off of her. She scurried up the bed with a look of horror on her face.

I had the Punkyfucker in a headlock and in the hallway by the time I ripped my eyes from her tits. Holding him upright enough to make it to the bottom of the stairs—I should have just tossed him down the flight, but hindsight is 20/20 and all that—I walked him in front of me. Trey and Corey came running into the foyer from either side as I escorted the naked asshat out of my house.

"Who the fuck is this guy?"

"Josh, what are—"

"Josh! You son of a bitch. Let him go!"

Two flights of stairs was apparently how long it took Hadley to throw some clothes on and come after me. I ignored her. And since neither Corey nor Trey was in a big rush to wrestle a naked dude away from me, they parted to clear my path to the front door. I threw the guy on the porch. He stumbled on scrawny legs down the front steps.

"Memorize my face," I growled at him. "The next time you see it or her, run the other way."

He stood cupping his junk at the bottom of the stairs, his feet unsteady on the loose dirt and gravel of the driveway. I slammed the door before he could speak. Hadley was right behind me, dressed in a pair of shorts and a T-shirt.

"You're out of your fucking mind!" she screamed at me.

"Are those his clothes?" I nodded at her hand holding a wadded mess of denim and white cotton. I grabbed them, opened the door without looking past the threshold, and tossed them out. "There," I snapped at her. "Better?"

"No, shithead! I can't believe you'd—"

"Would and did." I leaned against the door, crossing my arms over my chest. "I have witnesses. Go, spread the word, and let it be known throughout the land—"

She slapped me. Hard. Smacked the callous, sarcastic remark right off my lips. My entire body went rigid. My face was hot from where she'd hit me, fists clenched with rage. Trey jumped between us and put Hadley behind him. Corey grabbed my shoulder in one strong hand, planting me in place. She fought against Trey, screaming at me, but I didn't hear most of it past the anger and blood rushing between my ears.

"I'm never going to forgive you for this," she swore. "You did this to yourself, you bastard. You! Remember that, Josh." Her eyes were dark and deadly as she stared right through me.

She couldn't know how much that one stung. Yes, I had let her go, but for reasons I had no control over. For a moment there, I almost blurted it out. The reason I'd never be good enough for her. Maybe just to hurt her.

"Let's go." Corey opened the door behind me, poking his head out to make sure the Punkyfucker was gone. "Come on, man. Let her cool off."

He wrapped his arm over my shoulder, pushing me out the front door barefoot and shirtless. We hopped in his Jeep, and I let Corey cart me off, my brain fried and my heart dissected on the floor of the foyer.

* * *

We were silent as Corey drove down the two-lane road surrounded by the dark forest on either side. The only sound passing my ears was the wind rushing through the vehicle and the echo of the barbell in my tongue flicking between my teeth.

With the windows down, I sucked in as much fresh air as my lungs would take, but my chest was tight. No matter how I commanded my body to relax, I couldn't pry my fingers from my clenched palms. My eyes burned as I fought not to close them. Not that it mattered. Open or otherwise, all I saw was the bastard levered over her, Hadley's legs around his hips and her head tossed back with her lip between her teeth. My stomach turned, cold sweat coating my skin.

"Pull over," I demanded.

"Josh, I think you need—"

"Now." I unlatched my seat belt and grabbed the door handle. "Pull over, man."

He drifted to the side of the road, coming to a stop in the darkness with only his headlights illuminating my path to the tree line. I bolted from the Jeep, bracing one hand on a tree and the other on my thigh as I vomited. My stomach heaved, tossing out its full contents in two, three, four forceful convulsions. I stood there for a while, gasping for air and spitting the vile taste from my mouth. My head pounded, throbbing at my temples.

"You okay?"

"Yeah." I nodded and stood upright. "I just—"

"I know. No worries."

When I turned around, Corey tossed me a rag and a bottle of water. I wiped off my mouth and chin, stuffing the rag in my back pocket. Taking mouthfuls of water, I swished and spit until the taste was gone. My muscles were still tense, my skin too hot and too cold at the same time, but I was feeling somewhat better.

"Thank you."

"You got it, brother."

Together, Corey and I leaned against the side of his Jeep, both of us staring at the black forest ahead.

"What do you want to do now?" He glanced at me from the corner of his eye. "The range is still open for a couple hours."

"Probably shouldn't give me a firearm right now."

"We could hit up the bar by my place. They won't card us."

"Nah. I'd start a fight and you'd have to jump in and save my ass."

"You could go take a freezing dip in the Pacific."

It wasn't a bad idea, all things considered. Sitting by the water and clearing my mind would be the most peaceful way to get my head on straight. But seeing as how it was still a bit crooked and discombobulated at the moment, I opted for something completely fucked instead.

"Take me to Bear's shop."

"You want to get inked now? Isn't there a rule about that or something?"

"Probably," I agreed. "There should be."

Never get something engraved on your body with a broken heart.

I jumped in the Jeep. "But I'm not getting a tattoo."

* * *

We stood in the fluorescent lobby of Pins & Needles. The walls were covered in rows of hanging portfolios displaying each tattoo artist's favorite works. The two glass cases that separated the waiting area from the artist stations held body jewelry along with hats and T-shirts with the shop's logo.

"As your friend," Corey said, his hands gripping both my shoulders, "I'm telling you not to do this. It isn't worth it."

"It's cool." I was a little drunk on the idea by that point. "She's a professional. Mia's going to take real good care of me."

"You're going to regret this. Let me get you drunk. Fuck, I'll get you high if that will make you feel better. I'll take you out back and knock you around a bit if you just want it to hurt. But don't go back there with that chick and let her do unnatural things to your dick."

"I can hear you," Mia shouted from the back of the shop. "You want to be next, Corey?"

He shivered, cupping his crotch and backing away. "I'm not watching this."

"Good," I laughed. "I don't need an audience."

"I'm going outside. Maybe across the street. I don't want to hear the screams."

Corey shoved through the front door, the bell overhead signaling his retreat.

Time to soldier up.

I walked to the room at the back of the shop and reclined in the cushioned chair. While Mia closed the door and yanked on a pair of latex gloves, I pulled open my jeans and slid them with my boxers down enough to pull out my cock. She opened the plastic packages, taking out her sterile torture implements and preparing them on the cart next to her stool.

Mia's eyes landed on my dick. "I need to measure so I can choose the proper length for the piercing," she told me.

"Yeah. Go ahead."

"I need you to be erect. If the barbell is too short, you're going to be in a world of pain the first time you get hard."

"Right. That makes sense." I watched her face for a moment. "Do I just—"

"I'll step out. You call when you're ready." She walked out and closed the door behind her.

I was left with my flaccid dick hanging out of my pants, a lost look on my face.

I had considered getting the apadravya for a while and had done the research on healing and care after the fact. I must have skipped over the part where I had to jerk off in the shop. Had other men sat in this reclined chair—like at a dentist's office—and tugged it? That launched me right off the thing.

In the middle of the small room, I stood with my pants open

around my hips. Every black wall was covered in sketches and various photos of happy customers; among them were a few images of disembodied breasts with rings or barbells in them. Those weren't bad. In any case, I had to just get this over with.

Trying my best to clear my mind, I reached down and massaged my limp cock. I closed my eyes, breathing deeply as I stroked myself with one hand and cupped my sac with the other. For a brief moment, I felt the recent disaster try to invade my mind, but I shoved it aside. Instead, it was me spread over Hadley's naked body. It was my lips at her neck, my back that her nails dragged down. I pumped myself, imagining the warmth of her pussy as I slid in and out, filling her on every thrust.

Yep, that did the trick.

I hung hard and throbbing, no release in sight. Shoving it back inside my boxers, I poked my head out the door and called Mia back in. She was now only the second chick I'd ever let see my junk—a profound moment for me at nineteen. Except this woman was about to put a new hole in the head of my cock. I had to remind myself that I volunteered for this.

She glanced at my hard-on as she closed and locked the door behind her. Unwrapping a marker-type thing from a plastic package, she sat down on her rolling stool and slid over in front of me. I reached in and pulled it out, letting it hang in front of her face. It jumped a little. Fucking embarrassing. But Mia didn't react, just went about her business to measure the distance from the underside of the head to the top. With the marker, she drew two tiny points on either end.

"This is going to look good. I promise." She fiddled around with her instruments for a bit before sliding her stool over again. Holding up a cotton swab soaked in alcohol, Mia gestured at my junk. "You want to do this part? The area needs to be cleaned."

"Have at it," I told her. "Let's just get it over with."

She swabbed around the head of my dick and then up and down the shaft. I winced when she headed for my scrotum next. It was cold, the antiseptic tingling the hypersensitive skin.

"Okay. This is going to hurt. A lot. But I'm quick," she said. "It's just like your tongue piercing. Go ahead and lie down."

I swallowed down a mouthful of nothing and hopped onto the dentist chair.

"So..." Mia rolled her stool over and looked me in the eyes as she gave me the rundown. "I'm going to place a clamp over the head of your penis. I'll use this needle to pierce through the marks I made, then slip the bar through. That's it. Fast and painful."

Her smile was light and encouraging. I laughed out a nervous breath.

"You want something to bite down on?"

"No. I'll suck it up."

"Don't bite your tongue, because I promise you, you'll chomp right through it. And if you kick me, I'll stab you in the eye."

"I'll keep my shit together." Preparing myself, I adjusted in the chair once more. "Ready."

"Okay. Deep breath. And let it out," she said, applying the clamp. It was uncomfortable but not too painful.

Mia lined up the needle to the marks she'd made. "This is the worst of it. Lock it down, MacKay."

I steeled myself.

"Deep breath."

I filled my lungs.

"And let it— "

"FUCK!"

* * *

"Don't worry," Mia said after I came to. "A lot of guys pass out."

I chugged a can of soda to get my sugar up and tried to avoid looking at the bloodstains on the front of my boxers. Why was this shit legal?

"You know the drill: keep it clean, don't remove the piercing." She handed me a printed sheet of paper with the usual care instructions. "Everyone's different, but it could take up to six months to heal. I wouldn't recommend a lot of activity in that area until then."

That wasn't going to be a problem.

A few minutes later, I was cleaned off, bandaged—my cock had bled like Carrie in the shower scene—and putting my pants back on. In the lobby, I found Corey sitting with his knee bouncing. He looked like a terrified about-to-be daddy who'd been kicked out of the delivery room.

"You did it?" Corey wouldn't look at me, afraid I was strutting around with my cock hanging out and a huge, angry piece of metal sticking from both ends.

"Piece of cake. Didn't hurt a bit."

On the way home, we stopped at an overlook off the highway that had a fantastic view of the Pacific shore below.

"I bet you want that drink now," Corey laughed. "I can't believe you went through with it." He spoke over his shoulder, not looking at me while I stripped out of my jeans.

The ride from Bear's shop had been brutal on my wounded dick.

Every pothole felt like a hammer going to town on my shit. My cock throbbed, and not in a good way. I questioned the wisdom of the sadistic act I had allowed Mia to perform on me. Fucking bitch. I didn't mean that, of course, but just the same. Fucking cock-stabbing bitch.

Now dressed in only my boxers, I sat next to Corey on the bench that overlooked the beach below. It was windy and I was almost naked, but freezing my ass off was still better than going home. The barbell in my tongue clicked against my teeth as I contemplated what awaited me there.

"They say it's supposed to feel pretty goddamn great when you have sex," I offered up in my own defense.

At the moment, however, I questioned whether my cock would ever function again. Just the thought of getting a hard-on and trying to stick it inside a tight space, pushing and pulling, was enough to make me nauseated. Life as a monk started to look good.

Corey eyed me with pity.

"Don't do that," I warned him.

He didn't have to say it, so I'd rather he not.

"I'm just saying eventually. At some point."

He stared at me, which was worse than pity.

"Oh, fuck it." My fingers ran through my hair and scratched at the back of my neck. "I'm not there yet, okay? It's been—"

"Two years," he answered. "You told her to move on, and she did. Maybe you should stop kicking yourself and do the same."

"That wasn't moving on," I grumbled. "That was—I don't know—punishment. Where the fuck did she even find that guy? For that matter, why would she bring him to the house if it wasn't to shove him in my face?"

"Those are all good questions. But I think you should stop and consider for a minute that maybe it isn't about you."

"Of course it's about me. It's about us, what I did to her, and the fact that she's stuck with me when she'd rather use my skull as a decorative vase."

"What Hadley said was harsh," he admitted. "But you know she didn't mean it. She was pissed. Dude, you were out of hand back there. Seriously, Josh, what got into you? And why the hell would putting a hole in your dick be the answer?"

"I'm in love with her."

It was the first time I had said the words out loud to anyone except my parents. I had never told her.

"Pretty much always have been."

"So, you want to tell me the real reason why you two used to be Bonnie and Clyde and now you're...whatever the fuck you are?"

I locked up, shut down, and retreated back behind the gates. Corey didn't push the issue, but I knew he was disappointed.

* * *

I walked inside the house with my bare feet covered in grime and my jeans in my hand. When I managed to hobble my ass upstairs, Hadley was sitting against my bedroom door.

"What happened to you?" She grimaced at my appearance.

"I let Mia pierce my cock." I opened the door and stepped around her.

She got to her feet behind me as I went straight for the bathroom and started the faucet in the tub to wash my feet and get some feeling back in my frozen toes.

"You did what?"

"You heard me."

"Yeah, I heard you, but I don't believe it."

I turned around and pulled it out to give her a glimpse of my dick with a gauze cap on it.

"Shit, Josh. I didn't need to see that."

I tucked myself back inside my boxers and sat on the edge of the tub while I let the water run over my dirty feet. Hadley reached past me to grab the bottle of body wash and squeezed it under the faucet until bubbles started to erupt around my feet. She sat down next to me, facing the sink behind my back.

"Why did you do this now?"

"Seemed like a good idea at the time."

"Josh." Hadley sighed in exasperation.

"I don't know." Because I hoped if I ever did use my dick again, maybe the sensation of a piece of hardware would chase off the panic attacks. Something, anything different to disrupt the pattern. "Why do I do any of the stupid shit I pull? I'm fucked up."

"Stop it." She grabbed my bicep, twisting me until I looked at her. "You can't use that excuse with me. Honestly, I'm sick and tired of hearing it. Tell me the truth."

I glared at her, those accusatory eyes that saw right through me.

"The same reason I asked you to draw this." I pointed at the raven on my chest. "The same reason I got the fucking tattoo. The same reason I pulled that sweaty dipshit off of you. What magic truth do you think there is?"

Hadley bowed her head, exhaling as she closed her eyes, and took her hand from my arm. "You should go back to therapy."

"Pass."

"I mean it."

"You first."

That had escalated quickly, as was typical. Any time we tried to make up and play nice after an argument, it just turned into a worse fight. We taunted each other, picking at the scabs that only we knew how to find. It was our pattern, and the same reason why we had never—probably would never—get to the part where we talked about the night I'd left her.

I couldn't fathom a day that I'd ever be able to look her in the eyes and give her the real reason. For that matter, I think her patience with hearing a reasonable excuse had long since evaporated. I'd missed my window of opportunity a long time ago.

"I'm sorry I slapped you, Josh."

"I deserved it."

"No, you didn't."

"Oh, yeah, I did. Because I'm sorry I hurt you and made you feel embarrassed in your own home." I looked up, meeting her eyes. "I deserved it, because I'm not sorry about him. I'd do it again. That's just the truth."

"It still bothers you that much?"

Watching some guy screw the girl I loved? "Yeah. It really fucking bothers me."

There. That was honesty. That was opening up. And it made me nauseated.

"And you won't go back to therapy?"

"Not a goddamn chance."

"Then maybe it's time you try."

Hadley slid her hand to the back of my neck and rubbed her thumb back and forth under my ear. There was an odd expression on her face that I couldn't read. It was sort of solemn and hopeful all at the same time. My heart started to pound against my chest, because for just a second, I thought she might kiss me.

Just like that? All could be forgiven, and she'd just take me back if I stopped acting like a jackass all the time?

"How?" I asked.

I'd do anything if we could sweep it all under the rug and pretend it had never happened. Fuck, if she took me back, I guess I could consider going back to therapy if only so I could make love to her without wanting to tear my skin off. I couldn't go through that with her again. I couldn't put her through that.

"Open yourself. Meet someone. You deserve to be happy. Don't let *him* keep that from you forever. Maybe if you tried, you could find a way to get past whatever it is that you're afraid of."

She got up, squeezed my shoulder, and walked out. I stared after her for a while before it sank in. Hadley wasn't offering me a way back to her; she was pointing the way out. I would have preferred she slap me again.

So that's how it happened. Hadley set me loose. After the four months it took my dick to heal, I started trying to find anything compatible in any other woman that would take my mind off her. But my heart wasn't in it. Instead, I found a parade of coeds willing to engage in hollow sex while I tried to put back together the fractured pieces of myself.

Chapter 14

There was no desire in me to go to class today. After sitting through another self-aggrandizing lecture from Dr. Richardson, I was just fucking bored by the idea. Besides, I needed to head over to Vaughn's shop to pick up the new pedal I'd ordered and the drumheads that Corey had been waiting on. So I blew off the rest of the day. My pocket buzzed as I crossed the lawn toward the parking lot. It was a text from Hadley.

I'm over it for the day. Lunch?

Sometimes that girl could read my mind.

Me too. Meet at the car.

When Punky arrived, I was waiting in the car with the radio on and the engine running. She tossed her bag in the backseat, collapsed into the passenger side with a huff, and slammed the door behind her. I watched, careful not to laugh at her, while she wrestled with the seat belt. She was in rare form, and I worried for the well-being of whomever had pissed her off today.

"You okay?" I turned down the radio, looking her over to figure out what kind of angry this was.

"Dr. Shaw called my charcoal collection plebeian and pedantic. I'm not even sure those two things can happen at the same time. It's fucking charcoal. I'm not using a lightsaber to carve statues, for fuck's sake. But maybe I should have put a bigger set of tits on the trees in my landscape. Maybe then he'd appreciate the view. Oh, but Natalie is a genius, because she wears short skirts, flashes her baby cave, and leans over her drawing desk with her enormous tits hanging out!" Hadley punched the dashboard. "Damn it!" She grabbed her fist, curling her entire body around it.

"Easy there, Thundercat." I pried her hand away, holding it in both of mine while I inspected her knuckles and fingers. "You might want to think twice about doing that again. You're not much of an artist without your dominant hand."

"Same goes for musicians."

"Touché."

I kept rubbing her hand between mine. She didn't try to pull away, and I didn't offer to surrender her appendage.

"So why did you call it quits for the day?" she asked.

"Professor Monroe called my jazz composition plebeian and pedantic?"

Punky scowled and stuck her tongue out at me.

"Bored. And trying to write my jazz composition for the final gave me a headache."

"How's your set coming?"

"It isn't."

"How come?"

I shrugged, watching my fingers trace over hers. "I guess I just suck at it."

"Wish I could suck that well at anything."

I looked up, raising an eyebrow to Hadley's choice of words.

She rolled her eyes, pulling her hand back from mine. "Shut up, stupidhead. I want Thai food."

"Perfect."

Hadley turned up the radio. Jack White blared just for her like the universe had aligned to help alleviate her bad mood. I gunned the engine and tore ass out of the parking lot as the breeze filled the car. Punky bobbed her head, chanting along with the lyrics. Watching her out of the corner of my eye, I felt my own irritation subside.

* * *

Jupiter sat in a small strip mall, sandwiched between a Thai restaurant and a sketchy massage parlor. Vaughn, a weathered roadie who had toured with almost every major rock act since the end of disco, was the only man I trusted to work on my guitars.

Vaughn had sold me my prized Gibson Les Paul. The same one he'd taught me to play on. My dad had brought me in here almost every Sunday for lessons as a kid. At first, Vaughn had terrified me, a big man covered in tattoos. I was afraid of most men back then. But I grew to trust him. It was a bit like therapy, which perhaps had been my father's intent all along.

The door chimed as Hadley and I entered. She didn't wait for a word from me before she took off toward the back of the store to browse on her own. Jupiter carried everything. The front of the store held guitars, drums, and the usual suspects. In the back were the makings of a full symphony orchestra. If Vaughn didn't have it, he'd find it for you.

At the front counter, his seven-year-old grandson, Kyle, sat flipping through a copy of *Rolling Stone.* Every inch of wood was covered in scrawl and Sharpie graffiti. My name was on there somewhere, along with Hadley's and a drawing she'd done of us as cartoon lobsters when we were ten.

"Hey, little man." I gave Kyle a high five as I leaned against the front counter. "What's the good word?"

"I can play 'Smells Like Teen Spirit,' but my mom says I'm too loud." Kyle reached up and pushed his curly black hair out of his eyes as he fingered the callus builder in his palm. "She says I'm not allowed to sing that song."

"Why not?"

"She says *libidio* is a bad word."

"You mean *libido*?"

"Yeah. That."

I laughed, looking up at Vaughn as he pulled my new pedal out of the packaging. He was a huge man with long gray hair pulled back into a ponytail—but bald on top—and a beard to match. Faded old-school tattoos covered his hairy arms, the black ink having turned green some time during the Clinton administration.

"What does *libido* mean?" Kyle asked.

"Uh-uh, MacKay." Vaughn pointed one thick finger at me. "You fill his head with this shit, and then I have to hear about it from his mom. Lock it up."

"Sure, but you say *shit* in front of him."

Kyle was a damn guitar phenom. His grandpa couldn't have been prouder. Vaughn's only child, however, was less than thrilled. The metalhead was cursed with a daughter who was more Beyoncé than Joan Jett. Such a shame.

"He hears worse than that at school. Save the vocabulary lesson for puberty, okay?"

I winked at Kyle, taking a moment to inspect the pedal. Vaughn set it back in the box and put everything in a bag for me.

"You still looking for a replacement in your band?" Vaughn asked.

"Why, is Kyle ready to start gigging? I'm not sure I can afford him."

"Can I? That would be awesome!"

"You can't play in bars until you're thirteen," Vaughn answered.

I bit back a laugh as Kyle deflated.

"Why aren't you in school, little man?"

"Dentist appointment. Mom let me skip the rest of the day to hang out with Grandpa."

"You busy supervising, or you want to jam for a while?"

Kyle's eyes lit up.

"Whatever you want," Vaughn told him. "Pick something off the wall."

Kyle knew what he wanted. He went straight for the baby blue Fender Mustang, the same kind Kurt Cobain had often played. This kid had been born in the wrong decade. I pulled down the Jag hanging next to it. Together, we found a spot in the amp room and plugged in, sitting on a pair of stools. By ear, Kyle tuned his guitar until it sang in perfect pitch. Then he cranked up the distortion.

"You take lead," I told him. "I'll do rhythm."

He propped one foot on the rung of the stool and counted us off.

It amazed me to watch him. He never looked at his fingers, knew where they were at all times. They slid so effortlessly over the strings.

I sang as we played together. It felt good, jamming for the fun of it with a kid who was still just discovering the music and learning about himself as a musician. He had that awe about him. Everything was still fascinating and new. I envied that. It was the way I had felt when I was first discovering the piano.

"I wish I could sing like you," he told me. "I don't sound that good."

"Practice. In rock, you don't have to have a good voice, just an interesting one. Besides, your voice is going to change as you get older."

He plucked at the strings, looking around the room. "She's pretty," Kyle said, and nodded over my shoulder.

"Yes, she is."

Hadley had a blue bass guitar in her lap, the same one she always messed around with when we came in here. Her dark hair was tossed over one shoulder, her bottom lip between her teeth. She was beautiful. My fantasy incarnate.

"What's her name?"

"Hadley."

"Is Hadley your girlfriend?"

"No. She's my...We live together."

"But you like her."

I narrowed my eyes at the kid. "We're friends."

"So she's your girl...friend." He gave me goofy smile.

"What about you?"

"I'll let her be my girlfriend."

Clever fucker.

"She's too old for you." I set the guitar down and used the opportunity to steal another glance at Hadley while she wasn't looking. "And I think you might be too young to start dating."

"I think she likes you."

"Oh, yeah? And why should I take the word of a little kid?"

"Because she keeps looking at you and smiling," he said. "Or she's smiling at me and wants to be my girlfriend."

"You're a piece of work, you know that?"

Kyle laughed, pushing his hair back over his forehead. "You totally libido her."

* * *

On a stool in the garage, I sat staring at utter shitfuckery scrawled across the loose pages. When we'd gotten home from Jupiter, I had felt less irritable and disjointed. Something as simple as jamming with the kid, and a nice meal with Punky, had settled me somewhat. When I'd sequestered myself in here to work, I had every intention of making headway on my jazz composition for class. However, my headache returned with a vengeance, my eyes couldn't focus on the page, and the only music occupying my mind was the elusive tune I couldn't pin down.

Nothing. Hours of staring at black marks on straight lines, and I had nothing. Worse than nothing. At one point, I wrote sixteen bars of "Cocaine Blues" before it dawned on me that I was not Bob Dylan. Eighteen bars of some Thom Yorke song.

Was it possible that I had exhausted my supply of talent? Was there a finite number of notational combinations that my consciousness could produce?

In the 1850s, Robert Schumann believed he was transcribing

dictation from Schubert's ghost. He called the result *Variations on a Theme*. At night, he heard choirs and the orchestrations of Beethoven.

Didn't David Berkowitz claim that he received orders to carry out his murders from the demon that possessed his neighbor's dog? What was the difference between listening for the song stuck in your head and a psychiatric hallucination?

A .44 Bulldog revolver, apparently.

Fuck it.

I abandoned the music and walked back inside the house. From the kitchen, I grabbed a glass of water and popped a couple Advil for my headache. Still my vision was blurry around the edges. The shapes and colors in my periphery bled together in liquid waves. Maybe it was the Thai food, but my stomach fought me to keep my lunch down.

It was after 7:00. Hadley would normally have started pulling dinner together by now. Thinking that maybe she was in her own creative cocoon, I headed toward the stairs to check on her. Passing through the foyer, I glanced out the window and saw an unfamiliar pickup truck in the driveway.

"Andre, don't."

My attention jerked behind me to the hallway at the back of the house. It led to my dad's study, the master bedroom, and the music room. My breathing stopped as I listened for confirmation. I had learned this lesson once before: Thou shalt not barge into rooms at the sound of Hadley's voice. Thing was, sound carried in this house.

"I mean it. Don't."

I headed down the hallway.

"What's the big deal?"

"Please get up. We should—"

My feet stopped at the open door to the music room when I heard middle C ring out of my Bösendorfer piano. There he sat, the new Punkyfucker perched on the bench where my mother had died. I hadn't set foot inside this room, hadn't even looked inside, since that day.

Hadley's large brown eyes found mine like a startled deer. "Josh."

"Get out."

Andre turned around, looking me over. "Hey. I hope you—"

"Andre," Hadley warned. "Don't." Her eyes remained locked with mine, a tinge of knowing fear in her expression.

"Get out," I repeated. "Now."

"He didn't know."

Hadley stepped toward me, but I backed away.

"I just wanted to show him my—"

"No." I snapped my eyes shut and took a deep breath. My chest tightened. "What right do you think you have to be in here? This is my goddamn house."

"I'm sorry. I only wanted—"

"She was my mother, Hadley. Do you get that?"

"What's your problem, man? Take it easy."

I ignored Andre, leveling my glare at Hadley's shell-shocked eyes.

"You live here," I told her. "But this doesn't belong to you. You're just my tenant until you get your shit together and move on."

"Calm the fuck down." Andre stood, walking through Hadley's attempt to stay him. "She didn't do anything wrong."

"You play house with me, but this isn't your family," I said. "You cook and clean and pretend you're her, but you're not. Get over yourself, and get your dipshit fuck buddy out of my house."

"Listen, asshole—"

"Andre, no." Hadley turned her back to me and pressed both hands against Andre's chest. "I'm sorry, but you need to go."

"What? You're shitting me. No. Come on. I'll take you to Tom's."

"No," she said. "Please, just go. Please."

Andre scowled as he looked at me over her shoulder; then he stormed out. I waited until I heard the front door slam behind him.

"Stay out of here," I warned her. "And keep your toys in your own room."

* * *

During the hour-long drive into the city, I seethed with unresolved rage. I should have just hit the asshole. By restraining myself, I had exacerbated the symptoms. Without an outlet—the three orders of Jameson hadn't done shit besides dulling my headache—I was a walking bad decision in need of a trigger.

In the greenroom at the Nest, I held a fistful of her hair in one hand. With my back pressed to the drywall covered in posters and graffiti, and my jeans open around my hips, I closed my eyes while the blonde sucked me off.

There was no part of me that thought this was a good idea. I knew better. And yet...sometimes destruction begs destruction. Because Hadley knew what she'd done, she just didn't expect to get caught. Perhaps she'd been going in there for years without me knowing. And that was fine, so long as I didn't see it. But inviting an outsider to sit at Carmen's piano...How was that not a blatant slap in the face? I had never gone so far out of my way to hurt her. Well...except maybe every day for the past four years I hadn't told her the truth.

Fuck.

My head hit the wall with a groan as I felt the back of her throat constrict around me. I tried to come. Clenched my fists and squeezed my eyes shut. I was right there. So close. *Just fucking do it!* My muscles seized, skin crawling. Short, quick, stinging breaths choked my lungs.

I yanked her off me and zipped my pants. Then I bolted for the door, barely able to see straight.

In the alley behind the bar, I got ten feet before throwing up. The putrid brown slush that spewed out of me splashed on the pavement. Shaking, shivering, I stood doubled over against the brick wall, trying to get a handle on myself.

I don't know how long I was out there before I reasoned to go back inside and chase the memories away with another shot or three.

At the end of the hall, just as the door to the women's restroom swung open, I felt a strong surge of panic. Dark brown eyes and a disapproving scowl.

Oh, fuck me.

Trey pushed past Asha. He shoved me up against the wall and decked me right on the chin. I deserved that.

* * *

With a handful of ice wrapped up in a rag and held to my jaw, I sat back in a chair at our usual table. The Nest was far less crowded on a Tuesday night, and the jukebox playlist was shit. Asha glared through thick eyeliner with her arms crossed over her chest. Trey just looked disappointed. Well, disappointed and pissed off.

"Hadley called," he said. "Told me what happened."

"Help me out here. Did you sucker punch me because I went off on her for letting her dildo sit at my mother's piano or because I got a blow job on a weekday?"

I was met with a face full of ice water, courtesy of Asha.

"You've got a lot of nerve," she said.

I wiped my face, flicking the excess water off my hands as Trey settled in to let me have it.

"That girl gave up her whole life for you, and you tell her you're her landlord? The hell, man? That's Hadley, for fuck's sake."

"What part of 'my mother died in that room' is so hard to understand?" My hands shook. Under the table, my knee bounced.

"So that gives you the right to treat her like shit?"

"She knew better."

"Give it a rest," he shot back. "No one could live up to your rules and exacting standards at all times. There's nothing but eggshells around you."

"And yet, here you are, tracking me down." I tongued my lip ring, at least a little thankful that Trey hadn't aimed for my mouth.

"What's that?" Asha leaned forward, grabbing my hand.

"What?" I snatched it back. "Nothing."

"No." She looked under the table at my bouncing knee and then grabbed my hand again. "This. Why are you shaking?"

"It's nothing." I stuck my hands under the table and held my knee down. It was as if doing so forced the anxiety into my throat instead. "I didn't eat dinner. I didn't sleep last night."

"This is bad," she said to Trey. "Really bad. Why haven't you done something about it?"

"I'm right here, Tiny Tim. Talk to me."

"He doesn't want to hear it. Leave it alone."

"No wonder you and Hadley never talk unless you're yelling at each other." Asha planted her face in her hands. "Is this how it is? Everyone pussyfoots around you because they're too scared to call you on your shit or tell you that you seriously need help?"

"Hey, I thought we were on the verge of riding off into the sunset together. What happened to being nice?"

"Fuck being nice." She raised her head. "This is me being your friend. I'm guessing you have a pretty nasty anxiety disorder."

"Asha, you are astonishingly perceptive. Please tell me something I don't know."

Deflated, she sat back in her chair while chancing a glance at Trey.

"I told you," he said. "Reason doesn't work on either of them."

Asha looked down at the stained table. She picked at the nail polish on her index finger because her thumb was already picked over. "Hadley was crying."

"Punky doesn't cry." I flagged down the waitress as she passed by and gestured for another drink.

"You're an idiot if you believe that. But you know what's fucked up? She was mad at herself. Not for all the shitty, heartless things you said to her, but because she knew she'd touched a nerve. It was a mistake, Josh. Cut her a fucking break. She just wanted to show Andre—"

"Punkyfucker."

"—her paintings. Yes, I get it. He crossed an invisible line that he knew nothing about. You've got so many damn buttons that you might as well be mission control. But she didn't do anything to deserve the way you belittled and humiliated her." Asha tossed her hands up, exasperated and soaked in righteous indignation. "Oh, but you're the one who's suffering, so you come down here to drown your sorrows down some chick's throat. Classy, Josh. You're a real peach."

Well, that wasn't the plan when I walked through the door. It just happened that way. I only intended to get drunk alone until I was sure I could go home without breaking something.

"I suppose it's too late to claim she tripped and fell on my dick?"

The waitress came around and set a tumbler of dark liquid at my right, but my mind was still stuck on that one word: *humiliated*. I had humiliated Hadley. In front of an outsider, I had berated her, chastised her, and done my damnedest to hurt her.

Damn it.

I ran both hands through my hair, tugging at the roots. I stunk of Jameson, moldy hallways, and some kind of fruity perfume. The corners of the room sort of spiraled around my field of vision. My headache was back, or it had been there the whole time and I'd just been numb enough not to notice.

"She's hurting, man." Trey leaned forward, softening his approach. "But Hadley's more concerned about you. She only called me because she was worried. I don't know how many different ways I can say this. You need to talk to her. I'd start with crawling on your hands and knees, but then leave your bullshit at the door and have a conversation."

Between Hadley and I, Trey had always been closer to her. He tried to play the diplomat, the conciliator. Mostly, though, he took her side and never passed up an opportunity to tell me all the ways I was fucking up.

I turned my attention back to Asha. "How serious is this thing with Andre?"

Her eyebrows shot up. A secret smile curled up her Cheshire lips.

"Oh, honey. You have no idea. But I like that you're asking. That's good."

"Don't riddle me, Tiny Tim. Answer the question."

"They're very close. Either way, you're running out of time."

"What does that mean? For what? I'm not aware of a ticking clock."

"Then you two have a lot to talk about."

Chapter 15

The drive home was dark, quiet, and entirely too long. Turning down the hidden driveway, I held my breath as the house came into view. Security lights illuminated the exterior, but all was dark inside.

It took three tries to deactivate the alarm with my phone app. It occurred to me when I fumbled to get the key in the front door that maybe I should have let Asha and Trey drive me home.

Upstairs, I stared at Punky's closed door for a moment. There was no light peeking from underneath, just the sound of her moving around inside. A brave man would have knocked on the door and accepted her wrath head-on. For all we'd endured together—for all she'd put up with from me—I owed her that much. If she wanted to kick and scream and throw things at my head, I deserved to stand there and take it.

But I was a spineless shit.

Instead, I walked into my room and closed the door. I ripped off my shirt and tossed my jeans in the overdue pile of laundry, then collapsed against the wall with my head in my hands. Now that the anger and anxiety had subsided, I was left with only guilt.

I had overdone it this time. My verbal assault on Hadley was unwarranted. Sure, she knew my hang-ups about going into that room. She understood why letting some random fuck press his oily fingers to my mother's piano was unacceptable. But she hadn't done it maliciously. If I had stopped for just one second to accept her apology and reasonable excuse, I could have walked away without burning the whole house down with me.

I beat my head against the wall, as if doing so would kill the reactionary part of me that needed to lash out first and make excuses later. The compulsion was like a malignant mass that had grown inside me for too long.

Through the years of therapy during my childhood, I never felt that I was getting better. There was no great epiphany when I took a deep breath, opened my eyes, and saw a world that was less terrifying and threatening. Therapy, for me, had been about managing symptoms and learning to cope. For the most part, I considered the experience a mild success.

To show for it, I had a healthy relationship with my father, Tom, and Vaughn. I managed my anxious response to older males. With effort, I had developed friendships outside of Hadley. I hadn't had a suicidal thought in more than a decade, which was the most favorable endorsement I could offer. I had never turned to drugs to dull the ache; that right there ought to have earned me some sort of certificate of achievement. High school, for the most part, was a positive period in my life. I had my parents, friends, and music, and all looked bright. I should have known better.

My eyes drifted shut and my body went limp with exhaustion.

"Josh?" A voice called to me from the other side of my bedroom wall. "Are you okay?"

"Haven't been in a while." I pressed my ear to the wall. "You?"

"You're drunk."

"Yep."

"And you drove home. You know I should kick your ass for that."

"Don't. The wall is hard. You'll hurt yourself."

"You're an idiot."

"A brilliant idiot," I said. "All the opinions that matter say so."

"Oh, yeah? Your adoring and slobbering critics?"

"Nope. Asha ratted you out. She's Team Josh, you know. I have a mole in your operations."

"Might as well take out a full-page ad on *HuffPo*: I'm Queen Bitch of Your Anti-Fan Club."

I laughed, turning my body to grope the wall. I fucking loved her sassy mouth. "I libido you."

"What?"

"Kyle is a clever little fuck. I think he's smarter than I am. He might turn out to be the next great icon of the counterculture. Oh, and he wants to be your boyfriend."

"Uh-huh. Walk that back a bit. You libido me?"

"So hard," I groaned. "Tiny Tim is going to muzzle me, maybe a ball gag. Doesn't she strike you as the type that carries all sorts of kinky shit in her tool bag? She's afraid I'm going to go all carnivorous on your ass. Full cannibal."

"I...uh...Wow." She laughed, and the subtle vibration traveled through the drywall and tittered against my eardrum. "You're plastered."

"Half plastered, maybe. But you know I can't lie for shit when I'm drunk. It all comes out garbled and out of order, but it's all true."

"Even the part about turning Dr. Lecter on my derrière?"

"Especially that part. No, wait. Did he wear the skins or just eat the organs? I don't want to wear your ass, just take a bite out of it. A couple of bites, maybe. Would you get a tattoo of my bite mark?"

"You want to get one of mine?"

"Fuck yeah. You find a good spot of bare skin, and it's all yours, Punky. I'm your humble canvas."

"You're mental."

"I'm at peace with that."

She was silent for a while, and in the interim, I began to hum. I pressed my palm to the wall, feeling the gentle reverberation tickle my skin.

"I haven't heard that song in a while," she said. "I miss it."

"How can you miss something that belongs to you?"

"Josh, about Andre—"

"Punkyfucker."

"That's colorful."

"I'm rather fond of the term."

"About what happened earlier, I'm sorry. I only let him in there to show him my paintings. I told him not to touch it."

"I know. I lost my shit. But I didn't hit him. That was good, right?"

"Yeah," she answered without inflection. "That was good."

I took a deep breath, flicking my tongue piercing between my teeth. "Everything I said to you was bullshit. I'm a horrible bastard and a goddamn liar. I'd feel a lot better if you came over here and kicked me in the spleen."

"I'd rather knock out your teeth, rip out your tongue piercing, pull your nipple rings out with tweezers, and hook up your apadravya to my car battery. Your spleen is innocent in all this."

"Fuck, sweetheart. I might like it. In either case, I'm at your vengeful disposal."

"How did I know you were going to say that?"

"Because I'm disturbed and you know me better than anyone. Nothing I do surprises you anymore."

"Not true. You're an adventure. I've never been bored a day in my life."

"Glad to be of service." My fingers drew across the stippled texture of the wall between us. "You can punish me. I'll grin and bear it. Just know that I'm sorry and I didn't mean it. I'd take it back if I could. I've never looked at you as insignificant. You're massively significant in my life. If it weren't for you, I wouldn't have a house or a father. This is your home, too. This is your family, whether we share a last name or not. And I know that Carmen loved you like a daughter. She adored you, Hadley. She'd be so proud of the person you've become. There's more than enough of her memory to go around, so fuck what I said before. Fuck me for being a selfish prick. Hadley, I l—"

A ball of Hadley-scented weight dropped in my lap. Her arms wrapped around my neck as her head fell to my shoulder. With a face full of her hair, I held her close. She felt so fucking good in my arms.

Her breath sputtered against my neck. Without pulling away, I reached one hand between us to swipe under her eye. My thumb came back wet with tears. It was like a 12-gauge shell full of buckshot exploded through my chest.

Punky did cry. I made her cry.

"Shh, sweetheart. Don't cry. Not for me."

I held the back of her head and ran my other hand up and down her back, trying my damnedest to figure out which of the horrible things I'd said or done had broken her.

"I'm so sorry, Hadley. I suck. I'm a pathetic asshole who picks on girls because I'm a complete tool. Shh."

"Shut up, shithead. I hate your face."

"I know. It's a stupid, awful, terrible face. I'll happily place it under the tire of my car and let you peel out."

"That might help."

"Did you know that the smell of a woman's tears lowers a man's testosterone level? You get all weepy, and it turns me into a nutless gimp. In fact, I think your tears are especially potent. I can feel my balls receding. I think my hair might be falling out."

"No." She tugged her handfuls tighter.

Fuck, was that supposed to feel so good?

"I like your hair. The hair can stay."

"Okay. The hair can stay. But the testicles are goners."

"And your hands," she added with a little laugh. "It would be a shame to waste all that talent. And your voice. I like listening to you sing."

"I'm always singing to you, Punky. No one else matters."

This felt like progress. With Hadley's head on my shoulder and her arms around my neck, it felt as though we'd gotten over at least a small hurdle. I held her as tightly as she clung to me, appreciating that, for the moment, I had my best friend back. I'd fucking missed her so much, and it killed me to think of all the time I'd wasted.

"Hey, Punky. You feeling better?" I ran my fingers up and down her back, coaxing her to look at me.

"Yeah." She pulled back, sniffling as she wiped her hands over her eyes. "You know, you haven't called me that in years, but you've been doing it lately."

"Really? I call you that behind your back all the time."

"Huh."

There was that confounding syllable again.

"Sorry that—"

"Don't be," I said. "We kinda had a moment there, right? Listening to such a vivid description of my own torture was sort of cathartic."

"Yeah, well, I'm spent tonight. I'll kill you in the morning."

"The thing is, I do my dying after breakfast."

"Naturally."

My stomach growled.

"Did you eat?"

"No. But I drank a lot. Does that count?"

She slapped my arm. "Damn it, Josh. Why not?"

"I wasn't in the mood. Or I forgot."

"Come on." Hadley stood up, holding out her hand. "We can lock up, and then I'll make you something."

"You don't have to." My legs were all pins and needles as I got to my feet. "I'll just microwave something."

"Stuff it," she told me. "I'll make you a grilled cheese. I'm a little hungry, too."

"Lead the way."

* * *

"So," Hadley began as she heated up the skillet on the stove and I cut slices of cheese beside her. "When were you going to tell me about Alexei?"

Never. I hadn't yet come to terms with the fact that I had to attend the damn seminar. I was still holding out for an Ebola outbreak or a bomb threat to shut down the campus.

"What's to tell? He's coming, and the esteemed faculty has demanded my presence. My Friday night is pretty much fucked."

"I know you're stressing out about it."

"Sure," I confessed. I went to the fridge and poured a couple glasses of water for us. "But there isn't much I can do. I'll smile and nod and try to slip out of there as quickly as possible."

Hadley put together our sandwiches and placed them in the skillet. Just thinking about having to tolerate that arrogant bastard brought my headache back, so I popped a couple more Advil.

"Have you told Simon?" She put her back to the stove, crossing her legs as she appraised me.

"No. Haven't talked to my dad in a few days. Oh, I'm meeting Tom at the range on Thursday night. You want to grab dinner with us after that?"

"I would"—Hadley turned around and flipped the sandwiches—"but I've got plans."

"With Andre." Punkyfucker.

"He's picking me up after my last class. I won't bring him here."

I sighed, running my hands through my hair as I stared at her back. "It's fine. You can have guests over. This is your home. I meant that. Just—"

"I know."

"Something about him rubs me the wrong way. He smiles too much."

She laughed, pulling one sandwich from the skillet and turning to hand the plate to me. "Only you would see that as a flaw."

"I don't trust people who smile that much. Anyone that happy is hiding something."

We took our plates and sat at the counter. Hadley bit into her grilled cheese, offering me her full and amused attention as she chewed.

"He went away for a while a few years back, right?"

She nodded.

"Are you sure he didn't go to prison or a psych hospital? He could be a meth head or have killed thirty-seven people in Portland. Did you Google him recently?"

Punky laughed again, slapping her hand over her mouth as she all but choked on her grilled cheese.

"I don't think this is funny."

She swallowed, gulping a mouthful of water to help it all down the pipe. "Yes, you do. I think you like concocting these fantasies."

"Have you looked in the bed of that truck? If he's got an ax or a rifle back there—"

"That would describe most of the people in this town."

"Fine. But I don't like his face."

"You've been spending too much time with Asha."

"No shit."

As I took crunchy, chewy, delicious bites that were too big for my mouth, Hadley slid glances at my sandwich.

"Just take it." I peeled the corner of one triangle off and tossed it on her plate.

She smiled, popping the bite in her mouth.

"So, uh, about Friday," I said. "You want to come with me?"

"Sure."

"Cool."

Chapter 16

After school, I met Tom at the gun range. It was sort of our thing. We didn't meet up for coffee or sit and watch football together on weekends, but this worked. He wasn't much of a talker, and for most of the hour we didn't even look at each other. The two of us in separate stalls, expending frustration at paper targets.

In the years I'd known him, I'd never understood Tom. Not really. He didn't talk about himself or his life before Hadley. I wasn't even clear on how he came to be her godfather. But since the day the state brought the two together, he'd fashioned his life around hers. With that in common, we got along fine.

When my ammo was spent, I cleared my weapon and returned the rental to the checkout cage. No matter that I had never been arrested, everyone in the shop gave me the eye like I might steal something or load up a semiautomatic rifle and go on a merry spree.

Fuckers.

"Is Hadley meeting us for dinner?" Tom asked as we headed to the parking lot.

He leaned against his pickup truck dressed in the same green flannel jacket that I was pretty sure he wore the day I met him.

"I mentioned it, but she had plans with Andre."

"He's not a big fan of yours from what I hear. You two had some kind of run-in at the house the other day."

"Hadley and I had one of our spats. We worked it out."

"He's not a bad guy, Josh. Maybe you could put more trust in Hadley's judge of character."

His phone rang twice before mine buzzed in my pocket. Hadley's number lit up the screen.

"Hey," I answered. "Are your ears burning?"

"Don't freak out. I'm fine."

My entire body went rigid with panic as my pulse accelerated and my breath lodged in my throat. "What happened? Where are you?"

"Calm down. I'm at the hospital. We were in an accident."

My head snapped around to glance at Tom's concerned expression. "Hadley—"

"Are you still with Tom?"

"Yeah," I choked out. "He's right here."

"I assume they called him."

"Hadley was in an accident," I told him.

"One more time: I'm okay. I told them I didn't need treatment, but they shoved me in a room anyway."

"I'm on my way."

"I gotta go," she said. "The nurse is yelling at me."

Then the line went dead.

I was halfway in my car before I yelled out the open door to Tom. "I'm heading to the hospital. She says she's okay."

My tires were squealing out of the parking lot before I was sure he'd heard me.

* * *

I didn't have time to contemplate or obsess over the worst-case scenario. I considered only the distance between the other vehicles' taillights and my front end, my velocity as I turned the corner toward the ER entrance, and making sure to turn off the engine and take the keys before I ditched my car in the pickup lane.

I dared anyone to tow me or slap a ticket on my windshield.

Despite Hadley's reassurance that she was physically unharmed, I knew she had to be suffering. Her parents had been killed in a car accident. I couldn't begin to imagine the fear she must have experienced in those first uncertain seconds of impact. I needed something to destroy. I craved a target that I could punish for putting her through such a horrific ordeal.

She never talked about her parents. Neither of us had ever spent much time mourning our pasts once we had been given a second chance with our adopted families. However, that didn't mean she'd forgotten.

When I found her, Hadley was sitting sideways on the exam bed with her head bent over her phone. I lunged at her before she noticed me enter and wrapped my arms around her back with her hands trapped between us. Just the feeling of her against my body released all of the tension from my muscles. I breathed her in, exhaling in relief.

"Hi there," she laughed against my shoulder. "Miss me?"

"Are you okay?" I didn't move an inch, even as she wrestled her arms free to hug me back.

"I told you, I'm fine. A bump on the head and some bruising from the seat belt. No biggie." Her fingers gripped my back, curling the fabric of my T-shirt in her hands. "I knew you'd overreact."

I pulled away, taking her face between my hands to look her over. "Did they check you for a concussion? Are you in pain? Did they give you anything? What about an X-ray? I can call Simon. You know that sometimes symptoms don't—"

"Josh. Relax." She smiled as she grabbed my wrists and pulled my hands down to her lap. "There are actual doctors who work here and know what they're doing. Said I'm good to go once my ride got here."

I pushed her hair off her face, feeling around the side of her head until she winced at the raised bump. It wasn't that bad.

"A couple deputies came by to get my statement for the report. I haven't seen Andre since they brought him in."

"What happened?" I held both her hands in mine, amazed that she seemed so calm and unaffected.

"It wasn't his fault. We hit a patch of slick road. He was going a little fast, but—"

"Hey, Hadley."

Andre's voice snapped me upright.

Hadley's eyes lifted to look over my shoulder and then darted back to mine. "Josh, don't."

"I can't let this one go."

I charged at Andre standing in the doorway. Shoved him against the wall. "You could have killed her!"

"Back off."

"Fuck you. Do you have any idea what you've put her through?"

"Stop, Josh. Please. It's not a big deal."

"Me?" He pushed my shoulder. "You treat her like garbage. Always have."

"You don't know shit. I'm the one who's been here for her every day. Her entire fucking life, it's been me. You're no one."

"Josh, enough." Hadley wrapped her hand around my bicep and tried to tug me back. "It was just an accident."

"Don't defend him." Andre pulled at her, putting himself between us. "You don't need this guy. He's a train wreck."

In that moment, for a brief mad-rage second, I didn't want to hurt him. I wanted to dismember him. I wanted to destroy the thing that threatened to take Hadley away from me. Not because he had her affection, but because something so simple as riding in a car with him could have stolen her from me forever. And then what the fuck was I supposed to do?

"I'd do anything for her. I'd die for her. You can't even keep her safe for one fucking day. Her parents died in a car crash, and you—"

Andre cut a look at Hadley. She wouldn't look at either of us, her eyes on the floor. I knew that face.

"I guess you don't know her as well as you think you do," he said.

"Hadley?"

"Go wait with Tom."

* * *

On the ride home, I took care to drive at least five under the speed limit. For miles I bit my tongue while Hadley stared at the side of my face.

"Do you want to talk about it?" she asked.

"No."

One hand gripped the steering wheel while the other held tight to the stick shift.

The revelation that she'd misled me for so many years about her parents' deaths felt like a betrayal. I knew every scar on her body and how it got there. She knew the disgusting truth of my past. How the fuck had she lied to me about this? And she had lied.

Giving it some thought, I distinctly remembered asking years ago if she had kept a picture of her parents. She took me into the den at Tom's house—we were maybe ten or eleven at the time—and showed me one that he had framed. That was when Hadley told me with a straight face that they had died in a car crash. As the conversation replayed in my head, I felt the bitterness rise within me.

"Josh..."

"What's to talk about?"

"I'm sorry," she sighed. "I don't even remember—"

"I do. I remember everything, Hadley. You were my best friend."

"Hey." She turned in her seat, taking on a defiant tone. "The one has nothing to do with the other. We were kids and I lied. I'm sorry."

She remembered just fine.

"Forget it." I tongued my lip ring, my shoulders tense as I kept my eyes on the dark road ahead.

"I can't forget it if you're going to be pissy all night. I don't get why this is such a big deal. Just let it go. Please."

"The thing is, I don't think I can."

"So that's the way it is?" she asked. "The past two days, everything we said the other night, none of it means anything now? Perfect. I should have known."

I pulled into the driveway and shut off the car.

"Everyone knew but me, right? Tom obviously knew, and I'm betting Simon did as well. You've lied to me for years, Hadley. Don't make me the bad guy."

I got out of the car and slammed the door. Once inside, I went for the kitchen and the bottle of Advil. The nausea was back, competing with my pounding headache, and the corners of my vision grew dark and fuzzy.

"You are such a hypocrite," Hadley shouted from the foyer as she slammed the front door. "You're the one who shut me out. You're the one who stopped talking to your best friend."

"That's not the same thing." I rounded on her, glaring down at those dark eyes so full of fire. "Don't go there."

"Why not?" She shoved my chest. "I think that's exactly where this needs to go. Let's have it out. Right now. You ran from me without a word. You want honesty? Fine. You first."

"I'm not having this discussion." I turned my back on her, walking away.

My hands shook with anxiety. Sweat gathered at the base of my neck. My chest tightened, my stomach rolling with the memory of that night as it forced itself to the surface.

"Don't you walk away from me," she yelled. "Josh!"

I took the stairs two at a time until I reached my bedroom. I closed the door behind me, collapsing on the bed as my pulse raced. My skin crawled, palms sweaty. My clothes felt too tight, like the shirt collar was suffocating me. In a rush, I tugged and peeled at the fabric until I sat in my boxers. It still wasn't good enough.

In the bathroom, I turned on the shower and stepped under the spray before the water warmed. It didn't matter; I barely felt the temperature either way. One hand pressed to the tiles, I worked to get my breathing under control as I concentrated on pushing back against the images behind my clenched eyelids.

Turning my back on Hadley yet again was not the best course of action, not on a night I had come so close to losing her. Sure, she wasn't hurt in the crash, but a foot to the left or an inch to the right and maybe things would have been different. Nevertheless, I couldn't face her while my body succumbed to the torture of my mind.

For this very reason, I had never tried to explain. I had never bothered to make excuses. I had shut her out. No matter how much I loved her, I was never going to be well enough to be with her. Of course she deserved the truth. I owed her that much. But it was my inability to give it to her that made me a selfish bastard.

I hung my head under the pelting water until my fingers pruned up. After toweling off and dressing in a pair of lounge pants, I picked up the phone to call my dad.

"Josh, hello."

His voice was even, but I detected a stern note buried inside his usual tenor. I sighed, falling on my futon. She'd gotten to him first.

"Just tell me one thing. Did you know?"

"I did. I also advised her some time ago to tell you the truth."

"And she didn't."

"You can hardly crucify her for it. I understand your disappointment, but she has a right to protect herself."

"From me?"

"Whatever Hadley's reason for holding on to this secret, you have to respect her boundaries. I would think you could empathize."

"Don't do that. It's not the same thing. She knows everything about me. Not wanting to talk about the past and lying about it are two different things."

"So they are."

"Will you tell me?"

There was a long pause. My father expelled a breath.

"Forget I asked. It's fine. It doesn't matter."

I couldn't put my father in the middle of this. He loved me, but he loved her as well. Asking him to betray her trust just compounded the problem. However, another question occurred to me. Cryptic warnings had been lobbed my way over the past few weeks. If a change were imminent, Hadley would have informed my father.

"Is Hadley moving out?"

"Son, I think you should speak to her. Now that you've calmed down."

"She is." I sank back against the futon, the implied admission slamming into me. "When? Why now?"

"Josh—"

"She's been planning this for a while and hasn't said a word of it to me. What, was she just going to gather up her stuff one afternoon? I would come home to a note on the kitchen counter with her keys left behind?"

"I sincerely doubt—"

"Damn it! Dad, please. Tell me the truth."

"She's applied for a transfer to Emerson next semester to finish her degree."

My chest collapsed. I couldn't breathe. I'd finally done it. Years of pushing her away, and she'd finally had enough. The past two days hadn't meant anything. She was planning to leave me behind whether I had apologized or not.

"Josh?"

"Good. No, that's good. She should have gone in the first place. I'll apply for a transfer to Columbia and move to New York with you. We can sell the house—"

"We're not selling the house. That was never the plan."

"Fine. Whatever. It doesn't make a difference. I put my life on hold to accommodate her. If Hadley's ready to get on with her life, then so am I."

"Stop it."

"Come again?"

"Don't start with me, Josh. You've dragged this out long enough and we've indulged your behavior until now. Take the night to sleep on it if you must, but tomorrow I want you to sit down with that girl and work out your differences. Tell her the truth, son. I'm not giving you another option."

"Why would you say that? You know—"

"I do know. And because I love you and hate to see you in pain, I've tolerated your refusal to repair your relationship with Hadley. I watched you turn your back on the girl who brought us together and the woman who has been there for you every day since."

"Seriously?" I launched to my feet, at a loss for how this conversation had turned. "I gave up Columbia to stay here and babysit her because Hadley was going to throw her whole life down the drain when she turned down Emerson. I should have moved to New York with you. You're the only family I have left."

"She stayed behind for you."

That stopped me dead in my tracks.

"Hadley didn't turn down Emerson because she was too afraid to move to Boston. She stayed behind because I told her you didn't want to leave the band or the house where your mother died."

My mind filed through dozens of old conversations. The day I wrote my rejection letter to Columbia. Yelling at Hadley about ruining her life. Sitting down with the dean when I accepted my invitation to the university on the stipulation that they accept Hadley as well.

"It was all bullshit," I muttered under my breath. "You set us up."

"I did what I thought was best for you."

"You lied to me! What right do you think you have?"

"You're my son! Goddammit, Josh. You're my son and you've carried this demon long enough. If it weren't for that girl, I'd have nothing. No one. I love you with all my heart, but losing your mother destroyed me. There will never be another woman. I put my heart in the ground with my wife, and there it will remain. I'll never be whole again. I'll never be a complete person without her. I miss her every second of every day.

"I've done you a disservice. I should have put a stop to this nonsense sooner. Your mother wouldn't have let it get this far, but that's why she was the better of us all. You've always been an impulsive and prideful person, but this time it has carried on too long. You're hurting yourself. The two of you need each other. You won't be whole without her."

When I opened my eyes and finally took a breath, I found myself on the floor. My entire body shook and my head pounded.

"Dad..."

"I love you," he said. "You're all I have left. I will always do everything in my power to protect you and see that you are happy. Please, Josh. Don't let her get away. You know as well as I do that she doesn't want to leave."

"What can I say? It's been so long."

"Start at the beginning and just tell her the truth. Hadley will understand if you fill in the blanks. Trust her. She wanted to be there for you then and she will be again. You just have to let her."

I swallowed past the lump in my throat, trying to muster up the same confidence that my father so ardently held.

"I'll try, but—"

"Take the first step. That's the hardest part."

Chapter 17

My father's words echoed in my mind long after the call ended. In the dark, I sat on the floor with my back to the foot of the bed, eyes closed, face buried in my hands. The persistent headache that had plagued me for days returned, joined by the anxiety crawling under my skin and nausea turning my stomach.

I thought about going downstairs. I imagined the vacant black piano sitting almost invisible in the dark. Tugging at the roots of my hair, I watched myself take slow, tentative steps inside. Still far enough from the piano that I couldn't quite reach it, I pictured a younger version of myself sitting at the keys.

Beside me, my mother walked in and took a seat at the bench. She smiled while I played, brushing my messy hair off my forehead with gentle fingers. With an audience, I sat up straighter to assume a proper posture. My fingers traveled the keys. Carmen knew the tune well—I'd written it for her—and hummed along with the melody. She had the sweetest voice, a delicate and angelic soprano.

But the lighting changed. Where once it was daylight, the clouds coalesced around the house to shutter the sun and leave behind a gray wash. Her song transitioned. I sat taller, older. Carmen's skin turned pale. Glancing at her, I saw the discomfort in her unfocused eyes. Her hand reached out to grab mine from the keys.

"Mom?" I held her shoulders, searching her anguished face. "What's wrong?"

She didn't respond as the last remnants of color fell from her cheeks and sweat gathered on her forehead.

"Mom." I captured her face between my hands. Worry wrung my heart as I began to panic.

She fell limp and lifeless in my lap. Collapsed across my legs. Blood trickled from her nose.

"Mom," I pleaded again, holding her. "Wake up. Please." I wiped the blood from her nose, lightly rubbing her cheek. "No, no, no."

Caramel eyes stared up at me, but they were empty and unresponsive.

"Shit... shit..." I shook her, a futile struggle to reverse the damage and rouse her.

"Dad!"

The sound didn't make it past my lips. There was no voice behind it; my throat held a boulder too massive to move.

"Dad!"

"Josh. Hey, it's me."

My eyes snapped open and landed on the dark vision of Hadley's face inches from mine. Warm hands held my face as she crouched in front of me.

"What?"

"You were calling for your dad." Hadley's thumbs slid along my jaw. "I think you had an episode. How do you feel?"

I filled my lungs with another deep breath, letting my head fall back against the edge of the bed. She released me, dropping her hands to my shoulders, where she continued to run her thumbs over my damp skin.

"Exhausted," I said. "Sorry."

This wasn't the first time, but I hadn't had such a vivid flashback in a while.

Hadley's hands left me, and I sought her eyes. She couldn't leave me yet.

"Stay here," she said. "I'll be right back."

She walked into my bathroom and returned with a glass of water. I drank it in one mouthful.

"Better?"

"Yeah. Thanks."

She sat beside me, resting her back against the end of the bed with her knees curled up to her chest. "I didn't get in."

"Huh?"

"I heard you on the phone with Simon, and I didn't get in. That's why I haven't said anything. It was a long shot anyway. Turning them down once doesn't engender a lot of goodwill. I didn't want to tell you if it didn't pan out."

"When did you find out?"

"A week ago. I guess I'm still licking my wounded ego."

"Fuck 'em. Who needs Emerson? A bunch of pretentious elitists who wouldn't know talent if it shit in their shoes."

Punky snorted a laugh. "Unlike the unpretentious elitists at Columbia, right?"

"Well, yeah. They wanted me, so they have great taste."

"Jackass."

We were quiet for a moment, perhaps both struggling to figure a way in or out of this conversation as we stared out the windows and the black night beyond them.

There was one question I just had to ask. "Why now?"

Taking a deep breath, she rested her chin on her folded arms. "Nothing had changed. I sent off the application over summer break. I thought..." She paused and turned her attention away from me. "I thought maybe I was holding you back or just making it worse. That if I left, maybe you'd—I don't know—get better or go back to therapy or... something. Honestly, Josh, hitting rock bottom would be an improvement over the last couple of years. This pattern just has to stop. You're barely living."

And here I thought I was hiding it well. "You're right."

Beside me, Hadley deflated.

"But none of that is your fault. That's on me."

"I've felt helpless, you know? And I don't mean I want sympathy or anything. I just...I don't know how to help." Hadley shifted to face me, her eyes sincere and steadfast. "I don't know if you want me to try or if it's better that I keep my mouth shut. I don't know when it's the right time to push or if I'm making it worse. And then sometimes you just piss me off."

"I'm good at that."

"Really good."

"Maybe I pick fights with you, on occasion, just to get you to talk to me."

"That's the dumbest thing I've ever heard." But there was a little smile in her voice, and her eyes told me that she understood. "Maybe we're both idiots."

I wrapped my arm around her shoulder and pulled her closer until her head rested against me. As only Punky could, she'd chased off my queasy stomach and trembling muscles.

Now for the hard part.

"This is going to suck," I warned her.

"A big fat one." Hadley slid one hand across my abdomen and held my waist. "Three days ago we wouldn't have gotten this far."

"You're right. Maybe I should be drunk for this. That seemed to work out well the last time."

"You can be awfully charming when you're wasted."

"Noted."

Like two lungs of the same body, we both took a deep breath and held on tighter. I opened my mouth to begin. This was it. There wouldn't be another opportunity. I wouldn't get a better shot. But Hadley spoke first.

"My parents," she began. "They were murdered in a home invasion. In the middle of the night, my mom came into my room and woke me up, put me in the attic and told me to hide. I've never understood why they didn't come with me. Why wouldn't they hide and wait for the police?

"When Tom first brought me home, I'd lock myself in my room or hide in the attic for hours. When he took the door off the hinges, I started running away. I thought I could make it back to them somehow. Fix it. It wasn't until he took me to see Simon that Tom understood."

"What are you saying?"

"It's not your fault." Hadley sat up, meeting my eyes. "I've slept with my bedroom door locked ever since. I'd wake up in the middle of the night and check every lock in the house. Sometimes two or three times a night. I liked staying here when we were kids and Tom was on the road because nothing bad ever happened to me when you were there, in the foster home. I know that sounds horrible, but I always felt safe with you.

"Tom had me stay over with your family or let you stay at the house because he knew that I needed it. The way I am..." Hadley exhaled, looking down at her fingers picking at the hem of my sweatshirt in her lap. "It's not your fault. I know you blame yourself, that you feel like you have this obligation to me, but it started before that night."

"I made it worse," I argued. "There's no getting around that and I don't want you to make excuses for me. I abandoned you, Hadley. Whether I knew what would happen or not, whether I understood the history, I fucked up. I was supposed to be there. I was supposed to protect you. Tom trusted me." My voice rose until I was all but shouting in her face. "You needed me. I fucked you and left you there. Damn it, Hadley! Why don't you hate me?"

I shoved to my feet, unable to sit still any longer. My muscles twitched with the need to...I didn't know what. But I had to move. I paced the length of my room, the anger building until I stopped and rounded on Hadley now standing at the foot of the bed.

With all the confusion and fury coursing through my veins, I shouted at her. "Why are you taking the blame?"

"Why do you have to be the martyr?"

"Fuck!" I tugged at my hair, continuing to pace. "All this time, Hadley. Years. I've had this thing hanging over my head. I think about it constantly. Did you know that? I think about it until I'm sick to my stomach and then I lash out at you just to get a reaction. Just to get some kind of emotion from you. Hate me or yell at me or tell me I'm a sorry sack of shit. Don't stand there and rationalize that my fucked-up bag of crazy is somehow your fault."

"I took advantage of you."

I stopped short, snapping my eyes to her. "What did you say?"

"You weren't ready and I took advantage of you."

"Fuck off."

This was a bad idea. My fingers tingled like I'd sat on them too long and a chill ran down my spine. I was wrong; I wasn't ready for this.

"Josh—"

Hadley reached for me, but I jerked away from her.

"I was the aggressor," she said. "I instigated it. We went from first kiss to sex in the span of one night and I never stopped to think that maybe we should stop. I didn't take into account what it would do to you. I fucked up," she insisted, "because I wasn't looking out for you. I should have been your friend, but I was selfish and pushed you too hard."

"Are you fucking serious?" I stalked the short distance between us until I hovered over her much shorter stature and glared down. "You don't have that sort of power over me. No one does. I fucked you because you were warm, wet, and willing."

"Don't do that."

The sympathy in her eyes infuriated me.

"I don't believe that," she said, "so don't hide behind the act."

"What act? You've had a front-row seat to my highlight reel. I feel nothing anymore. Sex doesn't mean anything to me. I use women, I get off, and there's nothing more to it."

"I thought tonight we were going to be honest."

I couldn't handle it anymore. I felt claustrophobic. Cornered. My temples throbbed with a near-blinding headache.

"You won't convince me that you're really that person, Josh. If you think fucking through the pain is some sort of desensitization therapy, fine. But I know the real you. You're not as numb or uncaring as you try to project."

Her words, the tone of her voice, were like a blade peeling at my flesh. My legs went heavy, forcing me to step back and fall to the futon. I just didn't have any fight left in me.

"I can't finish at all with another person. I have this sort of mental block that won't let me get there no matter how good it feels. Then I dream about being with you our first time and it has me hugging the toilet in the middle of the night. Horrible panic attacks."

I felt so fucking pathetic saying it out loud. Somewhere in the back of my mind, I understood that I had never wanted to admit as much to Hadley because doing so felt like the final nail in the coffin. Her opinion of me mattered. I knew it was shit at the moment, but showing weakness in front of her was pretty much my least favorite thing. Short of having her, living with the far-fetched fantasy that there could be a future for us had been a small consolation that my heart held on to, no matter how improbable. It got me through the day.

Because I had nothing left to lose, and if I was going to present myself—naked, ashamed, and shivering at her feet—with all my scars and flaws, I looked up into Hadley's sorrowful eyes and said the words out loud. The truth this time.

"Making love to you is the happiest memory I can't stand to think about. Nothing has ever felt so perfect. I was right there, Hadley. I was with you completely. And then I wasn't. That night and every time since, I get to that moment of release and all I see is him standing over me and the things he made me do to him." The way he'd leave me like a used rag on the floor.

Hadley came to stand between my legs. She wove her fingers into my hair at the nape of my neck, anchoring herself there. My hands found their way to the backs of her thighs, skimming her bare skin.

"I pulled over for an hour on the side of the road that night I left you because I couldn't stop throwing up. I couldn't see straight. I damn near wrapped my car around a tree. Every day all I want is to lean on you and get as far away from you as possible. You were the only person I could talk to and the last person I wanted to tell." By the time the words fell out of my mouth, I was almost in tears. "My life didn't begin until I met you. I've loved you every day that matters. I'm so fucking in love with you and you scare the shit out of me."

That was it. I had nothing left. I'd bled my fears dry and felt all the more ashamed, embarrassed, and worthless for the experience.

"Are you scared of me now?" Hadley's voice was gentle as her fingers combed through my hair.

My head lolled into her palms. I was exhausted and unable to fight the simple fact that her touching me was a need I couldn't resist. I was greedy for her.

"No."

I didn't have the energy or good sense to be afraid while both of our open wounds sat exposed to the air.

Very slowly, Hadley hoisted one leg and then the other over mine. "Does this bother you?"

As she sat astride me on the futon, my hands slid up to her ass. I held her, just the lightest touch, but my temperature rose with the feeling of her straddling my hips.

"No," I responded past a mouth full of sand.

"I want to kiss you," she said. "I'm going to kiss you unless you tell me not to. You've got about three inches to make up your mind."

I looked at her, dazed, confused, and in awe. In the dark, Hadley's eyes were their own light. There was no sadness. No pain. She looked perhaps the most peaceful I'd ever seen her.

She leaned forward just a fraction. "One. T—"

I pressed my lips to hers.

My Hadley didn't live atop a pedestal. Neither of us was under any misconception that we were anything but flawed individuals with extensive backgrounds in mistakes and bad decisions. We'd both inflicted pain on each other and suffered our fair share. Despite all of that, and maybe because of it, her lips joined with mine felt like salvation. Her kiss was acceptance. Forgiveness that I felt I needed whether she agreed with me or not.

Hadley's fingers curled around the ends of my hair and tightened. That sensation, that awesome feeling of her asking for me, snapped me out of my own head. Every nerve, every ounce of my mental faculties became focused on reciprocating. I slid my hands up her back and held her closer, her chest pressing against mine. When her lips parted to suck in a quick breath, I was too overwhelmed to stop myself from scraping my teeth across her bottom lip and licking the plump flesh I'd fantasized about and obsessed over for the entirety of my sexually active life.

Hadley's seductive whimper did me in. That was it. That tiny, lustful sound was my breaking point at the very edge of sense. I flipped us over to toss her back to the futon. Hadley writhed under me.

I put up the faintest resistance against my instincts. One more needy moan from Hadley was all it took to break my thin resolve. I ground my cock between her thighs. Jesus Christ, I wanted to taste her. I wanted to slide my tongue along her cunt more than I wanted my next meal.

Shit. I needed to slow down. I hadn't even copped a feel of her tits and I was already eating her out in my mind while my cock looked for a secret passageway past the button closure on my pants and the seam of her shorts. This was how everything went pear-shaped in the first place.

First rule: Don't repeat the same mistakes.

"We should stop." Hadley captured my jaw between her hands, lips swollen and eyes bright.

We both panted as we caught our breath, but all I could do was kiss her again.

Plunging once more into her mouth before nibbling at her lip, I couldn't hold back a small laugh. Hadley forced my face away from hers. When I met her eyes, a confused crease appeared between her brows.

"What's so funny?"

"You," I said. "Me. Us. Get out of my head."

Hadley smiled, scratching her nails through the stubble on my jaw. Fuck, that felt good. My dick twitched against her thigh.

"If you keep doing that..."

"Sorry." Punky put on a contrite expression, though her fingers kept right on goading me.

I lifted one eyebrow.

"Okay, not sorry."

I lunged at her neck, holding her down when she yelped in surprise and pinning her hands above her head. I nipped at her skin, licking the slight flavor of salt from her warm flesh. Hadley arched up, a lustful moan reaching my ears.

"How about right here?" I spoke against her pulse. "My teeth imprinted on your neck."

"Not for all the dead presidents in your trust fund," she answered while shoving at my chest. "I'm not wearing the carnivore's version of a collar around my neck."

"Fair enough. But your ass is still open for discussion, right? Because if that's off the table..." I sat up, offering her my hand to help her stand.

"That's forward, don't you think? I mean you and my ass have hardly made the proper introductions and already you're proposing a permanent partnership?" Hadley shrugged, turning away to saunter toward the door.

So sue me, but I couldn't let her walk away like that. I smacked her ass. She jumped, spinning around with wide eyes.

My answering smile was anything but apologetic. "Nice to make your acquaintance."

Punky stuck up her middle finger and waltzed out of my room. I stood there feeling equal parts smug and uncertain.

"We still need to lock up," she called from next door. "And then I thought you could join me for a sleepover."

"Wait," I said, calling her back.

She stood in the doorway of my bedroom. "What's wrong?"

"Haven't you forgotten something?"

This pit in my stomach had been festering for years. Before we got any further, I needed to hear the words.

"I don't think so."

"Anything you want to say?" I hinted.

"Not that I can think of."

"Come on, Punky. Throw me a damn bone."

Hadley tackled me to the bed. She straddled me, her hands pinning my shoulders back. "You're an idiot."

My hands slid up her thighs to grab her hips. How many fucking times had I pictured this image? Hadley on top of me, her hair loose and soft around her shoulders.

"But you love me."

"Yeah," she sighed, and rolled her eyes. "I love you. The hell is wrong with me?"

I reached up and caught her face, running my thumb over her lips. "Not a goddamn thing."

"Is this still weird?" she asked as her fingers trailed over my shoulders.

"Less so."

"Now will you come to bed with me?"

I wrapped my arm around her waist and sat up. "We are in bed. On bed, at least."

"My bed."

"Does this bother you? It isn't haunted, you know."

Now was as good a time as any to get this ugly topic out of the way. If the subject was an issue for her, I'd set the thing on fire in the backyard, but she needed to tell me the truth.

"I'm not interested in punishing you for every random barfly you've brought home," she said. "I guessed the motivation behind it a while ago. Hell, it was my idea. Not exactly what I had in mind, but I shouldn't be surprised that you took the advice and ran full speed in the wrong direction."

"Not to get all dickish and clinical at once," I said, "but you're the only time I haven't used a condom and, being brutally honest, I couldn't give a fuck about anyone else who's been in this bed."

Granted, I had the market cornered on quantity in this house, but Hadley had never caught an eyeful. If I could get past the memory of Pencil Dick poking at her on the bed next door, surely she could adjust. Or was that the more dickish attitude?

Oh, fuck it.

"I'll get a new one," I conceded before I put my foot any farther down my throat and cockblocked myself for eternity. "New sheets and everything."

Hadley draped her arms over my shoulders, her eyes alight with humor. "No need to wake the AmEx right this second. I was jealous, sure. Can't help that. But it doesn't give me the creeps, like I don't expect specters of booty calls past to circle over my head at night screaming your name."

"That would be terrifying."

"It would. We'd have to move. At that I'd put my foot down."

"No argument."

"I just want you in my bed tonight. Nothing against this one. It was very good to me during the blackout."

I grabbed her hips and rolled us over, both of us lying on our sides. This wouldn't be the last difficult conversation we had, but she needed to tell me what she wanted, set boundaries. Without them, I'd run her over.

"How do we do this?"

"I'm not sure I have an answer for that," she admitted. "But here's what I think: In a totally bent sort of way, it kind of feels like we've been in a dysfunctional marriage for five years and just made up after we both realized we couldn't remember why we were fighting."

I couldn't help but laugh at that. "Go on."

"You're the philandering husband coming to terms with his

midlife crisis and I'm the frigid housewife—getting some on the side from the pool boy because my husband hasn't been in to flush the pipes in years—who set fire to your Ferrari because you asked if we were out of milk, but really because you left a birthday card on the dresser one morning but it wasn't my birthday, and I can only assume your mistress turned twenty-three that day and—"

I pinched her lips together, stupefied at the thorough and unfortunate history. "You've put some thought into this."

She pulled free of my fingers. "No, this shit just comes to me, rolls right off the top of my head."

"Extraordinary."

"I know, right?"

"But you said we make up. The remorseful husband who's recently pulled his head out of his ass and the arsonist wife who, if just a touch psychotic, knows he can't survive without her."

"Yeah," she said. "He comes crawling back with a château in Marseille and a fifteen-carat diamond pendant. The mistress has been indicted for fraud."

"Strangely," I said, "the missing sum is right about the going price for one French château and matching diamond."

"A remarkable coincidence."

"They reconcile over a bottle of fine Scotch and mind-altering sex."

"He's still middle-aged," she quipped. "He shouldn't get his hopes up. Boastfulness has always been one of her turnoffs."

"But they stay together for the kids."

"No kids. Those two lack the moral fiber to raise children."

"Then what's the glue that holds them together?"

"Love," she answered, because it was obviously the right answer.

"And even though he's older and has lost some of the stamina of his youth, he's still got a big dick. She's shallow that way."

I winked at her, but she refused to take the bait, even when it was still pointed right at her.

"And while she might have a thing for pretty flames and be just a touch different," she said, "they're both fucked in one way or another. They don't operate correctly with anyone else. They can't function alone and they don't want to. They are each other's preferred brand of crazy."

"Most people will say they're sick, hopeless."

"Most people are vapid imbeciles," she said. "Besides, they have to stay together for Tango and Cash."

"Tango and Cash?"

"The golden retriever and Chartreux."

"Ah, of course. He loves the damn cat that pisses in his shoes and the slobbering dog that has chewed a hole through every Italian leather briefcase he's ever owned."

"See?" Hadley threaded her fingers through the hair at the nape of my neck, scratching her nails against the grain.

This fucking woman knew exactly how to touch me.

"They're perfect for each other," she said. "And now, after the uncomfortable distance has been put behind them, they fall back into their natural routine, picking up right where they left off."

"That doesn't sound so hard," I said as I brushed her hair behind her ear.

"It doesn't? I was going for horribly painful and embarrassingly awkward. Shit. Okay, let me start again..."

Chapter 18

"I'm going to be late," Hadley mumbled against my lips.

I ignored her, replacing my tongue in her mouth to shut her the hell up. The morning had gone much the same while she attempted to get ready for school and again while she made breakfast. I'd have preferred to stay in bed.

Hadley went slack in my arms, letting me push her up against the wall at the end of a narrow corridor inside the art building. I'd made it two classes before I had to track her down. Now that we'd gotten it all out in the open, I couldn't think past the next time I could touch her.

"Seriously," she whispered. "My professor will have a shit fit if I walk in late."

"Which class?"

Since she was so determined to ramble on, I diverted my attention to her neck and slid my hands around to the small of her back, pushing up my Bad Religion shirt, which she'd borrowed this morning and tied in a knot around her waist. I'd had a hard-on all the way to campus.

"Pho-tah-graphy lab," she stuttered, her voice hitching as I nipped at her skin. "Asha and I are...uh...fuck...going shopping for my dress for the reception after that."

"Take my car," I answered, kicking her foot to the side so I could press between her legs.

I was done listening and slanted my mouth over hers, again claiming her lips. She bit my tongue.

"Fuck, Punky." I bit her lip for revenge and because I'd wanted to bite that damn lip for so fucking long.

"I'm not used to kissing you with a tongue piercing," she said with a smirk.

"And?"

"It's weird."

"Just imagine what it will feel like when—"

Hadley didn't let me finish, but she got the message. Her fists grabbed at my hair, tugging by the roots as she plunged her tongue down my throat. Her leg came up around my hip and I held it there, basically dry humping her like a rutting puppy.

"Smile!" A camera flash went off.

I snapped my eyes to the open end of the corridor and groaned.

"Shit, Asha. You scared me." Hadley dropped her hands and pushed me away. She arranged her shirt, making sure everything was where it should be.

My dick went into hiding from Tiny Tim. Cockblocking bride of Betsey Johnson's Frankenstein.

"Delete that," I snapped.

"Are you kidding?" Asha let the camera hang from the strap around her neck. "I'm having it blown up and framed."

"No," Hadley said. "Delete it or I'll dropkick the camera across the parking lot."

Asha's neon pink lips twisted in consternation and her eyebrows furrowed. "You're not going to let me enjoy this?"

"No," we answered in unison.

* * *

Tossing out the last of the orange chicken I'd bought for lunch—it was marginally better than eating my own shoe and I always regretted ordering from that place—I returned to my quiet corner of the student union reading room.

"MacKay, you handsome bastard, I'm going to kiss you!" Corey didn't have an inside voice. What he did have was the ability to draw unwanted attention for three square miles.

Every head in the room swung in his direction and watched as he came strutting over with Trey right behind him.

"You know you just tanked your chances of ever getting laid again," I said. "By a woman."

He grabbed my arm, yanked me from my comfortable and quiet seclusion, and then squeezed both sides of my face like a fucking goldfish as he smacked a kiss right on my lips. He then threw me back into my chair.

"I love this asshole," he exclaimed to the room dotted with people who looked equally surprised, amused, and irritated that their sanctuary had been disturbed.

"Okay, big guy. Sit your ass down before someone recruits you for a pride parade."

Corey's display of PDA didn't even break the top 20 on the list of most embarrassing moments I'd been subjected to in his company.

He and Trey took the seats across from me. A table of girls nearby appeared fascinated with attempting to discern how the three of us might play out in their homoerotic fantasies. I couldn't help myself.

"He's a bottom," I said.

"Please stop," Trey laughed. "I have a class with that girl." He nodded at the redhead with glasses. "Hi, Jennifer."

"Hi, Jenny." Corey turned in his seat, sliding on that easy grin that made chicks trip over their panties falling around their ankles. "He's kidding. I love tits."

"On that note," I announced. "Let's quit before we're charged with harassment. Yeah?"

"Says the guy who had a certain brunette up against a wall an hour ago," was Trey's retort.

"Thank you, by the way." Corey reclined in his seat, propping his foot up on the short table between us. "I made twenty dollars off Trey."

"For fuck's sake. Will you two please stop running odds on me?"

"Not betting if," Trey explained, "just when. We had a pool going."

"You two need lives. And you," I told Corey, "need a girl."

"Way ahead of you. I'm taking Grace out to dinner."

"I thought she hated you."

Sure, Corey was convinced that Grace was just playing hard to get, but so far Trey agreed with me that "hard" was more like impossible.

"Oh, she does. I'm wearing her down. I fixed her pipes."

I sat up, biting back a laugh. "I'm sorry. What?"

"She hasn't had a working kitchen sink for days. Asha mentioned that the manager at Grace's apartment was being a dick about it, so I went over there and fixed it for her."

"And that bought you dinner?"

"Yep. Tonight, since rehearsal is off. Ironed a shirt, ordered flowers, washed the Jeep—"

"You're going all out."

For Corey, ironing a shirt was a big step.

"She's out this afternoon with the girls on their shopping trip," Trey added.

"You and Asha have plans?" I asked.

"With you two situated for the night, I can get Asha alone for more than a couple of hours."

"Take her. I'm happy to be rid of her."

"So..." Corey propped his elbows on his knees and made the sort of dreamy face one would expect to find on a teenage girl compulsively ogling the flavor of the week on TV. "How'd it happen? What'd you say? How many rooms did you dirty and is it still safe to eat off your kitchen counter?"

"We talked," I said. "After I picked her up from the hospital—"

"Yeah," Trey interjected, "how's she feeling? Hadley texted me last night after they brought her in and I called Corey. We were going to head over there but she told us not to bother."

"She's fine. She's got a bump on the head and some bruises. Nothing serious."

"And Andre?"

"What's to say? If she'd broken a bone, I'd have broken his jaw." My fists clenched. I was suddenly in the mood to punt his face again.

"The way Hadley told it," Trey said, "it was just an accident. Unavoidable."

"And I should thank him for not killing her? Fuck that. I'd be in jail and he'd be in the ground."

"Hey"—Trey put his hands up in surrender—"I get it, man. We'd have helped you hide the body. I'm just saying, maybe cut him some slack."

"I've gotten Punky to and from home hundreds of times without a scratch on her. Why is that so hard?" I closed my eyes and exhaled. "Can we just drop it? I damn near shit myself when she called and I'd rather not think about it anymore. Besides, he's out of the picture."

Trey and Corey shared a pointed look.

"What?" I sat forward, examining them. "I'm not sharing. Hadley damn sure knows that. We put it all out there. She knows I'm in love with her. End of story."

"Everyone but you two idiots knew you were still stupid for each other," Corey said.

"So what's with the fucking look?"

"They weren't dating," he told me. "They're friends."

"She can't fuck her friends, either."

"No, dumbass." Corey rolled his eyes and sighed. "He wasn't sticking it to her."

I winced at his choice of words. "Please don't."

"They're really just friends."

"Bullshit."

"He's gay," Trey announced.

Once again, all eyes in the room turned in our direction.

He lowered his voice. "That's why he moved in with his mom a few years ago. He and his dad had some big falling out. Now his dad's sick, so I guess Andre came back to help take care of him."

"And everyone knew." This was happening an awful lot lately. I didn't care for it one bit. "Jesus fuck, guys. How long?"

"I'm guessing Hadley knew back then," Trey said. "They were close before he moved away. Asha, I think, has known for a while."

"But," Corey added, "I'd like the record to show that we found out this morning. I'd have told you if I knew Hadley had parked herself with a friend of Dorothy."

"Parked?"

"Yeah. Andre, according to Asha, isn't really out. More like he's got a toe out of the closet. So he gets Hadley as his beard to keep the peace with his dad and she gets someone safe that makes her look unavailable. Parked."

I let that sink in. Now it was funny. "I could kiss him."

Chapter 19

"You look fantastic," I whispered against Hadley's ear as I helped her out of the car I'd hired.

We still hadn't mastered the whole leaving-the-house-on-time thing, so we arrived on campus for the seminar just before it started. Hadley filled a flask for the occasion. I planned to have a good buzz going by the end of the night and was well on my way there when we pulled up in front of the music hall.

"You said that already," she answered with a smirk.

I wrapped my arm around her waist, appreciating the soft slide of her black dress under my fingers. It was tight, simple, elegant, and perfect against her tan skin.

"And it's worth repeating."

I maneuvered us to the far side of the courtyard that led toward to the main entrance, avoiding the others walking up from the parking lot.

"Well, you look pretty spiffy, too." Hadley adjusted my tie, tugging on the end. "I'd do you."

"Fuck, sweetheart." I tugged her hips against mine as I backed up against one tall pillar of the covered walkway. "Screw it. Let's blow this scene. What can they do to me if I bail?"

"Tempting." Hadley stared at my chest. She unbuttoned my jacket to sneak her hands inside.

Teasingly, her fingertips brushed over my pierced nipples. I exhaled, pressing my growing hard-on against her lower stomach.

"But then I would have gotten all dressed up for nothing."

"Not for nothing." My hands slid down from her hips, finding the bare skin of her outer thighs and trailing up to the hem. "Leave the dress on if you want. I can reach everything I need right where it is."

"You're awfully sure of yourself."

Fingers continued to glide back and forth across my nipples, making it damn near impossible to restrain myself from hoisting her up and pinning her to the pillar.

"Expecting me to give it up on the first date. What kind of girl do you think I am, anyway?"

"A sure thing."

I lowered my lips to her neck, kissing below her ear and biting at the skin there. Hadley hissed in response, fisting her hands in my shirt.

"I've thought about touching you, kissing you, running my tongue over every inch of your body, for so goddamn long, sweetheart." I licked over the pink skin where my teeth had been, speaking at her neck. "All I've thought about since last night is getting inside you."

"Josh." Hadley whispered my name like a plea.

Her head lolled to the side, allowing me access as I pressed my lips to her warm skin. I ran one hand into her hair, cupping the nape of her neck.

"I still remember what you taste like," I told her.

And I did. Vividly. Hadley shivered in my arms.

"Mr. MacKay!"

Dr. Richardson's sharp exclamation startled Hadley and she went rigid before pulling away. With flat indifference, I acknowledged my professor.

"I do believe that the attendance policy is predicated on entering the building. Perhaps you'd be so good as to escort your date inside."

He said the word like it left a sour taste in the back of his throat. *Date*. That got my back up and I stood straight, taking a step forward. Hadley stuck her arm through mine, holding me in place. I guess the idea to hit him or otherwise jeopardize my enrollment in this university had crossed my mind, but that happened every time I attended his class.

"Works for me," Hadley answered as she smacked a disingenuous smile on her lips. "I get paid either way."

With that, she tugged me along to the entrance.

"You're terrible," I whispered as I paused to hold the door open for her. "And I love you."

"I know."

Since we were among the last stragglers to file into the music hall, Hadley and I took two seats on the far right aisle in the back of the audience just as the dean took the stage. He prattled on for more than ten minutes about recent alumni accolades and the music college's tradition of blah, blah, blah. I tuned him out, instead entertaining myself with running my fingertips over Hadley's bare knee and tracing the goose bumps that blossomed over her skin.

We passed the flask back and forth—discreetly at first and then with an increasing lack of shit-giving—while a panel of two doctoral professors and a guest lecturer went on ad nauseam about the modern landscape for classical musicians and composers.

"Is it just me," Hadley leaned over to ask, "or does the one in the middle look like he could have been featured on *America's Most Wanted* in the eighties?"

I bit back a laugh, squeezing her knee.

"Seriously. Look at that mustache. He looks like a serial killer. You know," she went on as her whisper became less unobtrusive by the syllable, "they show a picture of a guy recently convicted on the news and you're like, 'Yep. He looks exactly like a guy who would cultivate rare orchids, raise chinchillas in his backyard, and keep severed human heads mounted on the wall in his basement.' "

"But he was always so polite," I stated with affected shock. "Willard was quiet and kept to himself. He brought his trash cans in from the curb on time and watered his lawn."

"I blame the schools. And violent television poisoning our youth."

"I heard," I began after taking a swig from the flask and handing it back to her, "that poor Willard's mama used to dress him up in skirts and make him serve tea at her book club meetings every Sunday afternoon."

"Well," she drawled in an exaggerated Southern accent, "I reckon that explains why his mama's head was found fixed atop a fifteen-foot stack of Oprah's Book Club selections on the front lawn of the public library."

"Shhh!"

We both glanced behind us at the chastising sound. It was one of those irritated shushes that came out louder, and therefore more conspicuous, than the conversation it sought to admonish. Hadley lost it; she burst into strangled laughter. I slapped my hand over her mouth, cradling her head to my shoulder to shut her up.

The senior citizen behind us—maybe a member of the faculty or just a local resident who had nothing better to do than attend the public event—could have passed for the unspoken but mutual vision Hadley and I shared of Willard's mother. It was fucking priceless. That face could drive a man to serial murder.

"She's very sorry," I told the woman. "My sister's a bit touched in the head."

She scowled, not softened by what I thought was a charming smile. Hadley tried prying my hand from her mouth, but I wouldn't budge.

"Her crib was lined with lead paint—"

Punky bit me.

"Ow. Fuck," I hissed, and yanked my hand from her teeth.

She'd gotten me pretty good, the feisty shit.

"Behave," I snapped at her.

Hadley's satisfied grin was wide and her eyes were bright with mischief.

"You know what Father said. If you can't control yourself, we'll have to send you back to the hospital."

"I'll be good." Hadley leaned toward me, propping herself up with one hand on the armrest between us. "Please. Don't tell on me. I'll do anything." Her other hand slid over my thigh just as her lips met my jaw.

Goddamn.

"Okay." I took the point of her chin between my thumb and forefinger. "I'll let you play with Mr. Rogers again, but this is the last time I cover for you."

Yes. In that scenario, my cock was named Mr. Rogers. There was no good reason for that.

Punky nodded, making a show to zip her lips and tuck the imaginary key into my breast pocket before primly settling back in her seat with eyes trained to the front.

The guy next to me leaned over. "That's your sister?"

I kept my expression flat, eyes on the stage, and barely tilted my head in his direction. My hand slid up Punky's thigh.

"Twin."

* * *

As the evening wore on, Hadley kept me amused and sauced through the remainder of the lecture and then the following talkback. When the dean again took the stage to announce Alexei, I found that I'd relaxed from my edgy demeanor.

Much to my relief, the dean made no mention of me. I wasn't sure why I had been so convinced that Alexei's presence meant that my name would be paraded out for the audience, begging that I stand for acknowledgment. I hadn't toured in years, and even then it was a small population who would have heard of me. I hadn't been a staple of the morning shows or fluff pieces on the evening news since I was a child. Interest in me was relegated to the audience that followed classical music. Shit, there were four-year-olds in China who were already surpassing my once-bright talent.

I guess that made me an arrogant prick, wrapped up in my own ghost. I wasn't here as a novelty. I wasn't special among this crowd. I was just another student attending a required function. The dean's personal invitation was just a matter of formality he felt obliged to uphold.

Hadley took my hand and entwined her fingers with mine as the audience applauded for Alexei. He crossed the stage, offering a tight nod before taking a seat at the piano. He looked the same—taller, thinner than the slightly overweight kid I'd once known and always despised.

Alexei launched into a selection from Stravinsky's *Petrushka*. It was a good choice, considered the last time Stravinsky was, well, Stravinsky. Alexei played it suitably. He lacked sensitivity to the inherent emotion of the piece, taking the song out of context from the ballet and therefore disarming it of meaning, and he favored his left hand in an obvious way. Alexei played the song for impact. He chose what the listener should feel and when, rather than trusting the intended meaning to come through from the original. And even that manufactured emotion felt inauthentic. His rendition was like asking someone who had never tasted saffron to somehow replicate the flavor. As a person and a musician, he lacked depth. He was emotionally sterile, which was perhaps the greatest offense he brought to the piano.

We were philosophically at odds. I doubted very much that he had any special affinity for music. He touched the keys as a student who had been instructed to do just so. His body was rigid on the bench, immune to the harmonies that poured out from his hands. It had always been my assumption that Alexei played for money, recognition, and because somewhere along the line he'd been told to do so and excel at it in the process.

Of course, one could say that it made me a hypocritical asshole to condemn a man's pursuit of fame and fortune when I had both and required neither. But I hadn't practiced twelve to fifteen hours every day for the checks it had earned me. I hadn't endured muscle cramps and tedious repetition for the satisfaction of my name on a marquee. I played because I fucking loved the piano.

The first time I set my fingers to the keys, I'd been fascinated, enthralled. The first time I performed onstage for a crowd that had paid to see me, I knew I'd found my purpose in life and nothing would ever fulfill me the same way.

I realized then, as I stared down at my leg, that the fingers on my left hand pantomimed the notes while my foot rode the imaginary pedal. My head pounded, either from the whiskey or the persistent agitation I'd felt for the last week. What made me sick? The memory of why I gave up my passion or the effort it took to abstain in favor of nursing my fear and anxiety?

"Baby," Hadley whimpered at my ear, "you said you'd take me to the Taylor Swift concert. There aren't even any words to this song."

I tried for a smile in return, though I'm sure I failed. To her credit, Hadley didn't let it show if she was disappointed that her joke didn't have the desired outcome. I kissed her temple, squeezing her hand tighter.

For the remainder of the performance, my fingers wandered through the air with my tongue piercing flicking through my teeth like a metronome.

* * *

The reception was dry: dry conversation, dry personalities, dry of anything mood-altering to imbibe. We'd finished off the last of the flask while trekking across the courtyard to the reception hall.

Hadley made a valiant effort to dig my demeanor out of the ditch, but I found myself distracted.

"Hey." She tugged the end of my tie, demanding my attention.

We stood off in a corner of the room, doing our best to survive the night unnoticed.

"If you don't at least pretend to stare at my tits or cop a feel of my ass, I will be forced to take drastic measures."

Okay. Now I was listening.

"I'm sorry. I don't mean to ignore you."

"I'm here to distract you and otherwise save you from yourself, right?"

"Essentially. And you've been great company. I'm just—"

"I know. But how can I charm you with my biting wit if you keep scanning the room like someone is going to jump out and attack at any second?"

"Good point."

"Ask me to dance."

"You hate dancing. More to the point, you can't dance. You sort of have this flailing, jerking, Elaine Benes thing that you do, but it definitely isn't dancing."

Punky fisted her hand in the waistband of my pants and tugged me against her chest. With narrow eyes and a low voice she said, "Listen, MacKay. When a woman gives you an invitation to handle her in public, you count your lucky stars and take her to the floor."

Fuck, I loved this girl.

I escorted her to the center of the room where faculty and a few students danced to the live string ensemble. As my mother had taught me, I took Hadley's waist and one hand in mine, leading her through the waltz. She proceeded to step on my feet on every third beat.

"Let me lead," I said.

"I am. I thought you knew what you were doing."

I pulled her body flush against mine, trapping her hand to my shoulder. I could and would command her body. Hadley sucked in a sharp breath, tensing before releasing her muscles to my control. As she relaxed, her head came to rest against my chest.

"Not half bad, huh?"

"This isn't even dancing anymore," she said. "This is just foreplay."

"Sweetheart, leaving the house was foreplay."

"May I cut in?" Alexei asked in a thick Russian accent.

Oh, for the love of Christ. How was it possible that in a single day I could be interrupted three times from wooing—yes, fucking wooing her panties right to the goddamn floor—the woman I needed to bed with a fiery urgency that threatened to cripple my dick?

Seriously. I wanted an answer.

Was this my punishment for years of inaction? Here. You finally have the object of your desire within your grasp. Now the universe will conspire against you and force you into eternal celibacy.

Fuck.

I closed my eyes, held Hadley against my chest, and didn't lose a step as I replied. "No."

"Not even for an old friend?"

Hadley hesitated in my arms. I squeezed her hand, urging her not to react.

"Touch her, and I'll break every bone in your hand," I warned.

Hadley's fingers closed around my lapel.

Chapter 20

Session 6

"And then what happened?" she asked.

I looked up from the ruled lines of my notebook with indifference. Sitting in the cramped office, Not-Doctor Reid appraised me. Not-doctor, because she was only a doctoral candidate assigned to the student counseling center. According to my father, she'd come recommended from my former therapist, who was a colleague of her advisor. Apparently, she was perfect for me. I had yet to figure out why.

"You already know the answer to that," I replied.

She was dressed in a plain casual shirt and jeans. That always bothered me. I hadn't dressed up for our appointment. I never did. Nevertheless, it seemed only proper that the therapist should attempt a look of professionalism. The least Not-Doctor Reid could do was wear a blouse with buttons and a collar while she listened to me confess my soul.

"You fractured his jaw."

"No."

"No? That's what I read from the initial complaint. Is it inaccurate?"

"Not Alexei."

"Right." She glanced down at her iPad. "Gregor. Alexei's mentor."

My fists clenched. I toyed with my tongue piercing, slipping it between my lips. "He approached us next."

"Gregor put his hand on your shoulder."

"Yes."

"That's it."

I didn't respond.

"He put his hand on your shoulder and then you fractured his jaw."

I remained silent.

"How?"

"How? With my fist. I punched him."

"I didn't know that was possible."

"Really?" It felt like she was toying with me, looking for a reaction. "Of course it is."

"One punch."

"Just one," I repeated. "That's all it takes if you do it right."

"Had you done it before? Fractured a man's jaw."

"No."

"But you'd considered it. You'd considered how to do it right."

"I knew I wanted to hit him as hard as I could. I did."

"You describe sex in vivid detail," Not-Doctor Reid observed, pivoting the topic. "Your recent encounters and personal thoughts."

I had no response to that worth lending a voice.

"But not your abuse. You refer to it often, though you hesitate to elaborate."

"And I won't."

The topic was irrelevant to this discussion. For that matter, it was not pertinent to the purpose of these sessions. To avoid criminal charges, I was to submit to counseling twice a week for the duration of the semester, at which point she would deem me fit to continue my enrollment or recommend expulsion from the university. We'd gotten the topic of my lack of remorse for the altercation with Gregor out of the way at the outset. The only question left to answer was whether I was, in fact, a loaded gun primed for violence, and therefore a threat to others and myself.

It was all a bit melodramatic for my taste. It wasn't like I'd attacked the man without a good reason. She was aware of my history.

"Why?"

She wasn't getting an answer to such a stupid question.

"I'd like to hear more." Not-Doctor Reid settled back in her chair. "Are you ready to continue?"

Chapter 21

I leaned against the window of the hired car for which I was now paying overtime after a trip to the hospital to have my broken hand set. Considering the damage and outrage Hadley and I had fled from at the reception, it wasn't that bad. I could still play the gig tomorrow night. It would hurt, but I could manage.

"Why did you lie about your parents?" I asked.

Hadley looked at me first with incredulity and then a scathing scowl. "Really? That's the question you want to ask? Right now? Fuck, Josh. Do you have any idea how much trouble you're in? We should have stayed. You know they called the campus police."

"Yes, I want to know. Yes, I have a pretty good idea to what degree I'm fucked. No, if we'd stayed, I wouldn't have hit him only once."

She slouched beside me. In the front seat, the driver kept his eyes on the road, ignoring us with professional ease.

"I was a kid," she huffed.

"We haven't been kids since we were five."

I had never mourned the loss of my childhood and innocence. It had never occurred to me to do so.

"That's what I told everyone," she answered after a weighted pause. "You didn't grow up like I did. You didn't go to school at first, subjected to other kids. When everyone knows you're adopted, they ask the same question: What happened to your parents? When you tell them it was a car accident, that's the end of the conversation. They assume it was a gory mess and then move on to pitying you in silence."

Hadley looked out the opposite window, her features cast in flickering shadows as we passed other cars on the highway. "What do you suppose they'd say if I told them my parents were murdered in a home invasion? You can't get out of that with a two-word response. 'Were you home at the time? Did you see it happen? Did you scream when you saw the bullet punch a hole in your father's head? Why are you still alive?'" She turned her eyes back to mine. They were cold, tired. "I had told the lie for so long that it was just a reflex. I'm sorry."

I took her hand, tugging her closer until she rested her head on my shoulder. "It's okay. I get it. I just needed to know." I exhaled against her hair, pushing it back over her shoulder. "I didn't care that you'd lied—yes, we were young and I can't hold it against you—but that there was something so important about you that I didn't know. That part hurt."

"Imagine how I felt when you stopped talking to me."

I deserved that.

"This amazing thing happened, and then something terrible, and I couldn't go to my best friend. And because it was you, us, I couldn't talk to anyone else about it either. I've never felt so alone."

"The car battery is still an option," I reminded her. "No time limit on that one."

"It wouldn't be very sporting now." Hadley knocked her knuckles on the cast that stretched up to my wrist. "I'll wait until you're back in fighting shape."

"You want to pretty me up?" I'd gone with a white cast so Punky could color me in.

"Sure." She ran her fingers over the coarse texture. "Maybe a scene from *Lethal Weapon*?"

"Funny."

"Or a design of yellow police tape." She looked up, smirking like child.

"You're a riot. Hysterical."

"So..." Hadley sat up, leveling her inquisitive gaze with mine. "Now that the ice has been sculpted into a lovely, steaming pile of shit, do you want to tell me what the hell happened back there?"

It had been a decade since I'd seen Gregor, but my instinctual reaction to him was just as potent. He repulsed me. Just the misleading smile on his tight lips was enough to incite me to rage.

"He's had it coming for a long time."

I might have been thirteen the last time I saw him. Gregor had been Alexei's mentor and manager for the entirety of his career. That relationship made me uncomfortable at first, for obvious reasons. As the years went on and we encountered one another on occasion, I became more leery.

Gregor was thirty years Alexei's senior, and I was certain now the man had taken a special interest in the boy for more than his musicianship. The last time I was in the same room with the man, he had put his hand on my thigh. It wasn't innocent and it wasn't meaningless. I ran to my father and told him what had happened. We were in Stockholm at the time. Simon canceled the rest of my scheduled dates in the region and we soon boarded a plane home. It was then my father agreed I'd never attend another event where Alexei's name also graced the program.

The ban had held until tonight. He'd put his hand on my shoulder. Hadley understood that much.

"Don't let anyone tell you that hitting never solved anything," I told Hadley. "I feel a lot better. Cheaper than therapy and the results are immediate."

"Simon is going to lose it this time. This is a lot worse than giving Nick a bloody nose in high school."

"Doubtful." I slouched back in the seat, draping my cast over Hadley's lap to trace my fingers along the bare skin on her knee. "I forgot to mention the seminar to my dad."

Hadley's head again lolled to my shoulder.

"He'll be more upset that I went at all. But it wasn't like I wanted to tell anyone why I shouldn't attend."

"Tom—"

"I'm throwing you to the wolves on that one. Run interference for me until I've talked to my dad's lawyers."

"Tell me the truth." Hadley slid her arm under my jacket and across my stomach. "How bad is this thing going to get? Because if they come for you with handcuffs, I might lose my shit and start a standoff."

I laughed, kissing the top of her head. "Gregor can press charges. I might get kicked out of school. Probation at worst if it goes to trial. I can afford to pay him off if needed."

"But you won't."

"No. I won't." I'd rather put a bullet in my head than give that vile bastard a dime or pretend to feel remorse for my actions.

"Josh?"

"Hmm?"

"Are you okay?"

"I am now."

* * *

I tried to sneak a peek at my cast, tilting my head just enough to look toward Hadley as she painted. She smacked my arm and used her body to shield her latest—albeit temporary—addition to her living canvas.

"I'm almost done," she whined. "Stop it."

I lay shirtless and sprawled out on my bed, an old towel under my arm, as Hadley went about her work. We'd gotten home well after midnight. I decided to put off damage control until morning. Instead, we holed up in my room after locking the house and pretended we hadn't a care in the world.

"I heard something interesting today," I said.

"Oh yeah?"

"Yep."

"Want to share?"

"I'm thinking about coming up with some sort of punishment for your secrets."

Hadley didn't miss a beat, just kept right along painting while I stared at the ceiling. I had a headache.

"As it turns out, Andre isn't the Punkyfucker of infamy he was purported to be."

"You drew that conclusion all on your own. I don't recall you ever asking the question outright."

"But you let me assume."

"You can make an ass of yourself all on your own, yes."

"Did you...back then...did you—"

"Turn him gay?"

I glanced in her direction again and got a streak of green paint across my stomach for the trouble.

"No. I can't take credit for that, but thanks for asking."

"That's not what I meant."

"We're friends," she stated as if she was sick of hearing herself say the words. "You could have just asked."

"I didn't have the right."

"Yes, Josh, you did. That's the point."

"Right. Sorry."

Hadley sprayed something over the cast before she shifted her position on the bed next to me. "Okay. Done."

Sitting up, I inspected the result. The landscape was spectacular in its detail, considering the small size and rough texture of the canvas.

"Hadley." I couldn't take my eyes off the painting, turning my wrist over to scan every inch. "This is amazing."

"Don't sound so surprised."

"No. I mean it. Fuck, Punky. You know I think you're beyond talented, but this is incredible."

She leaned closer, admiring her work. "It's the tree house. The one we found the summer after fifth grade."

"I know."

The scene was impossible to mistake. She'd captured the tiny structure nestled inside a massive tree to perfection. It was astonishing.

"You realize I can't ever take this cast off, right? This is too good to ruin."

"That day was the most fun I've ever had."

"Sure. We trudged for hours through the woods hunting for buried treasure. You twisted your ankle, I had some gnarly bite from fuck-knows-what, and then we got lost on our way home. Tom had to send dogs and half the town out after us. We were freezing and soaking wet by the time they found us that night."

"It was awesome. We had an adventure. And even though we never went back there, I held on to the memory."

Her eyes lifted to mine and I saw the glassy swell of tears that formed there. I reached out for her, sliding my hand to cup her cheek.

"For one day, this place was us. I never forgot about it."

"Neither did I. Never, Hadley." I touched my lips to hers. "I love you."

"Show me." Hadley pulled back just enough to look me in the eyes.

What I saw cut me open. She was so vulnerable in her bravery, so beautiful in her need.

I kissed her again and with every ounce of sincere meaning I could imbue into just two lips. I kissed her to say that she had always been mine, and I hers. We'd gotten all mixed up and separated along the way. I would be a better man than that. Hadley deserved someone stronger, someone dependable; I would become that man or die trying.

Freeing her of clothing an inch at a time, I worshiped every perfect surface of her body. Fingers followed lips over the expanse of her stomach. Hands held her breasts when each tight nipple met my tongue. I traveled the ridges and valleys of her collarbone and shoulders, professing my loyalty against her neck.

Hadley lay back on my bed while I descended lower, removing her little shorts, where I caressed her bare thighs and higher. Her entire body quivered as I laved at her sex. I devoured her, cupping her ass and lifting her to meet my mouth.

To every whimper and moan, I doubled my efforts; rubbing against her clit, sucking and tonguing the sensitive spot, watching in fascination when her back arched until she grabbed my head and forced me deeper. She came hard, tugging at my hair.

Climbing up the bed, I shoved my pants free of my legs. My cock strained for her, hard and eager. "Hadley—"

"Don't run from me again," she pleaded. "Just stay with me. Please."

Settling between her legs, I fisted my cock in my left hand and dragged the head through the slick lips of her cunt. I sucked in a breath and clenched my jaw, concentrating on keeping my shit together long enough to make this good for her.

"I'm ready," she said. "Please."

I pushed inside her, groaning through my teeth as she stretched to accommodate me. Fuck, it was too good. She was so goddamn soft.

We kissed and huddled close, her arms and legs wrapped around my back as I made love to my Hadley. Too soon, the need became too much. Tiny whimpers turned to throaty moans. I couldn't hold off any longer.

"Hadley, fuck, I'm coming."

With eyes clenched and my jaw locked, I pumped until I hit my climax. My stomach rolled as the inescapable images assaulted my mind. Every muscle tensed. My skin crawled.

"Josh, look at me. Please."

Her hands grabbed my face and I flinched.

"I'm here. It's just me. No one can hurt you. Look at me."

I barely cracked the seal between my eyelids. Just a sliver of Hadley's face made it inside.

"You're okay. You're okay. It's not real."

She continued to whisper reassurances as I caught my breath and swallowed down the bile on my tongue.

Hadley nursed me through the panic attack. She held me up while we showered together. Back in bed, she ran her fingers through my hair until my body gave up and I fell asleep.

It was better and worse than I had expected.

* * *

The next morning, I woke to the subtle stimulation of Hadley toying with one of my nipple rings. I pulled in a deep breath full of her scent, aware of her warm, naked body curled around mine. My right arm, however, had lost all feeling under her pillow. Perhaps forever. I'd have to learn to live without it, because I had no intention of moving.

"Hey," I greeted her.

"Hi." Hadley's dark eyes smiled. She pressed a kiss to my chest, her middle finger rolling back and forth across one piercing.

"Having fun?"

"These are sort of fascinating." She looked up from under her lashes with a coy tilt to her lips. "I've wanted to do this for a while now. Pretty much since the day you came home with them."

"All yours, sweetheart. Knock yourself out."

Hadley dragged her leg up my thigh, brushing against my erect cock. "You know..." She repeated the action twice more. "I haven't seen it yet. I sort of forgot to look at it last night. The hardware, I mean."

I stuck my tongue piercing out, to which Punky looked at me with confusion.

"It's like that, only it's in my dick."

"Does it...hurt?"

"No. Feels pretty goddamn fantastic."

"I'm not complaining."

She bit her lip. For that, I grabbed her leg and held it against my groin.

"You don't have to ask, Punky. You want to get acquainted, you go right on ahead."

She shrugged. "Eh. Maybe later."

Infuriating ego-basher.

I grabbed her by the back of the neck and claimed her lips, nipping at the bottom one. That'd teacher her. I didn't know what the lesson was, but she learned it.

Taking Hadley by the hips, I hauled her up to straddle me. "Fuck, sweetheart. You're wet."

"I had a very entertaining dream," she replied while pressing her lips to the base of my throat. "But you were still asleep."

"Hence the subtle wakeup call?"

"Something like that."

Her pussy slid back and forth over my cock. She skimmed my

chest, flicking her tongue at one nipple ring and then the other. I thrust up, grinding between her legs. Hadley raised her eyes to mine and I reached down with my left hand to grab my cock, ready to be inside her.

"About last night..."

I exhaled. Mission aborted.

"What do you want me to say?"

"Nothing. That's not what I mean. Just...are you okay? Is that what it's like every time?"

"Just about. Except I do it alone and sometimes I throw up before I can breathe again."

"Was it..."

The stops and starts were getting on my nerves.

"Don't be shy or embarrassed or whatever the fuck else. Just ask. I'll tell you the truth."

"Did I make it worse? By asking you to stay, not letting you handle it your way?"

"No." I pulled her lips to mine and brushed her hair back from her face. "No. Making love to you was the highlight of my fucking year. I'd like to do it again. Often. Now would be good. I can't promise you it is going to get better anytime soon. The panic attacks, not the sex. I mean, I guess that could get better. I thought it was awesome. You tell me what you want—"

She put her fingers over my lips and smiled. "Awesome covers it. By the way, you're a lot bigger than I remembered."

I squeezed a handful of her ass. "You brilliant girl. Now just tell me you didn't think it would fit and I can die a happy man."

"Nah." She pecked my lips and wiggled her hips on top of me. "I'll save that one for our first fight."

"First?"

She rolled her eyes. "First where makeup sex is an option."

"I think the first time was makeup sex. You did call me stupid-head, if I remember correctly."

"Huh." Hadley kissed along my jaw.

I turned toward her, taking her mouth as she mumbled through my efforts.

"I guess you're right. I'm pretty sure I forgave you, Punkyfucker, so I guess it worked."

"No, no," I protested against her lips. "You kneed me in the balls. That warranted reparations."

I slid my tongue along hers, my left arm holding her waist. And just like that, we were cracking jokes about the night that had ruined our lives for five years. Shit. I never imagined a day when such a thing could be possible. Then again, with Hadley naked in my arms, nothing else seemed important or so scary.

"Wait a minute." I pulled back. "You called me Punkyfucker." I laughed when it sank in.

"Sure did."

"I think I like it. I'm keeping it. Maybe I'll get that tattooed on my dick."

"The hell you will." Hadley tugged on one nipple ring.

I went still. That could go very right or very wrong real quick.

"No names. It's bad luck. You know that."

"Too late."

"What? You didn't. Where?"

She sat back, scanning my torso and arms. I raised my left arm. Hidden in the trash polka illustration she'd designed, Bear had inked her signature that he'd copied from a photograph.

"Josh." She ran her fingers over the image. "I don't know what to say."

"You've always had my heart."

She looked up, biting her lip and failing to hide her sweet smirk. "That's the cheesiest line I've ever heard."

"That? That's what you tell me when I profess my undying love for you? Fuck, Punky. You're killing me."

She laughed, grabbing two fistfuls of my hair and shaking my head. "I love you, dummy."

Our phones rang. We'd been content to stay in bed and put off the inevitable. The inevitable, however, caught up with us all at once. Resigned, Hadley and I turned to opposite sides of the bed and reached for the phones.

"Morning, Dad."

"Hey, Tom."

Hadley moved to get out of bed. I halted her, grabbing her chin to kiss her. She smiled, rolling her eyes to something Tom said, and then shimmied out from under the covers. I was distracted by watching her bare ass saunter out of my room.

"Josh?"

"Hmm?"

I rolled to my back, propping my injured hand above my head on the pillow. It was already starting to itch like a motherfucker.

"I just spoke with Tom," my father answered in that dry, reserved tone that I knew so well.

"Figured." Their tactic now was to divide and conquer.

"You sound tired. Did I wake you?"

"Not really." I decided to ease us into the topic with something more pleasant to start. "We were just getting out of bed."

There was a loaded pause. "I see. Well, I take it the two of you had a constructive conversation."

"Quite," I answered with a smirk.

"Good."

"My hand's in a cast." I brought it down, again scanning Punky's work. It was even better in the daylight. "Boxer's fracture. Fourth and fifth transverse necks of the metacarpal bones."

"The dean gave me a summary of the incident." Another uncomfortable pause. "You fractured Gregor's jaw."

"I had to leave, Dad. It would have been a lot worse if I'd stuck around."

"I understand."

Another uncomfortable span of silence ensued.

"I'm fine. Got it out of my system. Now I just need to know how much trouble I'm facing. Should I turn myself in?"

"Let's not get ahead of ourselves. I will contact our lawyers and they'll follow up. Tell me what happened."

I figured I had better get used to repeating the story. I did so, filling my dad in on the events of the previous evening.

"He touched you." Simon's voice was calm—that violent calm that concealed surging rage.

Yes, he understood.

"This will go away," he said in a clipped tone. "It happened on campus and quite publicly; there's nothing to be done about that. You'll get a slap on the wrist because the university has to act. But don't worry about this, son. That man wouldn't dare face us in a courtroom. Just do me a favor and keep your nose clean for a while."

"I can do that." I was relieved, sure. More than that, I was just so fucking grateful that Simon was my father. "Thank you."

"I'll have an attorney contact you Monday morning."

"Dad?"

"And I'm going to find out why Alexei was invited to campus in the first place. You should have told me. You shouldn't have had—"

"Simon," I interjected again.

He paused.

"I love you. I'm okay. Hadley took good care of me."

"I'm sorry."

"Don't. I would have told you, but it just slipped my mind the last time we talked." For obvious reasons. "He'll be sucking his meals through a straw for the foreseeable future. That makes me feel pretty fucking great."

"I love you, son. And, in this particular case, I'm proud of you."

What he meant was, *I don't condone violence, but I would have liked to run the bastard over with my car.*

"Thanks."

* * *

"Damn it, man. What the hell?" Trey took note of my cast and then leveled an exasperated look my way when I walked into the greenroom at the Nest thirty minutes before our set.

I put my guitar cases in the corner at the end of the couch, then took a seat on top of the counter that stretched along the far wall.

"What, you didn't hear?" Corey pulled out his phone. He swiped his fingers across the screen, taking a seat on the couch next to Trey. "Shit hit Facebook quick."

I had a pretty good idea what was in the video, confirmed by the accompanying background audio.

"That was a hell of a shot, dude. Wait, wait." Excited, Corey tapped the screen a couple times. "This is my favorite part. Right...here."

He stood and brought the phone over. The video was paused at the point of impact, showing Gregor's crumpled skin around my fist.

"That's one for the highlight reel," he said.

"Don't encourage him," Trey said. "Can you even play?"

"I'm good. I spent a few hours practicing in the garage this afternoon. I'm also a little hopped up on painkillers the ER doctor prescribed."

"Who was that guy?"

"Someone I never thought I'd see again. He deserved it."

We spent the next several minutes working out our set list, Trey and I tuning our instruments and getting into show mode. I had to take a piss before the show but found the toilet in the greenroom busted.

Fighting my way through the throbbing crowd, I headed to the restrooms. The mass seemed to inhale and exhale as one being, pulsing forward and back in waves. A cycle that churned people toward the bar counter and spit them back out.

In the hallway, a hand wrapped around my forearm and spun me around.

"There you are." Kate all dolled up in her tempting best.

I tugged my arm free. "I wasn't hiding."

"No, you weren't." She glanced over her shoulder, though we were obstructed from the crowd. "You and your roommate?"

"That's right."

"Won't that get messy?" She pressed her back against the wall, a flirtatious smirk on her glossy lips.

"Things are different now. I'm done with the hookups."

"Really?" She eyed me like a predator who found amusement in my discomfort. "I find that hard to believe."

"I couldn't give a shit. We fucked, Kate. Don't confuse that for knowing anything about me."

"I know you enough."

I turned to walk away, but she grabbed me by the waistband and pulled me back.

"Don't," I warned her.

"We're the same, Josh. That's why we have fun together. You're going to get tired of playing house with her."

"You're not the end all, be all of fucks. Get over it. I love her. Period."

"You can tell yourself that, but we both know you bore easy."

"Maybe we've been fucking the wrong people."

Chapter 22

Session 7

"Were you bothered by that?" Not-Doctor Reid sat in a black office chair that looked more fashion-forward than comfortable.

I'd had it with the stiff upholstered chair and now made my home on the small sofa. I wondered if that was the plot. Adorn the room with lumbar-killing chairs and eventually the reluctant client would be forced to submit to the cliché of the couch. Fuck that. I'd stand for the hour-long sessions before lying down.

"Which part?" My eyes drifted from my notebook to my cast, perusing the details of Hadley's painting.

"Kate's suggestion that you couldn't have a fulfilling sexual relationship with Hadley."

"No."

I pulled a plastic knife from my pocket and shoved it inside the cast, attacking the infernal itch on the underside of my wrist that wouldn't go away. There was something comedic or ironic about that, considering my surroundings, but I decided not to speak it aloud.

Not-Doctor Reid was silent too long. I glanced up, reading her patient expression, which called bullshit.

"Fine. Sure. Yes. It's a crock of shit, so it doesn't matter. We have great sex."

"How would you describe your relationship with Kate to that point?"

"Nonexistent."

"You carried on a sexual relationship," she insisted.

"We fucked. That's not a relationship. There was no relating. There was penetration and as few words as possible."

"But she was the only one you had sex with multiple times, correct?"

"What's your point?" I leaned back, rubbing my good hand through my hair. "Let's clear something up: I hate these leading questions when it feels like you have a particular answer you're trying to pull out of me. Just ask the question outright. We'll get along a lot better that way and our time will be far more productive."

"Okay, Josh. Why, if there was nothing special about Kate, was she the only one you fucked repeatedly?"

"Because she was zero maintenance. No hassles."

"And not because she fulfilled some specific need?"

Sitting forward, I leveled my eyes with the short, curvy woman. Reid had explained during our getting-to-know-you period that her area of study was modern sexuality; curious, considering that it was my anger issues that had landed me here. Thus far, our sessions had concentrated more on my exploits between the sheets than the many misdeeds of my fists.

"What do I need? The vast majority of my orgasms have resulted from the stimulation of my own hand, the exceptions being Hadley.

Even a warm body isn't a need. So, to answer your question: No, Kate did not fulfill a particular need for me that could not have been satisfied by anyone else."

"Then why do it at all?" Reid set her iPad aside, signaling we weren't close to a conclusion on this topic. "Was it only to appease your partner?"

"You overestimate my desire to please them. For that matter, you overestimate to what extent I gave a fuck. They were a means to an end."

"You cared enough to bring them to climax."

There was no smart answer for that. "I wanted to be good at it. That's entirely selfish and vain."

"Was it enjoyable? Fun?"

"Sex isn't fun."

"Not even with Hadley?"

"No. Making love to her is a lot of things, but I wouldn't call it fun. Foreplay is fun. Flirting is fun. Teasing and getting her worked up—those moments fall into the fun category."

"Then I return to my previous question: Why do it at all?"

Enduring childhood in a series of overstuffed foster homes taught me something about the nature of want versus need. We fought for toys, we fought for beds, we fought for food, and we fought for enough personal space to breathe. At five years old, the requirement wasn't much, and yet we still struggled to claim it.

After my first sexual experience with Hadley, I was terrified of sex. For a brief time, I thought maybe I would never have it again. In theory, I wanted to be balls deep in a girl. That fantasy centered around Hadley most often. The reality was far less appealing.

Imagine being a male in his late teens to early twenties. While the hormones went on about their business without any care for emotional sensitivity, I was this paralyzed person unable to act on the most natural instinct. My friends were getting laid. The girl I loved had scratched the itch. I shot loads of frustrated desire down the shower drain. All the while, I was a closeted freak walking among the normals and doing my best to hide the scar I carried.

Along the way, the want for theoretical sex turned into a need to break down the barrier of fear. I wanted to get past the psychological hurdle because I needed to feel whole again. I fucking required proof that I held absolute command over my body. I did it because I had to. I thought, maybe, I could fix myself.

"Kate is an emotional cripple. I had no responsibilities to her. She used me, and I used her because I couldn't hurt her."

Chapter 23

"Damn, sweetheart," I groaned, mumbling against Hadley's lips as she grabbed a handful of my cock through my jeans.

She shoved me up against the front door after it slammed behind us.

"Don't you want to lock up first?" I asked.

The drive home from the Nest had been long and difficult as I processed the evening after our gig, and Hadley did her best to distract me from getting us home in one piece.

She squeezed my sac, just on the narrow line between unbearable pain and fantastic pleasure. "If you don't get in the game, I'm going to start without you."

Shit.

She tasted of pineapple and coconut rum, her skin warm and salty. Punky dragged her teeth over my bottom lip and tugged; that was about all I could endure. I hoisted her off the ground and moved to pin her against the opposite wall. She wrapped her legs around my hips, using her thighs as leverage as she ground herself on my cock. My cast-wrapped hand held her ass while my left grabbed a handful of her tit.

Pulling Hadley from the wall, I carried her to the living room and sat on the couch with her straddling my lap. First, she was relieved of her shirt and bra. Right away, her hands roamed up my chest to my nipple piercings, where she rolled and flicked them between her fingers. Fucking hell, this woman knew how to touch me.

My shirt followed hers to the floor. Though I was enjoying her attention, I had to grab her wrists to restrain her hands behind her back so I could remove the obstacle between my lips and her tits.

"Shit," she hissed as I flicked my tongue over one tight peak. "Your tongue piercing. It's cold."

I did it again, flicking the ball on the end of the barbell back and forth.

"I want you," she demanded. "Now."

"I want your mouth."

I spoke without reserve or forethought. Hadley stared at me longer than was comfortable in this context.

"Or not," I offered instead. Really, it wasn't a deal breaker.

She blinked. A slow smile crossed her lips. Fuck, those lips and the many lewd ways I wanted to use them.

"No, I like the idea," she answered after what was perhaps the longest silence to follow a request for head in the history of fellatio. "I'm not morally opposed to it or anything."

"Morally opposed," I repeated as I wrapped my mind around the concept. "Interesting."

"That's a thing," she insisted.

"I'll take your word for it." Not like I was going to argue with her now. I needed her cooperation, and I wanted to get back to the part where she liked this idea.

"It's just that..." Her eyes dropped from mine.

I released her arms, her fingers wandering over my shoulders. I gave her that, not pushing too hard if she felt the need to retreat.

"I haven't before," she said.

"Good." What other answer was there?

She looked up and rolled her eyes. "You're such a guy."

"That can't be helped."

Yeah, it was a shitty double standard to want to claim the territory first or beat the living shit out of anyone who had gotten there before me. So what?

Hadley smirked. Her fingers traveled up and down my spine just at the base of my neck. I was damn near shivering.

"Is there a trick to it?" she asked.

"Just like a Popsicle."

Hadley's smirk grew menacing.

"Forget that. You chew your Popsicles. Do not bite it off," I scolded her.

Punky's answering pout was both adorable and frightening. "Just a nibble?"

"You have no levels between gentle and vicious—your elevator only stops at one and one hundred. No, sweetheart. You can't be trusted with teeth."

"You're no fun."

"And you're convincing me that I don't want my dick sucked."

She glared, perhaps taking my words as a challenge. "Well, what do you like?"

"There's no such thing as a bad blow job. Suck and use lots of tongue."

Okay, I had heard plenty of tales of poor performances. Short of throwing up while going down on a guy, how bad could those experiences have been? Something about a woman swallowing my cock just struck me as a fucking miracle every time it happened. Divine goddamn intervention.

"So..." Hadley's eyes roamed. "What, like now?"

"Do I need to make an appointment?"

"That would be handy. Gives me time to prepare."

"Prepare? Fuck, Punky. You know what? Forget I mentioned it." I moved to lift her off me.

"No, no." She pushed my shoulders back to the couch, insisting I stay put. "Now's good. I don't have plans. Well, I do, but I figure the one naturally leads to the other, so this is good."

"This is more than stupid. And you're drunk. I think you might be killing my wood."

"Is that like reverse psychology? 'Don't suck my dick.' And then I'm all like, 'No, I'm going to blow you and you're going to sit there and love it.'"

"Okay, seriously. This is the dumbest conversation I've ever had."

"No way," the crazy girl in my lap argued. "I can get way dumber."

"Damn, woman. I swear I'm not baiting you. Stop turning everything into a fight."

"So does that mean you want me to argue?" Hadley huffed, tossing her hair over her bare shoulder. "Honestly, Josh. I can't keep up with deciphering all of your mixed signals."

That was quite enough. Overpowering her, I laid Hadley over my lap and ripped her jeans and underwear down her ass in one swift movement. Her beautiful, soft flesh looked so inviting.

"Punky, shut the fuck up."

"Hey. That's not—"

I bit her ass cheek. Hard.

She yelped but didn't try to escape. "You're an animal, you know that?"

Holding her in place with one arm over her lower back, I reached down to free my cock from my jeans. I exhaled, the pressure finally relieved and yet not nearly gone. My dick lay against my abdomen.

Since my broken right hand was useless when it came to touching her in a pleasurable way, I used my left to slide two fingers through her slit. She was wet, her muscles pulsing as she clenched with need. One finger brushed over her clit and her entire body seized with anticipation. I worked my fingers back and forth, massaging her. Hadley whimpered.

I rubbed her pussy, increasing the pressure against her clit. She muffled a moan and pushed back against my hand. I leaned forward and dragged my teeth over her delicate flesh. I didn't bite hard, just a little tug. My dick twitched and I reached down to rub myself against her thigh. Hadley's back rose and fell on her deep, heavy breaths. I liked her this way: riled, needy, longing for my touch to get her off. No sense torturing her.

Palming her ass, I moved my fingers back to her cunt. I was gentle at first, priming her. But my intention wasn't tenderness. No, I wanted to see her leave claw marks in the leather.

With my right arm holding her still over her lower back, I plunged two fingers to the last knuckle with increasing severity. The harder I pumped, the more she tried to push back, fucking herself against my hand. I watched, enthralled by the sight of her ass bouncing across my lap, her thigh nudging at my cock.

"Faster," she whimpered. "So close."

Determined to get her there, I worked my fingers inside her, finding the spots that made her jump and her entire body seize and quiver. Her back bowed. I held her as she writhed through her orgasm.

"Lie down," she told me. Her hair was stuck to her face, a trickle of sweat down her spine, and her cheeks flushed red. "Lie down."

The goddess of blow jobs did exist and I saw her in that moment. I was her faithful fucking disciple.

I shifted around to rest lengthwise with my head toward one end of the couch. I didn't say a word or move a muscle as she pulled my jeans and boxers down to fully expose my cock. She took it in one hand, stroking me, then licked across the tip, dipping the end of her tongue along the slit. My hips bucked of their own accord. My cock knew where it wanted to be, but I told myself to hold back and let her get comfortable.

Hadley ran her tongue over the crown, along my piercing, and up the length of my dick from root to tip, tracing the thick vein. Without hesitation, she softly sucked the head, pumping me in her fist. Little by little, she took me deeper.

I had my first mild heart attack when Hadley lightly dragged her teeth over the head of my cock. I was so done for. She owned me. I was her eager man-slave. I was also about to come all over her if she didn't cut that out.

"You're too good at this." I held the side of her face, urging her to stop. "I might have a damn stroke, so let me fuck you one last time before I die."

Hadley crawled down the couch and pulled my pants from my legs. Undressed, she sat atop me, facing away. I gripped my cock in my left hand as I dragged the head through her swollen sex. I held myself in place and guided her with my other hand. She slid down, engulfing me in liquid heat and silky softness.

She was so damn tight, already squeezing my dick as she adjusted. I held her hips while she rose up and descended again—slow at first, rocking back and forth, and finding all the places I could touch buried inside her. I watched, enraptured, as her ass bounced on my cock. Content to let Hadley do as she pleased, I relaxed and enjoyed, gripping her round bottom to see my handprints emerge and fade.

"Josh," she whimpered. Hadley's pace increased. She dropped down on my dick with greater force, impaling herself in earnest.

"What do you need?"

"You," she panted.

I sat up just enough to wrap my arm around her waist and pull her backward to rest against my chest.

"Bend your knees," I instructed. "Spread your legs."

I draped my right arm over her abdomen, my other across her chest to grip her shoulder.

"Anything," I whispered against her ear, licking at her neck. "Everything I am, Hadley."

I thrust up, filling her in one strong motion. She moaned, writhing. Her hands fumbled to find somewhere to go, eventually coming up above our heads to grab the edge of the armrest. My hand over her stomach moved lower, rubbing her clit as her deep moans turned to desperate cries.

Feeling her muscles pulse around me, I pinched her clit as I thrust deep and held there, embedded. She tensed, her body seized by spasms, and my name pouring from her lips. Hadley jerked in my arms. I clutched her tighter while her cunt milked me.

"I'm coming," I mumbled, bracing myself for the pleasure and the terrible side effects.

My face buried in her hair, I clenched my eyes shut and held my breath against the visions that assaulted me. Still pumping in short strokes, my body disconnected from my mind, I spilled inside her while trying to force the sickness away.

I still flinched when her hands came up to cradle my face. Too warm and freezing at once, I wanted to crawl out of my own skin and into hers. I wanted to throw up. Really needed to. I swallowed over and over again in an attempt to stay the reflex. No matter what else happened, I wouldn't destroy Hadley and the gift she gave me by letting her see me empty my stomach every time we made love. That was too much to ask her to endure.

Chapter 24

I woke in Hadley's bed, the room dark, with that strange uncertainty if it had been a dream or reality that jolted me from sleep. Reaching over, my hand fell to an empty pillow. Her side of the bed was cold. I rubbed my eyes, looking toward the bathroom. Not there.

Sliding out of bed, I grabbed my boxers from the floor and slipped them on before walking out. Just as my foot hit the first step on the staircase, I heard the shattering sound of glass breaking on the hardwood floor.

On instinct, I darted into my room, pulled out the lockbox from my nightstand, and pushed the loaded clip into my Beretta. Hugging the wall, I descended the stairs. Streams of white poured into the foyer from the security lights at the front of the house, the backside likewise illuminated by floodlights.

In front of the sliding glass doors that led to the back porch, I found Hadley dressed in my sweatshirt, sitting in a constellation of broken glass and rocking back and forth. I clicked the safety on and lowered my gun, hiding it behind my back.

"Hadley?" I approached her from the landing at the base of the stairs, taking several tentative strides to reach her. "What's wrong?" I stopped, backing up to slide on a pair of shoes and grab her sandals from the foyer. "Punky? It's me."

She didn't acknowledge me, staring out the window into the yard. Close enough now, I recognized the blue shards of a vase that had once sat on the end table by the couch. Not a single knickknack of my mother's had ever been moved or rearranged in the house since her death. I forced myself not to react to the broken memento.

"Sweetheart."

When my shoe crunched on the glass, Hadley's head jerked up. I placed my hand on her shoulder and she tensed, flinching away.

"What's wrong?"

"I did it wrong," she replied in a tired voice. "I can't fix it. I can't finish and I can't go back." In a sudden fit, her fist launched at the wall. She didn't react to the pain, sitting otherwise motionless.

That explained the vase.

"I'm stuck."

"How long have you been sitting here?" I crouched down, rubbing one hand up and down her arm.

"I don't know." Her voice broke. "I can't fix it."

"Let me help."

I set the gun down to wrap my arms around her. The second it hit the floor, Hadley's attention snapped to the object. She jerked away.

"It's okay. It's okay," I insisted as she tried to get away. I slid the gun across the floor until it disappeared into the kitchen. "You're safe, Hadley." I shifted to meet her eyes, holding her face between my hands. "Do you understand? You're safe. I watched you, like I always watch. You know I wouldn't let you miss anything, right? All the doors are locked, the windows tight, and the alarm is set. It's just us, sweetheart. I promise."

"I have to check the rest of the locks," she insisted in a panicked voice, "but I can't move. Something's wrong with this one. I can't—something's different."

"What is it?"

"I don't know!" she shouted. The sudden outburst cut through the room and echoed off the walls of the empty house. "I don't know why this lock feels different. I don't know why it woke me up. I don't know why I have to sit here and stare at it but can't just check it and move on. I don't fucking know!"

"It's okay, Hadley. I'll help. We'll start again. I'll stay with you the whole time, okay?"

"No," she snapped. "This one is different. I can't— You don't understand. I know what every lock in this house sounds like, feels like when it clicks. This one," she enunciated, pointing with one rigid finger at the sliding glass door, "is not the same."

"I believe you," I answered. "Tell me what to do to fix it."

"I. Don't. Know!"

She aimed for the wall again, but this time I caught her wrist to stop her. One broken hand in this house was enough.

At a loss for better options, I took a deep breath and prepared myself for war. Giving her no chance to fight me off, I hoisted Hadley into my arms. She struggled, kicking and yelling at me to put her down. She fought me, but I suffered through it until I got up the stairs and dumped her on her bed. She ran for the door. I forced her out of the way to lock it, throwing all my weight up against it to keep her there.

"What are you doing?" she yelled.

"I needed my phone and I wasn't going to leave you alone."

We stood inches apart. Her chest heaved with frantic breaths. I knew I was torturing her, but it couldn't be helped.

"Hand me the phone," I said.

"Get it yourself."

"Damn it, Hadley. Fucking give me the damn phone. I'm not letting you out this door."

She growled, huffed, stomped, and then chucked my phone at my head. I caught it in my right hand and winced at the pain. She had quite an arm on her. Scrolling down my contact list, I made the call. It rang five times.

"Dude, what the hell?"

It was 4:00 a.m. after a gig. Corey was not pleased to hear from me.

"I need your help. Are you sober?"

He'd left the bar earlier than the rest of us, so I had hope.

"Yeah," he answered. He coughed over the sound of sheets rustling. "What's up?"

"I need a new lock for the sliding glass door. Can you go to Walmart and bring it over? I'll pay you back."

"What happened? Where are you?"

"Home. I'd go myself but I can't leave Hadley here and I can't take her out. We're fine, but this needs to be done now."

"Yeah, okay. Whatever you need. I'll see you in like an hour and a half."

"Thank you," I answered with relief. "I owe you big."

"No, you don't." He hung up.

Hadley sat silent on her bed, legs curled up to her chest.

"Will this make it better? You can watch us install it and test it out and everything. Is this is okay?"

Out of an abundance of caution, I texted Corey:

Get every kind of lock they have.

I looked back to Hadley, hoping I hadn't dragged him out of bed for no reason. She just stared at me.

"Sweetheart." I approached with caution. It was a real possibility that she'd slug me or kick me in the nuts. "I'll stay right here and wait with you. I'll do anything you want. But I'm not letting you go back down there to drive yourself crazy."

I waited, searching for any indication that I was doing something right or making a huge mistake.

"Hadley?"

"Play for me," she whispered. "Anything. Just sit here and play for me."

"As you wish," I answered with a wink. "Can I trust you if I grab my guitar from my room?"

She nodded. Because I wasn't convinced, I ran between rooms and back, closing the door behind me. Hadley sat against the headboard and pulled the covers over her legs. I sat facing her, one foot on the floor as I pulled the pick from the first fret and began to strum a guitar version of the first song I'd written for her. Hadley closed her eyes, her fists clenched in her lap so hard her knuckles turned white.

* * *

I had just slipped back into bed when Hadley stirred. Like a cat, she coiled up in a ball around me, then stretched the length of the bed. She looked up through red, tired eyes.

"What time is it?"

"A little after seven," I answered. "You fell asleep and I didn't want to wake you." I brushed her hair back from her face, letting my fingers slide down her neck. "The new lock is on. The old one was rusted out. Some pin in the latching mechanism broke and lodged in there."

"It's fine," she mumbled. She lay her head down again, closing her eyes as her hand skimmed across my chest. "Thank you."

"Of course, sweetheart." I brushed my fingers through her hair, content that the stress had passed.

"I don't want to do this anymore."

"Don't make vague statements that scare the shit out of me this early in the morning."

"Sorry." She draped her leg over my hip. Her fingers stroked down my abdomen and back again. "I don't want to do my thing anymore. I don't want you to let me do it."

That wasn't a fuckload of responsibility or anything.

"Okay." I didn't know what else to say.

"I mean it," Hadley insisted.

"I believe you."

"You're not going to say anything?"

"What should I say?"

"I think this is a pretty big deal. Don't you want to ask why or…something?"

"Why?"

"Forget it," she huffed. Hadley rolled over, turning away from me.

Oh, fuck that.

"Hey." I grabbed her shoulder and forced her to look at me. "I'm right here. I'm listening. Tell me what's on your mind."

Her expression softened, but not as much as I would have liked. She'd woken up in a bad mood.

"I had to move out of Tom's house to feed this thing," she said. "I invaded your house and forced myself on Simon."

I was about to tell her she was an idiot for thinking any such thing, but her glare told me to hold my tongue.

"You spent a fortune rigging this house like Guantanamo, and on top of that you spent years rearranging your whole life to fit my habits. I hated that. I hate it now. Depending on how much of a dick you were being that day," she said with a smirk, "I hated it a little less."

That was fair.

"But dragging Corey out of bed at four in the morning is seriously the last straw. I'm sick of myself, you know? I don't want to be this way anymore."

"That all makes perfect sense to me," I said. "But don't spend a second worrying about Corey, my dad, and especially not me. Screw that noise. We love you. Four in the morning or two in the afternoon, it doesn't fucking matter. If you're serious about this, I'll do whatever you need. I just want you to make this decision for you and not anyone else."

Hadley nodded, biting her lip while she seemed to contemplate that for a moment. "I've thought about it for a while. There was a chance I was going to move out."

I didn't need the reminder.

"I figured I'd just go cold turkey. Maybe it'd feel different in a new city." She sighed, looking away. "Anyway, it doesn't matter. Point is I want to quit."

"What do you need from me?" I wrapped my arm around her

waist to pull her closer. "I can talk to my dad. He'll help us find a therapist."

She shook her head. "No. I can't do therapy. I don't want pills and stupid breathing exercises or whatever else. That would just be substituting one crutch for another. I have to do this my way."

"Okay."

"Don't let me," she said. "No matter how bad it gets—I'm going to have shitty days—don't let me cheat. Don't let me beg or bargain and guilt you into backing off."

"Straight detox is it, then?"

"Yep."

"Will you still love me if I have to tie you up and sit on you?"

Hadley smiled, weaving one hand into my hair and scratching her nails over my scalp. "Will you still love me if I turn into a raging bitch?"

"If?"

She tugged my hair hard. Hadley rolled over me, straddling my hips. "You'll pay for that one."

"Do your worst, sweetheart." I grabbed her hips, pressing her down on my groin. "I'll lie here and take it like a man."

"Damn right."

"Punky?" I took her face in my good hand, running my thumb over her cheek. "I love you. I'm proud of you. And no matter what happens, I'm always here."

"Fuck, MacKay. Go fish your balls out of my backpack, will ya?"

"That's my girl."

Chapter 25

Session 8

"Neither of us slept that night," I informed Not-Doctor Reid. "She was anxious. We had to establish ground rules. Hadley wasn't allowed to touch the locks. None. I would go through the house and check the doors. And she wasn't allowed to follow me. But that night after I'd set the alarm and we were watching TV in bed, Hadley was agitated. She didn't throw a fit or anything, but I saw that she was just shy of losing it. So we stayed awake. I played my guitar for her, we played cards—anything to keep her mind occupied."

"And the next morning?" she asked.

"She waited outside in her car. We had to drive separately so I could meet with my attorney." I smirked, stretching my legs out as I sat back on the sofa. "But you already know how that went."

Reid gave me a polite nod.

She wore a blue button-up blouse and dark gray dress pants with a pair of black heels. It was a vast departure from her usual jeans and T-shirts. I didn't spend a second thinking she'd dressed up for me.

"You got a lunch date or something?" I asked.

Her brow furrowed.

"You look nice. What's with the outfit?"

"I'm presenting the first draft of my dissertation to my advisor."

"What's it about?"

"We're getting off topic." Reid woke up her iPad and crossed her legs.

"I had just left the attorney's office with word that Gregor wanted a payoff. I refused, of course. I walked into Dr. Richardson's class and was promptly sent out to see the student disciplinary board. It was just a preliminary hearing. Since Gregor hadn't filed charges, I was there for them to tell me I was on academic probation pending a formal hearing."

Once Gregor realized I wouldn't part with a dime, he chose to leave well enough alone rather than risk my attorney dragging his name through the mud during a full trial. Above all, Gregor valued his professional reputation, and he didn't want to find out what skeletons I could coax from his closet to parade for the press.

"In the end, you were referred here. Why was counseling an absolute last resort for you?"

"You dress like shit," I told her. When she wasn't all dolled up for her professor, at least. Loose clothes that hid her figure and said to everyone, *Don't look, I'm ashamed of myself.*

Reid didn't look up from her iPad.

"How does someone with body issues decide to study sex?"

She wouldn't so much as glance my way.

"Dressing like you usually do, you don't present the image of someone qualified to tell me all the ways I'm going wrong."

"I'm sorry you find me offensive," she replied as her eyes met mine.

"No, you're not." I leaned back on the sofa. "You couldn't give a fuck what I think of you. You're the one in the leather chair and I'm over here. There is a power structure to this arrangement."

"So it's my implied power that angers you?"

"No. I'd have to fear the consequences to care about the outcome here. Because I don't, you have no power."

Reid sighed, putting her iPad down. "Then why are we here, Josh?"

"Am I wasting your time?" I smirked, tilting my head.

"It's your hour." Reid countered with that bored look she must have practiced in a mirror because it was too damn effective. "I get credit either way."

"You clean up well. The outfit's nice, but it's all wrong on you. Like you're dressing up, playing a part. You don't know what the professional, powerful, polished Not-Doctor Reid looks like."

"Why do you call me that?" She uncrossed and recrossed her ankles as she sat up in her chair.

"You tell me."

"Because it allows you to walk out of here after every session and dismiss our conversations, dismiss me, as total bullshit."

That was the first time she'd cursed while not quoting me. I liked it.

"You assure yourself, seek to remind me, that I don't really know you—no one does—and am therefore not to be taken seriously. We're irrelevant, obsolete. You exert the absolute minimum effort and strive for nothing. You covet nothing. You have no goals, ambitions, or aspirations. You're bored, Josh. And, frankly, you're boring me with your narcissism."

"Just a minute, lady. I can claim many vices and personality disorders. Take your pick. I'll own it. But narcissism isn't one of them."

"With few exceptions, you tick off every characteristic on the list," she informed me with an even tone. "Excessive preoccupation with control, personal adequacy, prestige..." She paused, looking me over. "Shall I go on?"

"You're on a roll. Don't stop now. I love hearing about myself."

"Within the general population, you believe you're better than others, fantasize about power, refer to your past achievements with conceited hyperbole, and expect constant praise and admiration from others. If you don't get it—for instance, not being publicly recognized at the seminar—you rationalize away the expectation and then resent the perceived adoration.

"You state that you have no fear of consequences, which was brought on by a lack of adequate punishment for infractions during your childhood. You miss the emotional cues of others—Hadley most of all—in favor of your own misguided notions. You take advantage of the tolerance of others. You're jealous and assume you are highly envied, have fragile self-esteem, and when you're not assaulting or physically attacking another person, you default to a state of unemotional stubbornness."

"That was a mouthful. Feel better?"

"No," she huffed. "Because it isn't real, and you know that. You really are too smart for your own good. So smart you've conned yourself into believing the lie."

"Which is what, exactly?"

"That for all your ill-conceived endeavors to rectify or normalize your behavior, you are still essentially a victim. You're terrified, Josh. You are more the scared five-year-old boy curled up on a dirty mattress, discarded and crying, than a grown man and a survivor."

My fists clenched and my jaw locked. It took great concentration to keep my knee from bouncing.

"Name one fear you've overcome in the last eighteen years."

"Sex," I hissed through my teeth. "Rabbits fuck like me."

"And you can't ejaculate without curling into a ball and regressing to that same little boy."

She revealed no pride in pulling the trigger on that well-aimed shot. Instead, she resembled an owner putting down a dying, pathetic animal. I stared at her in silence. As if every second I didn't tell her to fuck off and then slam the door behind me proved her wrong.

"I dress the way I do," she added, "because we're here to discuss your sexuality, not mine. You're obsessed with the topic. With good cause. What you endured was abuse, Josh. Not sex. Subjugation. But what if you could change the way you think about your trauma? Let's work toward that goal."

It all came back to fear.

My natural instinct when confronted with fear was to demonstrate power, to exert control over the situation. Depending on the circumstances, control manifested as manipulation, retribution, the need to inflict harm—physically if possible.

"You wouldn't hit a woman, right?"

"Of course not."

"Why?"

That struck me as an unusual question. The answer was obvious, though she wanted something else. I didn't understand what.

"Proper manners aside," she continued, "why not hit a woman who has threatened you or someone you want to protect? You've struck men for less."

"Because..." I was stuck. I didn't have a good answer.

"Would you hit a child or an elderly person?"

"No."

"What do they have in common in your mind?"

I rubbed my hand through my hair and slumped sideways on the sofa, exhausted. "You don't pick on someone smaller, weaker."

"So you view women as weaker."

"No," I groaned. "Don't make me a chauvinist."

"Not at all. But consider that for a moment."

I did. Closing my eyes and laying my arm over my forehead, I went round and round in search of the response Reid intended me to offer.

"I was the only one. I don't know if that's in the notes. Other kids came and went from that foster home. Including Hadley, there were three or four others at any given time. But I was the only one—at least I'm pretty sure—that he abused while I was there. I was also the smallest. It wasn't until I was thirteen that I started to grow into my body, you know? All this"—I gestured over myself—"happened all at once. One day I woke up six inches taller than everyone else. Until Hadley got there, I was also the youngest."

"Go on."

Sliding back farther on the sofa, I exhaled and took a minute to gather my thoughts in some kind of logical order.

"He picked on the runt. And what could I do, right? I had no choice but to take it. And I hate the word *helpless*. So one day I wake up and I'm not so helpless anymore. I got in a lot of fights when I was a kid. Sure, I had anger issues. Have anger issues," I corrected, "but that wasn't the only reason. I picked some of those fights. I started a few. I was the bully. Because I could. Because one great fucking day I woke up and realized I was bigger and stronger than the other guys my age and I didn't have to take shit."

"You ran from Gregor the first time he touched you," Reid said.

My eyes still closed and my cast resting over my face, I nodded. "I was still a kid back then and he was an adult. Not so much the second time around."

I opened my eyes and dropped my arm to the side. It was at that point I realized I'd gone horizontal on the sofa.

"Breaking his jaw wasn't impulsive or an act of sudden rage. I told myself a long time ago I'd make that bastard pay if I ever saw him again. I was just making good on a promise."

Reid closed the cover on the iPad and set it aside. "I neither approve of nor condemn your actions. That's irrelevant. What's important to discern is if you understand where the motivation for violence in these situations originated. Logically, you do. You also understand the difference between rage and reasoning."

"I've got a headache and I haven't slept for shit," I groaned. "Give it to me straight."

"You don't have an anger-management problem, Josh. Neither are you prone to excessive violence as your sole means of conflict resolution. You know what is considered acceptable behavior but do not temper yourself when there are no consequences. There are specific circumstances under which you feel frightened, threatened, or motivated to protect. When you are afraid or perceive a threat, you get angry; that is not unnatural. Rather than treating the symptom, you would be better served by working to eliminate the fear while also retraining your brain to mediate your anger response. Medication can help."

"Right," I exhaled. "I'm just a big pussy."

"So," she continued, "as far as I'm concerned, you can walk out that door a free man. I'll write up my evaluation and recommended that your enrollment continue."

I sat up, wary. "That's it?"

"Not nearly. Unless I told the disciplinary board that you were likely to come back with an assault rifle and five hundred rounds of ammo, you were never in real danger of expulsion. You know that. We're all going through the motions here."

"So what now?"

"Keep our appointments. Come back for our next session and let's really go to work. Commit to meaningful therapy and digging into the topics we've skimmed so far. Do it for yourself and not because anyone is forcing you."

I placed my elbows on my knees, studying Reid as she swiveled back and forth in her chair by the tip of her shoe, just a couple inches to each side. She was too damn excited by the prospect.

"And why do you care either way?"

Reid smirked and then let out a heavy breath. The pretense came down. Like this whole time—weeks now—I'd only met a character she played on TV. A persona she put on just for me.

"I like you. You're fascinating. And I want to help you. More than that, I know I can help if you're willing to work at it." Her back-and-forth swiveling became more animated, teasing and excited. "What's your answer?"

"Well, if I'm so fucking fascinating…" I stood and gathered my stuff.

Reid raised an eyebrow.

"See you next week."

Chapter 26

Thursday evening I stayed late on campus while Hadley went out to dinner with Asha and Trey. When I'd asked my Jazz Composition instructor what it would take to win some time in the music department's recording studio, I thought it was a major favor. Instead, he said he'd sit at the console and give me a few hours.

"Come on in and I'll play it back," Professor Monroe said through the intercom.

I set my acoustic guitar in the stand. In the control room, I took a seat on the couch.

Charles Monroe was a legit jazz and blues authority and underappreciated legend. Though he wasn't a household name outside the scene, the sixty-year-old had played with or mentored some of the greatest contributors to the genre since Art Tatum and Benny Goodman were at their peaks. Basically, the man was a certified badass and a seriously wicked musician.

He leaned back in the rolling leather chair behind the vintage Neve recording console. Together we listened to the recorded playback of the tracks I'd just laid down. Monroe wore about six different varieties of the same plaid shirt with dress pants and leather loafers. Every day. He was a little guy, too. About five foot three and maybe a hundred pounds dipped in solid gold.

When Monroe laughed, which he did often, the sound was harmonic and infectious. His cheeks crinkled up so high his black eyes were nothing more than tiny slits below thick eyebrows. In class, I always preferred to picture him behind a piano with a blue spotlight sparking off the lacquer top and a lit cigarette resting in an ashtray beside a shot of bourbon.

He swiveled in his chair to face me with a hard look. I fidgeted, flicking my tongue piercing between my teeth. One look and I was a nervous fuck.

"Why are you bringing that weak shit to my class when you can write music like this?" he asked with not an ounce of humor.

I was at a loss. In fact, I just stared at him like a deaf moron until he spoke again.

"That"—he pointed toward the recording stage on the other side of the window—"is some serious passion, man. That is music. I'm sitting in here getting chills and thinking about girls I kissed in tenth grade and thirty years ago when my pop died. Where does that come from and why ain't you bringing it with you every time I see you?"

"I..." No, that was much better. A full syllable that time. Frustrated with myself, I ran a hand through my hair. "I've been stuck."

Monroe rolled his chair toward me and leaned forward on his elbows. "It ain't stuck, son. What you laid down in there is all heart and hate and deep soul-searching questions that only have answers in the notes. That sterile bullshit you shill in class is—"

"Bullshit," I stated for him. "Yeah. I know."

"So?"

I leaned back, stretching my legs. "I am stuck. I haven't written anything halfway decent in weeks. But this stuff is old."

"Written for the piano."

"Yeah."

"It shows." Monroe relaxed back in his seat and crossed one ankle over his knee. "But that's how damn good it is. Because those songs still rumble your gut on six strings. What changed?"

I looked up, debating whether to answer the loaded question. Ordinarily, I would have dismissed the topic and shut down. Telling Monroe to fuck off would have made me an ungrateful prick.

"My mom died," I said. "She taught me to play. And some other bad shit happened around the same time. It was a rough period."

"So you quit?" His brow furrowed and Monroe looked at me like I'd told him I'd cut off my own nose to appease the Lord of Daffodils that resided in my anus.

"Well, uh, yeah." My knee bounced. I forced it still with my broken hand and went about tonguing my lip ring instead. "She died on the bench while we were playing together."

He exhaled, shaking his head. "That is rough. I get ya. And grief like that is the best damn reason to keep writing, keep playing. Man, we all got shit. I grew up in the South in the fifties," he told me. "You don't think I got sadness? The world is fucked. Life's a bitch. And music makes it worth repeating every day. Damn, Josh. The best music is written from sorrow. If you don't know that," he said while shaking his head again, "I ain't taught you nothin'."

"It's this." I held out my left hand. The right was no different except it was wrapped in a cast. Suspended in midair, my hand vibrated. "Thinking about my mom, thinking about playing, remembering how she died, this is what happens."

Monroe watched me shake with a critical eye until I dropped my arm in my lap, defeated. I wasn't a musician if I couldn't control my hands.

Following a long silence, he spoke again. "Rusty Grabe said he couldn't play sober. He had stage fright so bad he tossed up in a mop bucket until he passed out before his first set at The Cooler. The man threw fists and would have bit your ear off rather than get dragged onstage without three shots of whiskey. So, one day, the boys and I mixed up some nasty shit. It was black as tar, tasted like charred pig turds, and shoved it down his throat." He laughed, making me smile despite myself. "He got up there and killed.

"And Joey Connor developed Parkinson's. Shook like a leaf from head to toe. So he comes to me after fifteen years and says he can't play live anymore. He can cut records, the engineer can always piece together the good takes, but Joey was too embarrassed to get up in front of a crowd. Well, I told that sumbitch that we'd put his piano on springs and get some big fellas to shimmy the floor underneath him. That way the whole thing balances out."

Monroe turned around and faced the console. "Come by my office after two tomorrow. I'll have this ready for you."

* * *

I missed my father the most when he was home. That logic was all backward, yes. I rarely thought about it during the months we spent talking on the phone. When he came to visit, it was then that I recalled how good it was to have him around. I missed the gleam of fatherly pride in his eyes. The way he hugged me as if every time I let him touch me was a gift. The sincere tone of his voice when he said he loved me. Every time he got on a plane to return to New York, I almost went with him.

My fingers pressed to the frets and my cast-wrapped hand strummed across the strings. I played the same incomplete, disjointed bars of the song that had consumed me for weeks. The chord echoed off the cement wall of the garage, mocking me.

I felt Simon standing behind me in the doorway.

"You can come in," I said. "I'm just messing around." I set the acoustic guitar aside and cleared off a chair for my dad. It was well past midnight. I'd left Hadley asleep in her bed upstairs an hour ago.

"Actually," he said as I turned to face him, "I was hoping my son would have a drink with me." My dad smiled, leaning against the doorway. "Perhaps a cigar."

"Doctor," I said, "I'm surprised at you."

"Little vices, Josh. They're good for the soul."

"You'll get no argument from me."

With a bottle of brandy and two cigars, we retired to the back patio. The air was crisp, a slight breeze carrying the fragrant smoke away. We reclined in the matching Adirondack chairs.

"That one is new," he said. Simon nodded at the tattoo over my ribs.

"Yeah. Got it a few weeks ago. What do you think?" I raised my arm, leaning forward so he could examine the image in the glow cast by the security lights.

"It's...creative."

I laughed, resting back in the chair. "I figured as much."

"Hadley drew it?"

"Of course."

"Any new holes I should be aware of?" The corner of his mouth turned up in that way he had, trying not to appear too amused with his eccentric son.

"Nope. All accounted for since your last visit."

Telling my father about piercing my cock had been the most awkward part of the entire episode. I must have asked him a dozen times over the ensuing months if it would ever fully heal. I blew a ring of smoke, watching the circle of opaque particles widen and dissipate as it traveled. The brandy burned my tongue and warmed my throat, the perfect complement.

"Hadley seems well," Simon said. "She's happy."

"She's glad you're home. It's been a tough week. Some days are better than others."

"I might have noticed a few new dents in the walls."

"There's that. But she's trying really hard. She'll get there."

"And you?"

"I believe in her. I know she can beat this thing. I'm just working to keep it together, you know? Be supportive."

"I have no doubts on either count."

That right there was perhaps the most significant of all the many reasons I loved my father; he had an unwavering faith in me, even if I didn't believe I deserved it. That sort of faith has a way of influencing a person. A man as good and honorable as Simon inspired me to be a better person, if only because letting him down was such an unappealing prospect.

"I'm happy you've agreed to therapy."

"Let's not make a thing of it," I said. "It was a reasonable course of action, considering the circumstances."

"You made the right decision." Simon puffed on his cigar, closing his eyes as his head tilted back. "I miss it here the most when I return."

"I know exactly what you mean."

We sat in comfortable silence until our cigars were only stubs between our fingers and our glasses held more air than liquid. My headache, which had been a constant annoyance lately, dissipated with the tension in my shoulders. I felt relaxed for the first time in a while. Enjoying my father's company, appreciating the serenity of our remote property, was just what I needed.

"Is this a private party?" I looked over my shoulder to see Hadley stepping out to the patio in those damn little shorts and my sweatshirt. Bless that girl. "Menfolk doing men things and all that."

"Come here, sweetheart." I held the cigar between my teeth and grabbed her around the waist, dropping her in my lap. "See? The view just improved."

She rolled her eyes and smiled, embarrassed. "Your son is shameless," she told Simon. "I don't know where he gets it." Hadley yanked the cigar from my mouth and pressed a quick kiss to my lips before taking a drag.

"Never stop courting," he answered. "A touch of charm will earn a lot of forgiveness."

That was my new favorite discovery about her. Punky had always been shit at taking compliments—she used to punch me in the arm for saying she was pretty—but now a few sweet nothings had her blushing like the Pope at a Boy Scout jamboree. It did good things for my ego.

"You love it," I told her.

"You're only half as clever and a third as charming as you think you are," she said. Punky gave me back the cigar, then swiped my brandy snifter.

"That's still twice as good as the next guy."

"Well, I should get to bed," my father announced. Subtle.

"Good night, Dad."

"Night, Simon."

He patted my shoulder as he passed, bending down to press a kiss to the top of Hadley's head. "Good night," he answered. "See you in the morning. And happy birthday." Simon stepped inside and closed the door behind him.

"That's right. It's after midnight." I set the cigar aside and took the glass from Hadley's hand. Taking her cheek in my palm, I brought her lips to mine. "Happy birthday, Punky." She tasted like cigar and brandy, and it was the hottest fucking flavor on her tongue.

"What'd you get me?" Hadley draped her arms over my shoulders, her eyes bright and expectant.

"Not telling. You'll have to wait." I cradled her to my chest, running my hand up and down her bare leg.

"It's officially my birthday. I want my present now."

"Too bad."

"Josh."

"Hadley."

"I want it now," she repeated with a bit more demand in her tone.

"Say it again."

"I want it."

"Oh yeah?"

"Yeah, baby. I want it so bad. Give it to me now." Hadley put on her best porn-voice impression, cracking me up.

"You naughty thing." I squeezed her ass. "You know I can't resist when you beg."

"So I can have my gift?" Her smile brightened with her excited expression.

"No. But I'll give you a ride on my cock."

She smacked the side of my head, pouting. "You suck."

"I'll suck, lick, bite...whatever you want, sweetheart." I pulled her closer. Hadley swerved when I went for her lips, so I attacked her neck instead.

"A hint?" she begged.

"You'll have to wait and see." I kissed along the underside of her jaw and down the blue vein while my left hand moved inside the front of her sweatshirt to capture a handful of her breast. "This isn't the liquor talking," I said, "and I'm not just flattering you because I'd like to get inside you in the immediate future." I brushed my thumb over her nipple, feeling it constrict under my touch. "But you have my favorite set of tits in the world, Punky. Museum quality."

She jerked away. "Did you really just say that?"

"Goddamn right I did." I hoisted her up and sat her astride my hips.

"How do you do that?" she asked with a sweet smile. My smile.

"Do what?"

"Be so perfect all the time. You're not living up to your reputation as an insufferable prick."

"I am that," I admitted. "And I'm not perfect." I urged her lips to mine again. "I only need to be perfect for you."

"Shut up and screw me," she laughed, nipping my lip. "You've earned it." I gripped the underside of both thighs, sitting forward to lift us up. "No," she said. "Here."

I sat back, appraising her. "Here? Really?"

"Mmm-hmm." Hadley kissed my jaw and traced her fingers over my shoulders. "I like it out here."

"Simon—"

"I seriously doubt your dad is going to come looking for us."

"Can you keep your voice down?"

I pinched her nipple. She yelped and the sound turned to a deep moan when I tugged on it.

"That's a no."

Hadley was a loud lover. A fact I rather enjoyed, but my father didn't need the soundtrack. We were much closer to his bedroom out here than upstairs in one of our rooms. Although, the way sound traveled through the house, it might not matter where we were.

"I'll be good," she whispered. Hadley sat back on my lap, dipping her head to flick her tongue over one of my nipples, teasing the piercing. She looked up from under her lashes. "Promise."

"You'll do no such thing." I tugged the sweatshirt over her head and pulled her forward. She arched her back, shoving her tit in my mouth.

Hadley writhed in my lap, grinding her hot cunt over my erection. With my right hand around her hips, I encouraged her movements. My teeth scraped the tight peak of her nipple. Her hands went to my hair, tugging and holding me there. I tended to the other breast, flicking my tongue piercing across the sensitive tip.

"Damn it, Josh."

Her hands dropped to my jeans, ripping at the buttons until each one popped open. Punky's greedy fingers found my dick and pulled it free. I thrust into her hand, then pushed Hadley back until her feet met the floor.

"Off," I said as I snapped the elastic band of her shorts with one finger.

With my left hand, I stroked my cock, appreciating the view of her half naked in front of me. Teasing me, she slipped her shorts and underwear to the floor in a slow, deliberate movement.

"Come here," I said, and tugged her to straddle me.

Hadley grabbed the back of my neck with one hand, the other fisting my cock to guide me in. I groaned and pressed my forehead to hers as she sank down, my dick prying open her tight channel. Cradling her ass in my lap with my broken hand, I moved my left between us to rub circles over her clit. Hips working back and forth, she didn't lift one inch, just sliding her ass across my thighs with me burrowed deep inside her.

I found her lips, kissing her hard. *I love you,* they said. *I worship you. You fucking own me and please don't ever take this away from me.*

Hadley's forehead fell to my shoulder and she held on. Muffled noises of anticipation were concealed behind her clenched teeth and clasped lips.

"Hang on to me," I said.

Hadley's arms closed around the back of my neck. Hoisting us up from the chair, I took two strides and pressed her back against a pillar. Bracing her there, I swept both her legs over my arms. With more freedom to move in this position, I slammed into her. Again and again our bodies collided in a speedy rhythm. Her muscles tensed. I felt her snug hole clench around my cock.

"That's it, sweetheart."

A tiny scream burst from her lips. The sound lasted only a split second before her teeth clamped down on my shoulder, silencing her announcement of completion. The sharp sting of pain shocked my system. I came hard, unable to stop myself. Bracing my body against Hadley, her back to the pillar, I panted in exhaustion. Every muscle tingled and shook. I was barely fucking standing, so I backed up and took her with me as I fell into the chair.

"Fucking hell," I hissed. "Punky?" My hand combed through her hair. "You can let go now."

Her teeth retreated, leaving an impression in my shoulder. "Sorry."

"Don't be." I stroked my fingers up and down her spine. My dick twitched inside her. "That was fucking spectacular."

She nuzzled against my neck and ran her nose along the sweaty column, her lips leaving kisses along my throat. "Are you okay?"

"Yeah," I answered. And then I opened my eyes to the black spots still littering my vision. "Actually, yeah. Really okay."

So fucking beautiful with her cheeks flushed red, her eyes sleepy, and her hair a wild mess.

"You didn't have an attack."

"No."

"That's good." Her lips turned up and stopped before they revealed a full smile. As if she was reluctant to celebrate this fact. "Why not?"

"No idea. And I'm not going to linger on the thought." I swiped my thumb over her bottom lip. "Maybe we'll just have to make love standing up from now on."

She laughed, burrowing her face against my neck. "I feel like I just got punched in the uterus."

My head fell back and I laughed with a full voice. "Goddamn, Punky. Such romance. Such poetry."

"Fuck off. That thing needs a warning label."

"I'll do it. I'll get a surgeon general's warning tattooed on my cock."

"Will you stop it with that?" Hadley sat up, grabbing my jaw. "I like your dick just the way it is. No more ink or hardware on that part. Okay?"

"Whatever you say, sweetheart. He is your humble servant."

Chapter 27

In the alley behind the Nest Saturday night, I walked my father to Hadley's car after our show. The birthday girl inside was down for an all-nighter, but traveling cross-country had taken a toll on Simon.

"Are you sure you don't want me to drive you?" I offered.

"No need." He unlocked the car with the key fob, the headlights illuminating the small lot. "Stay and have fun. And please eat something. You barely touched dinner, and you're looking a little thin since the last time I saw you."

"Yeah, sure. Just haven't had much of an appetite recently." It seemed every time I looked at food my stomach went a bit queasy these days. I'd probably caught a bug or something. "I'm glad you came. Means a lot that you could see us play."

"I thoroughly enjoyed myself." Simon opened the passenger door and turned to face me. "Your mother would be proud to see everything you've accomplished. The way you've grown."

My eyes fell to the fascinating scuffmarks on my leather boots. "Thanks."

"Josh, if there's anything to take away from the girl you had tucked under your arm all night, it's that a passion so strong has no substitute."

"Yeah. I got that part figured out. I'm not letting her go. Tom issued the requisite threat."

"I'm not talking about Hadley." He slipped inside the car, lowering the window as he shut the door and started the car. "Love you, son. Be safe. I'll see you in the morning."

I took a step back as my father pulled away. In his wake, he left me perplexed. Oh, I understood his meaning just fine. Was it really so obvious?

I loved music. It was the only damn thing I was good at. The band, while a necessary distraction and suitable creative outlet, wasn't a passion. Nothing against Trey and Corey. I loved those guys. No matter how much I threw myself into this hobby, though, I saw it more as a stagnant, failing relationship: She was safe, comfortable, and nonthreatening. She didn't give me a hard-on when she walked in the room, nor was I overcome with the irresistible urge to mount her when she slipped into bed beside me. Days were not consumed with thoughts of her to the point of obsession, infatuation. Worse, she enabled my lazy complacency rather than inspiring growth.

Well, now I just wanted to throw Punky against a wall and fucking eat her.

Such deliberations only exacerbated my headache, which now had a side of tinnitus from the amplifiers. Tonight was for Hadley. Everything else could wait.

Back inside the bar, I went into the greenroom to use the private bathroom. It wasn't pristine, but it got less use than the rotting petri dishes the customers used.

As I came out, Scott was waiting for me in the darkened hallway. With greasy, limp hair and a patchy growth around his jaw, he was almost unrecognizable. Small red scabs speckled his pallid complexion.

"I told you—"

"I want my money," he said through chapped, split lips. His eyes were stained by broken blood vessels.

"You need to leave right now. I'm done with this shit."

"Man, I'm not playin' around. You owe me." He was jittery, anxious, glancing down the hallway as if afraid to be seen.

"Scott, go home. Get yourself some help. I'm not doing this anymore."

I tried to walk away, but he wouldn't let me pass. Scott lifted the hem of his shirt to flash a small-caliber revolver stuffed in his waistband.

"I told you I'd be back. Just give me the money and we'll call it square."

"The fuck is that for?"

"So you know I'm serious."

"You're going to shoot me? Really? Who are you anymore? Look at yourself, Scott. You should be in a fucking hospital. You're killing yourself."

It was one thing to exchange a few blows and broken knuckles. Pulling this shit was goddamn insane.

"I'm done with your bullshit. You come at me with a fucking gun? Shoot me, you nutless fuck. Or go crawl back into your hole and fuck off."

"Coming through!"

Scott backed off as one of the bar-backs came down the hall wheeling a cart of overstuffed garbage bags toward the Dumpster outside. Scott circled me, and for a second I thought he was relieved, like he'd been given an excuse to walk away and pretend this never happened.

"We're not done," he said, and darted into the alley.

Scott wasn't there yet, but he was working up to becoming a dangerous man. I would have to go to the police, if only to protect Hadley and save Scott from himself.

But not tonight.

Hadley deserved to have fun, and I refused to let anything ruin her birthday. So I slapped on a smile and returned to the group.

I arrived at our table just in time to see Asha and Hadley slam blue shots of I-didn't-know-what.

Hadley grimaced, shaking her head. "What was that?"

"I don't know," Tiny Tim laughed. The escaped member of Alice Cooper's sideshow took a swig of Trey's beer.

"You trying to poison my girl?" I asked.

Hadley turned around, smiling with a lopsided grin and glassy eyes. "Hi, handsome."

"Sabra told me it was the birthday special," Asha said. "I thought bartenders liked you here."

Sitting down, I pulled Hadley on my lap. "Save any for me?"

"None for you." She tapped my nose, blinking a lot over her dark, dilated eyes. "Someone has to get us home."

Winding my hand into her hair, I caught the back of her neck. "Just a taste, then." My lips met hers. She opened for me, allowing my tongue to lick inside. "Wow," I said as I pulled away. "That's fucking awful."

Punky laughed and grabbed my glass of water. "I know, right? What did I ever do to Sabra?"

"Just so you know," Corey said from across the table, Grace beside him. "Hadley offered to cook me dinner for a week if I spilled the beans on your gift."

"Is that so?" I looked to Punky, arching my eyebrow.

"Yeah," she said, without remorse. "And he wouldn't tell me. How's that for loyalty?"

"You already cook him dinner three times a week," Trey said. "It's not much of a bribe."

"Speak for yourself," Corey replied. "Sorry, Hadley. Bro code."

"Bro code?" Grace scoffed. "Really? Can we please retire the phrase with popped collars and visors?"

"Screw that noise." Hadley shifted in my lap and almost fell over. "I've known you longer. Doesn't that count for anything? Trey?" Hadley leaned across the table. Everyone reached for their drinks to save them from the incoming calamity. Trashed, she was so damn adorable. "We're tight, right? I know you like me better than Josh." She sat up, grabbing my face and staring hard. "Sorry, babe. It's true. I'm Trey's favorite."

"I'm crushed," I mumbled with her hands squeezing my cheeks.

"Hadley."

We both turned to see Andre standing on the other side of the railing that separated the table deck from the rest of the floor.

"Just wanted to come by and say happy birthday. Can I buy you a drink?"

"Thank you," she said. "But I'm already getting them for free."

"Right." Andre gave us an awkward smile.

"Have a seat," she offered. "You here with the guys?"

"Yeah. By the bar."

"We've got room. Join us."

The others started shifting their chairs around to clear some space at the table. I wasn't thrilled with this idea, but what could I do? It was Hadley's birthday, and that meant I had to suck it up and deal.

Andre gave her a nod and went back into the crowd.

"Be nice." Hadley placed a kiss to my lips. Her eyes were soft, smiling.

"Anything. It's your night."

"So can I have my present now?"

"When we get home."

She turned to the group, a plea on her face. "Anybody?"

Silence.

"Traitors," she snapped. "All of you."

* * *

The ugly lights popped on overhead to usher the drunk and stumbling out to the pavement. Right about the same time, my headache kicked in full force. Like I had a golf ball lodged behind my eye. Across the room, Trey and Corey were dodging dart ricochets as Asha and Hadley hurled them at the board. Or the vicinity of the dartboard.

"You know," Andre said. "Right?" He sat across the table picking at the label on his empty beer bottle. It was just the two of us now, and I sensed a man-to-man was unfolding.

"Know what?"

"That I'm batting for the other team."

"Yeah. I heard." I leaned back, using Hadley's straw to try and soothe the itch under my cast. "That has nothing to do with everything else. I wasn't picking on you."

"No." He smothered a smile. "I figure you like me better this way. I get it. She's not my type."

Like was a strong word. I hated him less.

"You were close?" I asked.

"Are close."

Okay, now I hated him a little. Whether he liked dick or not didn't seem to matter within the realm of my possessive nature toward Hadley. He was still a man, still not a fan of mine.

"Help me out here. She never talked about you. Suddenly, you're back in the picture."

"I don't see how I owe you an explanation," he said, and crossed his arms.

"Listen, Andre. You and I will probably never get along. I'm good with that. But you're going to have to accept that I'm not going anywhere. Hadley is my whole life. Like it or not, this is permanent."

Looking away, Andre surveyed the room. A line of patrons waiting to close out their tabs crowded the bar. A dozen more filled the hallway waiting for the bathrooms. Veiled in darkness, this place was a dump. Under the unforgiving glare of fluorescent lighting, it was far less appealing.

"My dad sent me away." Andre sat rigid, his attention aimed in the distance. "That's why I left. I asked the wrong question and that was it. Called me a fag and told me to get the fuck out. He didn't have a son anymore. Sent me to live with my mom. Hadley was the only one who ever called. So when you tossed her aside, I was there."

"Whatever you think you know, Andre—"

"She protected you. Every day you ignored her and Hadley called me crying, she wouldn't tell me what happened. Just because she's forgiven you doesn't mean I will."

"I'm good with that." I stood, tossing a few twenties on the table for the waitress. "You need a ride home?"

"I'm fine."

"For what it's worth," I said, offering my left hand, "thank you for being her friend when I wasn't."

He accepted the gesture with reluctance and squeezed my hand harder than necessary. "If she calls me crying—"

"Look for me to be tied to her rear bumper."

* * *

"You're enjoying this too much," Hadley slurred.

I held her in my arms as I climbed the stairs to my bedroom. During the ride home, she'd fallen asleep and didn't wake until I carried her through the front door.

"Be nice to me," I warned. "You're completely at my mercy tonight."

"Every night."

At the stop of the stairs, I nudged my bedroom door open with my foot and crossed to the bed, where I laid her down on top of the duvet. "You want anything? Water?"

"Present." Hadley sat up against the headboard. "Gimme." Like a child, she held out her arms, fingers wiggling in anticipation. Fucking adorable.

"It's not your birthday anymore." The clock on my nightstand read 3:25. "I missed the deadline. Guess you'll just have to wait until next year."

Her lips turned to a playful pout. "Please?"

"Ah. There it is, the magic word." I went to the closet. "Close your eyes. And don't fall asleep."

The restraint she'd shown in not rummaging through my room to find the hidden gifts was commendable. When we were kids, Hadley had exercised a remarkable talent for finding, opening, and then resealing Christmas presents. She was nearly impossible to surprise, the curious thing.

"Keep them closed." The first gift, the recording of Hadley's favorite songs I'd written, went into the CD player. I set the second one upright against the opposite side of the bed. Sitting on the edge beside her, I placed a card in Hadley's hands. "Open."

She looked down, scanning the generic birthday card with a sassy raised eyebrow. "If there's a gift card in here—"

"Ingrate. Just read it." I reached over and flicked on the bedside lamp.

" 'Something big and something new, something small and something blue,' " she read. "A riddle? Josh, I don't have the energy for a scavenger hunt. Please tell me it isn't buried in the backyard."

"No. No digging." With the remote, I turned on the stereo. The album began in chronological order with the first song I'd composed for her. The song I'd played for her birthday so many years ago when things were far less complicated and our lives were only supposed to get better.

Hadley's expression dropped. A crease formed between her brows, her bottom lip trembling. No. No, no, no. Not the reaction I'd aimed for.

"Sweetheart." I held her cheek, running my thumb over her lip. "What's wrong?"

"You made me a CD?"

"I thought you'd like it. I laid down your favorites. You've been asking me to play for you and..." Shit. "It's everything I've ever written for you." Her face turned pink and tears fell to my fingers. She crawled onto my lap to bury her head against my shoulder, clinging to me. "Don't cry, Punky. Please don't cry." I rubbed her back. What the fuck had I done wrong? And why the hell didn't someone stop me? "Say something." I pressed pause on the remote.

"No." Her head popped up. "Don't stop." Grabbing the remote, she pressed play. "It's perfect."

"Really?"

She nodded, smiling and sniffling. "I love it, Josh. It's the best thing you could have given me."

Hadley pressed her lips to mine; they were warm, tender, and tasted of salt. Pure panic subsided into relief and immense pride as we kissed, and I realized I hadn't strung her along all day just to fuck up in epic fashion.

"I get the old and small part," she said. Hadley pulled back and wiped the tears from her cheek. "Something big and blue?"

I reached to my side of the bed and grabbed the bass guitar by the neck to place in her lap. Her eyes lit up.

"Are you kidding me? Josh. This is— How did you know?"

"I was always watching you, Hadley. I never stopped noticing." My fingers trailed the side of her face and down to her neck, brushing her hair over her shoulder. "Trey said he'd start giving you lessons. I can teach you the basics."

Enamored, she plucked at the strings, experimenting with the steel under her fingers like I'd seen so many times at Jupiter. I wanted to share this with her. To have something we could discover together. Those dark, gorgeous eyes looked at me with an expression I wanted to bottle and retrieve at will. I could bench press a Volkswagen on that look.

"Thank you," she repeated, and set the bass on the floor against the nightstand. "For everything." Her hand found mine, entwining our fingers. "Today was perfect. It means so much to me, Josh. I can't even tell you."

"You don't have to. I love you." I brought her fingers to my lips, kissing her knuckles. "I'm going to make it up to you—all the birthdays I wasn't the friend I should have been."

"No." Hadley tugged my hand to her lap. "I don't want to play that game. We're skipping over all the bad stuff and picking up where we left off with the good parts, remember?"

"You're right. I'm rehabilitated from my midlife crisis and my little arsonist isn't setting any more fires."

Punky smirked right before a yawn stretched her mouth wide. "Sorry," she laughed.

"Go ahead and get ready for bed. I'll set the alarm."

Hadley hesitated. She held my hand tighter when I tried to get up.

"You can do this. I'm trusting you. Get ready for bed. Don't touch the locks while I'm gone. When I get back, I expect to find you tucked in tight."

She took a deep breath and nodded as she released my hand. I pressed a kiss to her forehead and left her to it.

I'd learned that the expectations of those you love are powerful motivators and strong deterrents. To make my father proud of his son, to be a better man for the girl I cherished, I put forth a greater effort than I might have otherwise. I made different choices than I would have if left to my own devices. So I hoped the same would work on Hadley. But if it didn't, I'd do my best to be what she needed. Hell, maybe she'd never get over it and push past the needs of her disorder. All I wanted was her happiness. I'd take her any way I could have her, scars and all.

* * *

Sunday evening, after we took my dad to the airport, Hadley and I were sequestered at opposite ends of the house. Like me, she had a portfolio due at the end of the semester.

While she worked in Simon's study, I returned to the garage to get started on that composition for my jazz showcase. My head hurt. That fucking incessant song wouldn't leave me alone. My broken hand was sore. My stomach was revolting against the few bites I'd managed to eat all day. Nevertheless, I ignored the multitude of excuses and sat with my notebook open on the music stand and my guitar across my lap. By 1:00 a.m. I had made some headway. Not a revelation by any means, but enough to call the evening productive.

"You don't think I can feel it when you walk into a room?" I looked over my shoulder at Hadley standing in the doorway with my sweatshirt hanging over lean, bare legs. Lovely. "My Punky sense tingles if you leave the town limits."

Hadley smiled, rolling her eyes. I used to think that move meant I was irritating her. I now realized it was a response to finding me pretty damn charming. Oh, the conversations that might have gone quite differently if I'd had that bit of insight.

"Time for bed?" I said as she crossed the garage to where I sat.

"I can't see straight anymore." She grabbed my hair, tugging my head back. "I should have majored in philosophy or something."

I slid my fingers up and down the backs of her thighs, marveling at how fucking soft she felt. I grabbed the backs of her legs, tugging her to stand between mine. "What, and give up the secure and lucrative future of a degree in art?"

"And what are you working on? Jazz? Maybe you didn't get the memo, but jazz is dead." She leaned forward, kissing along my jaw and down my neck. Hadley dragged her teeth, biting lightly.

My hands moved under her sweatshirt to grab her ass. No shorts, just a tiny pair of black panties. "Did you come in here to seduce me?"

"Do I have to try?"

"Hell no."

I stood and attacked her mouth. My hand fisted in her hair. Hadley stretched on her toes to meet me. With one arm under her ass, I hoisted her up until her legs locked around my waist. We bumped into every wall and counter through the garage and past the kitchen. Damn near took a header down the stairs as I carried her to her room.

Inside, I threw her on the bed. She bounced, laughing. My cock strained at the image of this amazing woman spread out, waiting for me and the savage things I'd do to her.

"Show me something," I said, rubbing my erection through my jeans.

Hadley reached for the bottom of the sweatshirt and pulled it over her head.

I climbed over her, first tasting her lips before traveling her throat with my tongue. On seven million separate occasions I had fantasized about licking every fucking inch of her. From her shoulders, I lingered with her breasts, massaging them, sucking her tight nipples until she whimpered, then biting for a scream.

Hadley writhed beneath me, grinding against the ridge of my cock. Manipulating the heavy flesh of one breast, I applied my mouth to the other. I listened to her body, alternating between hard and soft. Her noises grew louder, more desperate as I moved my attention to her other breast. With my tongue piercing, I lashed at her nipple, flicking the cold steel over the little peak. I worked on her until she was quivering beneath me.

"Scoot up," I told her.

She slid up the bed to rest against the pillows, giving me room to settle between her legs. I knelt above her and held her right leg over my shoulder to kiss a trail from ankle to thigh, repeating the path on her left.

"You having fun?"

"Very much," I mumbled against her skin. "You are my dream come true."

Hadley looked up with a content smile and sleepy eyes. "I love you."

"Sweetheart"—I peeled her panties down her legs—"I'm just getting started."

I spread her thighs to reveal the Promised Land, my goddamn birthright as far as I was concerned. No lucky son of a bitch ever had it this good.

I devoured that girl. My tongue stabbed shallow into her as my thumb rubbed over her clit. Shoving two fingers inside, I sucked the sensitive nub, flicking my tongue piercing. Hadley's nails scraped across my scalp, and I thought I might come in my fucking pants from just her needy violence.

"Get there, Punky." I pumped my fingers into her cunt, harder and faster as she moaned.

Her walls clamped down. Hadley's hands fisted the pillow. Her entire body jerked. I pulled my fingers free and wrapped my mouth over her pussy, licking every drop of pure ecstasy.

As her body shuddered and went limp, she muttered under her breath. "I don't think I can take any more."

"Do you mean that?"

"No," she breathed. "I want a lot more."

"Good." I smacked her pussy.

Hadley slapped her thighs together around my hand, glaring at me.

"Bend over, sweetheart. I'm going to ride the hell out of you."

"Please?" she asked with a sassy inflection.

"If I have to say please, I'm going to tie you up and spank you."

Her mouth dropped open, eyes wide. "Rude."

"Hadley," I warned.

She took her sweet time sitting up, eyeing me all the while, like she was daring me to make good on my word. Another time. Right now, I needed to be inside her.

With Hadley on her knees, shoulders flat to the bed, I caressed her ass with one hand and pulled open my jeans with the other, shoving them down enough to free myself.

"Right here," I said, running my thumb over her pristine skin. "My teeth would look so nice."

"Keep dreaming."

"You'll cave. One of these days."

Positioned at her entrance, I held my cock in my good hand, rubbing the head through her slit. Every bit of friction against the piercing sent vibrations down my spine.

"Josh," she whimpered.

"Sorry. Getting myself all distracted."

"You're going to lose your topping privileges."

Inch by fantastic fucking inch, I slid into her. I spread her ass to watch my dick disappear inside her. Embedded to the hilt, I flexed my hips, holding deep. Hadley squeezed around my shaft.

"So good," I groaned. "Shit. You feel so—"

"Josh." Hair flipped over Punky's shoulder as she tilted her face to look at me. "Stop thinking about nailing me and do it already."

"Damn, I love you."

"I know."

I pulled out to the tip, gently sliding back in. At an easy pace, holding her hips, back and forth, I stroked myself with her warm, soft cunt. So fucking tight. Bending over her, my lips traveled Hadley's shoulders and down her back. I could have kept this up all night—slow, patient, just on the razor's edge.

"Faster," she whimpered. "I want more."

But Punky wasn't the patient type.

No matter that I had her nearly immobile but for my will, Hadley used every bit of leverage she could find to push against me, forcing her pussy to take me deeper. Faster. Harder. The urge to come was right there, but I wanted this to last. Leaving a kiss on her lower back, I encouraged her to roll over. She reached up to touch the side of my face as I settled on top of her.

"If you don't want to," Hadley whispered, "I understand. We can stop."

"No." I kissed her palm. "I can handle it. I don't want to miss a second of anything with you."

Covering her body with mine, with Hadley's legs wrapped around my hips and her arms clinging to my shoulders, I made love to her. And when the memories rushed my consciousness, I let her hold me tighter until the shaking stopped.

Chapter 28

Session 9

"What is it about that moment?" Reid discarded her iPad. She sat forward in the rolling leather chair, attention trained on my every frustrated, fumbling word.

Horizontal on the sofa, I didn't look at her. My legs were too long, one elevated on the opposite armrest and my other foot touching the floor. I fought to discuss the topic while evading the memories, the psychosomatic effects. There was a water spot on the ceiling that had grown four inches in diameter during the last week.

"If I knew, I wouldn't be here."

"Help me out, Josh. Explain it to me."

Eyes closed, I absently traced one finger over my eyebrow. "Fear. Panic. Revulsion. Coming feels great, yeah. Of course. But it's...it's like fudge covered in dog shit. I get the good stuff, the pleasure, but always coated in shaking, nausea, a putrid taste in the back of my throat. My entire body breaks out in cold sweats."

"And you see him?"

Through clenched teeth I answered, "Yes."

"Specific instances or a general scene?"

"Fuck." I tugged at my hair, trying to get a handle on my racing pulse. "Does it matter? What's the difference?"

"Try."

I'd fought her on this. I had agreed to her help, but asking me to go back into those memories, to talk about him, was something I had hoped to avoid.

"Do you believe you're safe here?" Reid asked.

"Here" was irrelevant. This room or a street corner, it didn't matter. The danger lived in my head. Why wasn't there a surgery for that? Well, a surgery more precise and reliable than a lobotomy. Reach in and scoop out only where the raven made his nest.

"I see him—you know—finishing." I hated saying the words aloud. My stomach turned. "I make a distinction between rape and molestation. He didn't rape me. The sick fuck used me. I was a prop. Might as well have been a porno mag with hands."

"And when you've been with someone," she said, "when you're with Hadley now..."

"What?" I demanded. "Ask the damn question."

"Do you see yourself as your abuser?"

"Fuck you." I jerked upright, fists clenched.

"You're angry at the insinuation?"

"Yes," I hissed. "And you're baiting me. Why?"

"I have a theory and it goes like this: You envision yourself as the victimizer. As a child, impressionable, you learned to associate sexual acts involving another person as perverse, abusive. Alone, masturbating, you're not hurting anyone. But in your mind, taking pleasure from these women, from Hadley, is something selfish and depraved. You think you're scarring them just as you were traumatized. What you're experiencing is post-traumatic stress, yes. More to the point, you feel guilt. Strong remorse for taking pleasure from what you perceive as Hadley's pain or subjugation."

"Bullshit," I scoffed. "We have great sex. I'm not—no. Fuck that. I love her."

"You do. Hadley knows that. Put aside logic, Josh. Your emotional responses in these situations are outside rational thinking. Consciously, you're making love with a consenting adult for mutual enjoyment. Deeper, in your subconscious, where that five-year-old boy lives, he doesn't understand the difference."

Reid looked at me. I looked at the floor. It went on like that so long I forgot I hadn't responded.

"Now what?" I muttered.

"Come to terms with the disparity."

Chapter 29

For the last forty-five minutes, Dr. Richardson had prattled on about the economic divide in America and its influence as reflected in popular music.

"I'm sorry," a girl on the other side of the classroom remarked, "but I don't get singers—like big celebrities—that write about being poor and having it so hard. I mean, hello, you're rich. What more do you want?"

"It's not like they were all born into fortunate circumstances," another classmate argued. "I mean, look at Jay Z. He was—"

"Rap doesn't count."

"Excuse me?"

"What? It doesn't."

"Wow. That's not racist."

"What does that have to do with race?"

"Like all hip-hop artists are black and therefore grew up poor, so it's okay for them?"

"Eminem is white."

"That's enough," Dr. Richardson said. "Ms. Fuller," he addressed the girl suffering from an abundance of stupid, "why don't we table that discussion?"

I tried not to laugh at the absurdity happening around me. At the very least, the participation of others in discussion meant I could concentrate on more stimulating tasks and be left alone.

My phone buzzed with a text from Asha.

Photo lab. Now. Hadley needs you.

I was out of my seat in an instant, ignoring the calls from Dr. Richardson at my back.

Sprinting across campus, rain pelted my face and soaked through my clothing. The clouds were mean overhead, threatening a storm that would last all night.

When I reached the photo lab in the art building, Asha pointed me toward the darkroom. Inside, Hadley sat huddled in the corner under a table.

"Hey, Punky. Is there room under there for me?"

She said nothing. Illuminated by the single red bulb in the center of the ceiling, Hadley sat with her knees to her chest, head resting on her folded arms. She was shaking. The anxious, terrified vibrations shattered my heart.

I crawled under the table beside her and pressed my back to the wall. "Who we hiding from?" I asked, not that I expected an answer. "Asha is gone. I think the game is over. So if you want to come out now..."

Hadley had spent the entirety of class secluded here. When Asha couldn't convince her to leave, she had sent for me to coax Hadley out.

"Sweetheart." I tucked her hair behind her ear as I looked for just a glimpse of her face. "Talk to me."

Nothing.

I waited, but the silence only served to make me feel impotent, insufficient.

"You used to let me sleep with your blanket, remember?" I let my head fall against the wall, closing my eyes. "The first time I saw you, that blanket was tangled around your arms and neck like a boa."

A rainbow of pink, blue, and yellow wrapped around a tiny version of Hadley.

"The first time I came to you after he was done with me, you gave me the blanket and said it would protect me. Every night after that, I slept wrapped in that thing like a cocoon."

Her shaking slowed, though Hadley still wouldn't acknowledge me. I did notice her hands, like tense claws, gripping her arms. She was fighting, silently and alone. Without me.

"Thing is," I told her, "the blanket didn't work. Just about every night it was the same thing over and over. Yarn wasn't much of a deterrent against monsters like him." I slid my hand over her thigh, squeezing her leg. "You know what did help? You did, sweetheart. In your own way, you fixed me up with my leftover pieces."

I constantly pondered what might have been if not for Hadley. What might have become of me if her parents hadn't died, sending her to the foster home. How long would I have stayed there, subjected to that man's vile attention? Without her, my parents would have been two people living a few hours away who'd never spared a thought for this boy, alone and covered in shame. But for their influence, for Hadley's friendship, I found an escape from the persistent nightmare that followed long after he was gone.

"How many different ways can I say that I wouldn't be alive if not for you? I'll never be able to square us on that one. So please,

Punky. Lean on me. Fight me. Slap me. Scream and throw things. Don't shut me out. Not when I know you're suffering. It kills me."

"It's like suddenly realizing I forgot to turn off the stove," she muttered without looking up. "And then I'm picturing the entire house burning down. Only the flames find me sitting in class. Like they're licking up my legs. I know it isn't real, but it burns. I feel it searing my skin while I tell myself it's just a delusion." Hadley's voice grew softer as her hands clenched, nails biting into her forearms. "I see someone inside," she continued. "And I'm not here anymore. I'm asleep in bed. I'm alone. He's coming for me and I don't—"

"You're not alone." I wrapped my arms around her waist, pulling Hadley against my chest. "You hear me? You're not alone. I'm right here, Punky."

Her hands fisted in my wet shirt.

"You're never going to be alone again," I whispered. "I'm not going anywhere this time. I won't leave you behind."

"How do you turn it off?" she asked.

"I don't know." I kissed the top of her head, holding her tightly. "But it starts with letting me get you out of here. You can't sit in the dark forever."

"The security video," she muttered.

"What about it?"

"It's not working. That's how this started."

I pulled out my phone, bringing up the app for our security system. An error message popped up. Well, fuck.

"Just a glitch," I told her. "I'm sure—" I swallowed the rest.

Any plausible explanation was irrelevant. No amount of empty reassurance would change the feelings of anxiety that had already taken hold in Hadley's mind.

"Let's go home. It's storming like a motherfucker out there, anyway. Better to get home now before the roads flood."

* * *

That night I did my best to distract Hadley. Even after we got home and locked up, she remained anxious, jumpy. The storm only got worse and had her flinching at every crack of lightning or creak and groan of the house when thunder clapped loud and violent on top of us.

It wasn't her fault. Her irrational behavior was something she couldn't control, no matter how hard she fought to hold it all in. Worse, there was nothing I could do about it. All the chicken soup and hot tea, blankets and silly cartoons, couldn't quiet the part of her brain that screamed, *Danger!*

It was after midnight when she finally nodded off in bed. We slept in my room, Hadley's body curled around me, tucked tight beneath the covers. I couldn't fix it, but at least I felt useful. She needed me, and wasn't that all anyone wanted? To have purpose. To have someone to take care of. Someone to miss you when you were gone.

As much as I had faith in Hadley's ability to conquer anything, there was a good chance she'd never fully recover from the trauma of her parents' deaths. And perhaps a selfish part of me didn't want her to change. Because I liked being needed, and both of us being a little messed up meant I wasn't alone.

* * *

My eyes snapped open. I looked down to see Hadley curled against me, her chest rising and falling with gentle breaths and one arm draped over my stomach. Outside, the storm raged on. Wind howled through the trees in a wild song as rain battered the glass.

The clock on my nightstand was dark. The power was out. It might have been the air conditioner shutting down or the generator kicking on that woke me. Satisfied, I closed my eyes.

Minutes later, under the noise of the storm outside, I became aware of a hissing sound—long, consistent. Fifteen seconds, I counted. It stopped for a moment and started again.

A series of clicks.

My body tensed.

My heart beat faster.

In an instant, my vision narrowed in the darkness and my senses focused. I climbed out of bed to press my ear to the door and listen for the noise under the violent storm outside. There was no pattern to the hiss and clicks. I knew every sound of this house; those weren't normal.

Pulling on a pair of jeans, I grabbed a flashlight and removed my pistol from the lockbox in the nightstand. I grabbed Hadley's sweatshirt from the floor.

"Hadley." I brushed my fingers across her cheek. "Wake up."

She didn't move as bursts of lightning lit up the room.

"Hadley. You need to get up."

She stretched under the covers as she came to.

"Don't speak. Don't argue. Get in the back of my closet. Call the police. Stay there."

Hadley shot upright. I took her face between my palms.

"There's someone downstairs. I'm going down. You're staying here. Call the cops. Stay very quiet. Do not come out no matter what you hear."

"No, Josh," she pleaded in a panicked whisper, grabbing at my wrists. "Don't go down there."

"Put this on." I shoved the sweatshirt at her. "Now," I demanded when she hesitated.

She pulled it over her head, climbing out of bed. "Please. Stay."

"The storm has gotten worse. We don't know how bad the roads are or how long it will take for the police to get here. The security lights are out. That means the generator isn't running. It isn't a coincidence."

"But—"

"Don't," I insisted, placing my cell phone in her hand.

My course was set. I pushed her toward the closet and into the darkest corner under my hanging shirts.

"I love you. I promise, Punky, I'll come back."

Prying her hands from mine, I stepped away, ignoring her pleas and closing the door behind me to encase her in protective darkness.

I crept out of my bedroom and locked the door from the inside. The intermittent hissing noise continued below. I descended the stairs. Halfway down, I paused. Flashes of white through the windows filled the open space, and I noticed a dark, contiguous line drawn across walls. It continued through the foyer and, as I peeked around the corner, into the kitchen and living room. Then the smell hit me. Spray paint.

I released the safety on my weapon and held up my flashlight.

As I continued downstairs, the next step creaked. It felt like an air horn in a museum. A sharp, shrill noise that pinched every nerve. I heard a spray can drop to the wood floor. Footsteps ran toward me. I rushed to the bottom of the stairs as a dark figure blurred past.

"Hey!" I clicked on the flashlight.

He darted toward the door to the garage, so I lunged after him, grabbing the hood of his sweatshirt. Scott fell to the floor. Sprawled on his ass, he stared up at me, into the barrel of my pistol as I pulled back the hammer.

Open black sores dotted his chin and jaw. In the blue beam of the flashlight, I saw nothing: He was no one anymore, eyes vacant. Weeks ago he was a whole person; now he was half dead.

"Fuck, Scott." I released the hammer on the gun and engaged the safety. "What the fuck are you doing?"

He shuffled back on his palms, scrambling to his feet. Scott squinted at the flashlight.

I stared at this hollow shell of my friend, a man I'd known for years, and realized how far he'd deteriorated. His unfocused eyes darted between my face and the gun at my side.

"Scott, why?"

But he wouldn't say a word. Across his face played a struggle of indecision.

"Look at yourself, man. This isn't you."

"Fuck you, Josh. You ruined my life, took everything I had."

"You chose this. You chose those pills over the band. So you break into my house? For what, a few bucks for your next score? Go home, Scott. Figure your shit out."

"Right, because you don't owe me anything. You treat people like shit and just expect them to stand and take it. But what gives you the right to judge me? You have no idea what I've been through. You're so wrapped up in your own bullshit that you don't even see the people around you. We exist. We have our own problems. Wake the fuck up, Josh."

He had a point. The sad reality was that I'd let this happen. We all had. If I'd been paying attention to anything beyond my selfish narrow view, I might have noticed when his spiral began. I might have seen the signs. At the very least, I should have been there for him. Tried harder. He had one foot in the ground, and only now did he have my attention.

"You're right." I tucked the pistol in the waistband of my jeans behind my back. "I should have been a better friend. I'm sorry, Scott. I pushed you out, but I can help. Let me help. I'll do whatever I can. You just need to get clean and then—"

"Do you hear yourself?" He scratched at his neck, shaking his head in disgust. "It's like you can't help but talk down to people."

"I'm trying, please. If you don't want my help, at least go to your family. They must be worried about you."

"Nah, man. I can't go back there. It's too late for that."

"So what, then? You can't run."

"What does that mean?" His head jerked up, eyes alert and accusing.

"The police are on their way. Hadley's upstairs terrified. You can't just run from this one. But if you let me help you—"

Scott looked toward the front window, then turned and ran. I followed him through the garage and into the mud, pleading with him to stay. Under the pelting rain, I watched him dive into his waiting car and fishtail through two inches of floating forest debris clogging the gravel driveway. I didn't breathe until his taillights became invisible through the trees.

When I turned around, I saw the barrel of a hunting rifle with Hadley behind it. She stood ghostly still in the center of the garage. Her face a placid surface betraying no emotion, like a sleepwalker blind to the world around her.

"Hadley," I said, my voice a timid shudder. "It's me."

She didn't acknowledge my words but flinched when I moved toward her.

"Punky, it's okay. It's just me. He's gone."

She crumpled to floor, clinging to the rifle pointed at the ceiling. I pried the gun from her hands and slid it across the floor.

"Sweetheart?" Kneeling, I set down the flashlight and took her face in my hands.

"I always knew it was there," she said, referring to the rifle I thought had been a secret since the day Tom stashed it in the foyer closet.

"Did you know it's unloaded?"

"Yeah."

"Come here." I sat back, bringing her into my lap and hugging her to my chest. "You never fucking listen to me," I said. Though she was perfectly calm, I felt my muscles tremble. "You're so goddamn stubborn."

"I couldn't let anyone hurt you."

"I'm so proud of you, Punky. I love you. So much. You're my fucking hero."

We stayed like that, clutching one another, until a barrage of lights and sirens splashed down the driveway.

Chapter 30

Session 10

"Did the police catch him?" Reid sat back, ever planted in the same leather chair with her tablet on her lap.

I couldn't decide if her consistency was reassuring or if it pissed me off.

"Yes, a couple days later." I rolled a quarter between the four fingers on my right hand, rehabilitating my dexterity now that the cast was off. "He got picked up trying to pawn my guitars. Aside from trashing the house, he made off with anything of value he could carry. Small stuff. Some mics. A couple of Corey's practice drums. Mostly just gear from the garage. He had shut off the generator and came in through the garage door. Busted the lock to get into the house."

"You took some time off from school," she said.

"Yeah, to get the house back in order. Painting the walls and stuff. Hadley got worse before she got better. She wasn't afraid, exactly. More like a live wire jumping on the pavement, shooting sparks. She had all this energy and nowhere to ground it. She didn't sleep, so neither did I. I would distract her, entertain her until she got sick of being babysat and shoved me away. So I wrote and she drew. Schoolwork and shit. Even back when we were still pretending to hate each other, I never saw so little of her."

"That disappointed you."

"Yeah, it did. I expected her to lean on me, crack and let me put her back together. I was prepared for her to completely break down. Instead, Hadley was retreating, while I was left..."

"What?"

"Feeling unnecessary. We stopped having sex," I admitted. I ran both hands through my hair, thinking back to that sense of isolation. "Most of our interaction took place in uncomfortable silences."

Reid glanced at the clock on the desk beside her. I rubbed at my eyebrow. Somewhere along the way I'd learned to read her mind, and she mine. We'd spent too much time together.

"Why are you stalling?" she asked.

"Am I boring you?"

"Actually, yes."

"I'm not sure I like your tone."

Reid smiled the way she did when she didn't want to find me charming. "Skipping ahead?"

"It's okay to say you enjoy hearing about my sex life."

Today's session had been heavy. I needed a reprieve, to decompress, because it was only going to get worse before I wound down the clock.

"You have no idea how far off base you are," she said.

"Oh, really?"

"Should we have a long and involved discussion about your avoidance tactics next?"

"Pass." I couldn't handle a dressing down today. "I'm still fragile."

"Whenever you're ready."

"She didn't seem to need me."

The first couple of days were the closest I'd ever felt to Hadley. Then weeks passed, and it seemed a shift had occurred while I wasn't looking.

Chapter 31

"Go relax," I offered. Standing at the sink, I helped Hadley clean up after dinner. "I'll take care of this."

"No. I can do it. Go make sure Asha isn't trying to seduce your dad."

I laughed, peering into the living room where the macabre mistress was talking my dad's ear off. They were fast friends, of course. I'd tested the hypothesis and found that it was impossible not to at least half like Tiny Tim. She was still fucking irritating, but that was all part of her charm.

It had been almost a month since the break-in. Simon had been staying with us while we got the house back in order, but mostly to keep an eye on Hadley. Likewise, Tom and our friends had been practically camped out in our living room. I wasn't the only one waiting for a major meltdown.

"I wish you wouldn't do all this," I said.

Hadley had been in full hostess mode since the cavalry arrived, constantly cooking, cleaning, entertaining. Wouldn't even let me order pizza. The one time I had offered to cook, she damn near took my head off.

"You're running yourself into the ground." I wrapped my arms around her waist, brushing my fingertips across her stomach. "I'm worried about you, sweetheart."

"Josh." She set the dish down and turned on me. "Stop. No more hovering. You're driving me insane. Tom's breathing down my neck. Simon is pushing pills on me. I don't need another dad. Please," she said with a sigh that might as well have been a smack to the face, "leave me to it and find something else to do."

I could have taken that better. I should have. Instead, I stormed into the garage like a royal fucking prick and proceeded to bash on Corey's drums like they'd insulted my mother.

"Hey, hey!" Corey shouted above the noise after I'd been at it for over an hour. "You break it, you buy it, brother."

He and Trey shut the door behind them as they stepped into my angry cave.

"Bill me."

I kept at it, hitting the tom harder. I beat on that thing, kicked the shit out of it. Then the drumstick went right through the head.

"Motherfucker!" I hurled the stick at the garage door, where it snapped and fell to the floor. Surveying the result, I felt like a teething child. "Shit, Corey. I'm sorry. I'll replace it."

"Eh, screw the kit. What's with you?" He took a seat on Trey's amp, hands folded in his lap.

Trey grabbed the stool. "You want to talk?"

"Not for the first time," I said, "but I've got no clue what's going on in her head."

"Hadley."

"Yeah. She's all quiet one minute; then I open my mouth and she snaps at me. I mean, I get it. She has every right to lash out and lose her shit. That's fine. I don't mind. It's just—what the fuck, you know? I'm trying to be supportive. Why is she shoving me away?"

They were quiet for a long time. Dread welled up in my chest as I expected one of them to say something I didn't want to hear.

"I forget that you didn't see what she was like back then," Trey answered.

"Wow. Okay. Right for the jugular."

"Hadley deals with things in her own way. Give her some time. You're doing fine."

"Doesn't feel fine."

It felt like every day she was slipping farther away. The more I tried to hold on, be attentive, the more she retreated.

"We'll tell you if you're fucking up."

"Why'd you stop?" Asha appeared in the doorway. "It was just getting good."

"What do you want, Tiny?"

"Did you know your dad has never seen *Labyrinth*?"

Huh. No, actually, I didn't know that.

"Neither has Tom. We're going to watch it."

"Start without me."

"You sure?" Trey asked.

"Yeah. I'll be there in a minute."

They left me to my thoughts, which were nothing positive. My head throbbed with a constant pulsing behind my eye. Everything in that eye became sporadically blurry, like trying to see underwater. Despite my best efforts, I hadn't eaten much during dinner. Sometime later, my father walked in to find I hadn't moved a muscle.

"Would you believe I'm too scared to go in there?" I asked.

He approached me, taking to the stool that would henceforth be known as the *What's Wrong With You? Throne.*

"Yes," he answered. "And then I'd ask why."

"She's frightening." Punky terrified me. "She's punishing me."

"I find it unlikely that Hadley would feel the need to punish you for recent events."

"Maybe she should."

"Why is that?"

"For kicking Scott out of the band instead of trying harder to help him. If I hadn't been sleeping around, Stephanie wouldn't have had an ax to grind. Hell, if I'd just paid him off, he would have gone away."

"Son, listen to me."

He stood, and the man before me had never looked so little like the patient, gentle, coddling man I'd known as my father. His demeanor changed to something I would have avoided at all cost had he ever punished me a day in my life.

"Did you cause Scott harm? Perhaps. And you shouldn't dismiss that concern. Guilt can be healthy. It teaches us what behavior to avoid in the future. It rights our trajectory. But succumbing to remorse rather than learning from it is a fruitless endeavor. It's a bottomless pit, Josh. Frankly, it's beneath you."

Oh, but it was so easy. Such an attractive state of being when light turned to dark and feeling good became nails on a chalkboard.

"Did you spend even one second under the misconception that what that man did to you in the foster home was your fault?"

"What?" My fists clenched. "What did you just say?" Because surely I'd misheard Simon.

"Did you," he repeated, "ever operate under the misguided belief that you deserved to be abused?"

"Fuck you!" I shouted. I shot to my feet, smashing my cast against the cymbal. Pacing, I tugged at my hair. "I can't...I can't fucking believe you'd say that to me. What the fuck is wrong with you?"

I wanted to hit him. I wanted to hurt him.

"This is not your fault!" he yelled. The sound was all wrong coming from him. "Whatever Scott's troubles, whatever your involvement, he lost the right to make you the bad guy when he threatened you, then broke into this house. We are not responsible for the behavior of others."

I kicked something, whatever was in my way. "I should have been more careful. I have a responsibility to Hadley. What the fuck was I thinking?"

"Does it matter?"

"Yes!"

"Is there a danger of a repeat performance? Will you make such a mistake again?"

"I don't want to, but—"

"You'll do everything possible to support and protect her. She doesn't blame you for anything."

"Wait. She's talked to you? What does she mean that you've been pushing pills on her?"

"Yes, we've spoken. I understand she hasn't been sleeping. I prescribed something and I'd like you to make sure she's taking it."

"Damn it, Dad. Don't do that. Don't go behind my back."

"With all due respect, Hadley was my patient before you became my son. Her health isn't dependent upon your permission."

"I'm sorry." I sat down, taking a few deep breaths. "I'm edgy. I know. I have a headache—"

"You haven't been sleeping, either."

"I'll sleep when she does."

"And Hadley tells me that you get a lot of headaches lately. I'd feel better if you saw a physician. You've lost weight, and she says you're not eating much."

"It's nothing. Stress."

"Josh, please."

Meeting his eyes, I knew better than to argue. "I will. Yes."

* * *

Simon went back to New York a few days later. Hadley finally had enough of everyone's constant surveillance and politely told our friends and family to go the fuck home. I tried to talk to her. To sit down and have an honest conversation about how she was feeling since the break-in. I approached her a dozen different ways to get at anything like an honest answer, but all I got was "I'm fine." Four fucking weeks of "fine" and "don't worry about it." What the hell was I supposed to do with "fine" when her side of the bed was empty in the middle of the night?

My dad thought it was all in my head. That I was so bent on taking the blame I concocted a conflict to feed the guilt-thirsty part of myself. The guys insisted Hadley just needed time to process. When she had, everything would get back to normal. But they didn't know her like I did. Whatever bullshit she was feeding the rest of them, I wasn't buying it.

"You ready for bed?" I had a splitting headache throbbing behind my eyes, but tonight I wasn't leaving the living room unless she came with me.

Credits scrolled up the television screen. An entire edited-for-cable movie had gone by since the last time I'd asked her. Hadley sat at the opposite end of the couch with her legs in my lap and a book in her hands. It was almost midnight, and we had to be up by 6:30 for school tomorrow. Before the break-in, I'd have been making her come by 10:30 and we'd be out by 11:00. But sure, it was all in my head.

"You go on up. I want to finish this chapter," she said. Hadley propped her elbow on the back of the couch and drummed her fingers along the top of the cushion.

I hadn't seen her flip a page in twenty minutes. "I can wait."

"Really, I'm not tired." She offered a stiff smile. "Don't let me keep you up."

Flicking my tongue piercing between my teeth, I flipped through the channels on TV. She hated that noise: a *tat-tat-tat-tat-tat* that made her eyebrow twitch. Hadley's chin began to work back and forth as she chewed on the inside of her cheek.

"What me to grab you a glass of water to take a sleeping pill?"

"Nope." She drilled her eyes into the pages of her book as if willing me to leave the room.

"You told Simon you were taking the pills."

Her eyes shot up. Hadley closed the book and dropped it in her lap. "Are you setting my bedtime now?"

"The bottle's full, minus the two I watched you take before he went back to New York."

"Now you're counting my pills? What the fuck, Josh?" She yanked her legs from my lap.

"We never go to bed at the same time anymore. You're getting up in the middle of the night. You're lying to Simon. I mean, shit, we haven't had sex in two weeks."

She rolled her eyes and picked up her book, opening it a quarter inch farther in than where she'd left off. "I'm on the rag."

"Bullshit. Your period doesn't start for six more days."

"Seriously?"

"We've lived together for three years. I'm perceptive."

"So that's what this is about? Your dick feels neglected? Sorry, Josh. I'm not coin-operated."

"Why are you lying to me, Hadley?"

"Piss off." She chucked the paperback at my head and stood up.

"Uh-huh, sweetheart." I grabbed her hand. "I want a fucking answer. This shit stops right now."

"I don't know what you're talking about."

Yanking her hand from mine, she stormed off. I chased her as far as the landing and spoke to the back of her head.

"Damn it, Hadley. Stop. Just stop. Because if you lie to me again, I'm not sure we're coming back from this one. We made a promise: no more secrets. After all the shit we've put each other through, that's the one rule that has to mean something. Otherwise...what the fuck are we doing together?"

At the top of the stairs, she spun on me, glaring down. "Okay, you know what? I think I should go stay at Asha's tonight before one of us says something we can't take back."

"Does she have an attic?"

"Well done, Josh. You're an asshole."

"I love you, and you're breaking my fucking heart. Please."

"What? What do you want from me?"

"To stop sneaking around. Stop treating me like a fucking stranger you can manipulate into believing everything's normal. I've trusted you with the ugliest, most humiliating parts of me, but you sit there night after night for a fucking month and you lie right to my goddamn face."

"What are you talking about?" she shouted, clawing her hands through her hair.

"I watched you. Creeping around the house last night. Over and over. Flipping the latches and turning the locks."

"You've been spying on me?" Hadley stomped down the steps to meet me at the bottom, eyes full of fire.

"Because you won't talk to me. Let me help."

"What right do you think you have to monitor my every move? Forget about how fucked up that is. Do you understand what a hypocrite you are? Until very recently you were screwing half the undergrads on campus, but you don't see me checking your phone or hassling you over every drunken groupie who flirts with you at the bar."

"I have never, would never fucking cheat on you, Hadley, so don't—"

"Is that what it is? To you it's like I'm cheating on you because you don't get to watch the OCD girl fidget and count and pull her fucking hair out because she hates herself just a little more every time she twists the lock? Well, I'm sorry, but that's sick. Really. That's some kind of perverse fascination you have."

"You could have told me you were back on your ritual. You should have talked to me instead of letting this thing fester inside you. We're supposed to be partners."

"Man, you just can't help it, can you? This self-righteous bullshit just comes naturally to you. But if I so much as leave a fingerprint on the door to that music room, you'll rip my ass a new one. We all have shit, Josh. The difference is, I don't shove your face in it."

"Is that what you want?" I turned my back on her and headed for the music room.

"Josh, what are you doing?"

The door swung open, smacking off the wall behind it. Then I got a really stupid idea.

"Stop it, Josh. You don't—"

I hovered over the piano. Until then, I'd thought it was the thing I feared most. A massive black memorial sitting silent in a darkened tomb. The bench was over my head and ready to come crashing down.

"Josh, don't. You're going to regret this. Put it—"

I slammed it down, filling the room with the deafening sound of my pathetic rage. The legs hit the floor and my ass met the seat. Fingers to the keys, the melody came effortlessly. Easier than breathing. Like my heartbeat. I closed my eyes and let the notes slide down my arms, into my piano. Behind me, Hadley let out a sigh of relief.

"Why are you doing this?" she asked. "You don't have to be in here. This isn't what I wanted."

"Because right now this simple fucking thing is taking all my concentration." It felt like two bony hands tightening around my neck, squeezing the air from my lungs. My hands trembled. They vibrated over the cold, slick keys beneath my fingers. Behind my eyes, my headache protested every note. "And when I play this song, I see the blood running down her lips. I see the look in her eyes when she realized she was taking her last breath."

"Stop. Please. You don't have anything to prove to me."

"Apparently I do."

"Enough!" She slapped the cover over the keys, damn near snapping my fingers off. "Why would you think you have to do this for me?"

"Because I need you to trust me. If that means tearing back another layer of skin, so be it. You've hit bone. I have nothing left you haven't seen."

"I do trust you. It's just..."

"I love you, Hadley. I'm not capable of ignoring you. And I've tried to be what you needed. I've never tried so hard at anything in my life. So I don't know what the fuck to do with myself when you hide and won't tell me what's hurting you."

"I don't blame you for what happened with Scott, but I can't control this thing. It eats at me every day."

"Then why not let me help? Anything. Let me feel like I matter."

"Because I knew you'd beat yourself up thinking it was your fault. No matter what I said to convince you otherwise, all you'd hear is that you'd broken me. It's like you crave burden. You don't know how to behave unless you're living under a cloud of contrition. But I love you," she said, skimming her fingers across my shoulders, "and I can't stand giving you one more reason to hate yourself."

Wrapping my arms around her, I pulled Hadley onto my lap and pressed my forehead to hers. "It drives me crazy when you keep secrets from me. I don't want that to be us."

"I'm sorry. I just didn't want to let you down." Hadley draped her arms over my shoulders. "I was afraid you'd be disappointed in me."

"Never, Punky."

Pushing the hair from her face, I pressed my lips to hers. This complicated, infuriating woman had never been easy. Our lives would never be simple. I didn't love her because it was painless. We were a fucking mess and sometimes it hurt. But she understood me the way no one else could. And I'd never give up on her without a fight.

"For the record," I said, brushing my fingers along her cheek, "I apologize for being a prick."

Hadley arched an eyebrow. "And..."

"And for resorting to covert tactics. Maybe that was a step too far."

"Hmm." Nodding, she pursed her lips. Sassy little shit. "Maybe. You certainly know how to overdo it." She grabbed my face and planted a rough kiss on my lips. "But I love you anyway."

White light burst in the center of my vision. Electricity shot through my body, hot and violent. My arms clenched around her. My jaw locked. It was a sudden, terrifying burst like being struck by lightning.

"Josh?"

Hadley pulled back, but I couldn't let her go.

"What's wrong?"

I tried to speak, but my lips wouldn't move. Sharp pain flared behind my eyes. The room slid sideways. Her face blurred in two. Her voice became a loud, high-pitched ringing in my ears.

"Josh!"

The last thing I remembered was falling to the floor.

Chapter 32

The myth of my invincibility had been greatly exaggerated. I woke with a splitting headache and a bitter taste tinged with blood on my tongue. Like the worst hangover that ever drove a man to sobriety, I felt nauseated, disoriented.

Opening my eyes, a blurry collage of color filled my vision. The too-bright room smelled like latex and antiseptic. Despite my diminished capacity, I felt her. I squeezed her hand entwined with mine. Her presence alone could wake the dead.

"Punky."

"Hey," she answered as she leaned closer. Warm lips met mine. "How do you feel?"

"Like shit. What happened?"

Fingers swept over my eyebrows. "Can you see?"

I looked in her general direction and found only a pale blob with a dark frame hovering above my prone body. "You're fuzzy. Come closer."

"This better?"

"A little closer."

Long hair brushed my cheek. "Here?"

"Just a little more."

Her mouth caressed mine. I sucked on her bottom lip, licking across the soft flesh.

"Get in," I told her.

"The bed?"

"The bed. My pants. Yes."

"Can you even feel your dick?" Her fingers wove into my hair.

"I don't know. Reach down there and find it for me." I took her hand, sliding it down my chest.

Hadley backed away. "Josh, do you know where we are?"

"Can we pretend I don't?"

"Not really." She put her hand in mine. "You had a seizure. An ambulance brought you to the hospital. You've been unconscious for almost an hour."

"Well, fuck."

"How much do you remember?" Hadley dug her thumb into the pressure point between my thumb and forefinger, massaging the nerves.

Girl was fucking magical.

"I made a mess."

"That you did."

"But we're not fighting anymore, right?"

"Not at the moment," she said with a sweet smile. "I'm sorry."

"Let's not do that now."

As a rule, healthy men in their twenties did not fall to the floor, flopping about and foaming at the mouth. Our pattern of lurching from one emergency to the next wasn't nearly over.

"Just be here with me."

The doctor entered minutes later. Then it was tests and waiting and the resignation that I had pissed away too many years of not creating a life with Hadley. Not delivering on the promise of my parents' aspirations for me. I was sick of being the erotic wasted talent.

My mind was elsewhere as the doctor delivered the results of my MRI. The finer points of my state of health were not enough to hold my attention. Perhaps because I had never been especially interested in myself as a topic.

* * *

"Josh, this is insane. Stop."

Towing Punky behind me by the hand, I dragged her through the dark, thick forest. I followed only a memory and the narrow beam of the flashlight.

"Josh."

"This is important," I told her.

I wasn't sure what we'd find—if anything—but it was imperative that we seek it.

"Now?" Our boots crunched over dead leaves and squashed mounds of mud and moss under our soles. "It's freezing. It's the middle of the night."

"Morning, actually."

We'd spent all night at the hospital. The sun was due soon. I walked in front of her, holding back hanging branches from her path.

"That makes all the difference."

"Really? How so?"

Her snarky tone was a thin veil at best. She'd come willingly. Out of curiosity if not absolute terror that I'd drop dead should she take her eyes off me for more than a second.

"You should be resting. You need to call Simon. You—"

"Sweetheart." Pausing, I turned the flashlight up to illuminate her face. "I appreciate your concern. Rest assured that I am aware of the thirty-seven tasks of dire importance that I must carry out in due time and precise order."

"Uh-huh."

No one did unimpressed like Punky.

"But"—I stroked my thumb along her jaw—"I've earned the right to fuck off any damn way I please. That starts with you, me, and our very own Neverland."

"Now would be an awful time to develop a Peter Pan complex."

I aimed the flashlight into the distance to her right.

Pressing my lips to her ear, I whispered, "Close your eyes."

After a skeptical glance, her eyes shut.

On the trip home from the hospital and without any particular instigation, a memory poked me right between the eyes. Not following would have driven me fucking mad.

"'If you shut your eyes and are a lucky one,'" I recited, seeing as how she'd given me the cue, "'you may see at times a shapeless pool of lovely pale colors suspended in the darkness; then if you squeeze your eyes tighter, the pool begins to take shape, and the colors become so vivid that with another squeeze they must go on fire.'"

"How do you do that?" she asked.

Peter Pan was one of her favorites. As a child, she never understood why people kept telling her she couldn't fly away and join the Lost Boys.

I waited, siphoning every necessary second from the universe. "Magic."

I doused the flashlight just as the first shades of color rose up like high tide over the trees.

"Open."

Watching the light touch her skin and the sparks ignite her eyes, I viewed the gentle sunrise in the slow dawn across Hadley's face.

"Impossible," she whispered.

"I no longer believe in any such thing."

Tugging her forward, I led Hadley through the tall grass. Our tree house. The lost adventure. Overcome by vines and time, the rotted remnants still occupied the center of its massive tree. We stared toward the east while I held her against my chest, arms wrapped around her stomach.

"Do you like it?" I asked.

"It's hallucinatory." She wiped her eyes as her chest rose and fell to a staccato rhythm. "I can't believe you found it."

Sitting among the wet grass and the bird songs, we watched the world transform. The sun overtook the sky, painting night into day. I wanted to write it all. The melody of her heartbeat. The chorus of her awe. For the first time in months, the music in my head sounded nothing like the distorted, puzzled meandering of a hapless neophyte. But it would have to wait. Item number 17.

"You spent the last few weeks waiting for me to combust," Hadley said.

"And you didn't. Why?"

"The same reason you waited so long to tell me what happened that night you ran away. How selfish would I be if I heaped my crazy into your lap? You had your own shit to deal with."

"Like what?" I asked, incredulous.

What possible "shit" did she think was more important than her well-being?

"You pulled a gun on someone." She brought her legs up to her chest and wrapped our arms around her knees. "Because of me."

"And I'm pretty fucking okay with that."

This was the conversation we should have had weeks ago. Then again, I hadn't come right out with it either.

"No one lays a hand on you, Punky. Ever."

"My parents. Tom's house. Every time something bad has happened, I've been alone. It felt like too much to ask of you."

"Get rid of that thought." Gripping the back of her neck, my nose pressed to her temple, I willed Hadley to accept my sincerity and put to rest this debate for the last time. "Seal up whatever self-destructive, self-conscious crevice of your head that idea crawled out of and never open it again. I love you. Shit like that just pisses me off."

"I'm scared." Her grip on my hands tightened.

"I'll dig a moat and build a fucking wall around the house, if that's what it takes. If you don't want to move—"

"Damn it, Josh!"

Hadley got on her knees and turned to face me. Either she was going to tackle me to the ground and mount my dick as if it were a Thoroughbred, or Punky was about to beat the living shit out of me.

"I didn't set the alarm when I went chasing after the ambulance. I didn't check the locks. I'm not sure I even closed the front door behind me. They put you on a gurney and drove off. What if that was it? You can't leave me to do this on my own. That wasn't the deal."

"Come here, sweetheart." I pulled her into my lap and tucked her against my chest. "I made you a promise. I always keep my word."

"You could go blind."

"But I won't."

"You could end up a vegetable."

That was expressly against my wishes, but a conversation for later. Item number 26.

"You could die."

"I will die. It's unavoidable. But not before I'm old and senile."

"Don't do that. Don't make it a joke."

No. The mass of tissue and calcium deposits festering near my optic nerve and pituitary gland were not a joke. I'd seen nothing amusing in the image of the tumor inhabiting my brain. Item number 4: Schedule supraorbital craniotomy. But it was my tumor and I'd take it any way I pleased. With grace, if possible. Dignity.

"Things are going to be different," she promised. Combing her fingers through my hair, she cast her eyes downward. "No more doomsday bunker and flailing to fool-proof life. After you beat this, I'll get help."

"You think we should try normal for a while? See how the other half lives?"

"Let's not go to extremes."

"Fair enough." I placed my lips to hers. "I'm going to be okay, sweetheart. Don't start burying me yet."

"If you don't wake up from surgery, I'll make sure they can't give you an open casket."

"That's my girl." I took her lips, embedding in the kiss everything I hastened to explain. "Hadley, I'm not done yet. I just got everything I ever wanted."

* * *

I spent hours avoiding the call to my dad. At my mother's piano, I played at the keys and scribbled notes. It felt imperative, a fever of creative energy. As if years of abstinence now begged to be sated, the music released. It all came so easily, pouring out of my fingers, rushing to be realized before...

Anything could happen. Step outside and have a tree fall on me. Get struck down by lightning on a clear day. But music wanted to be heard.

I felt her there. My mother. Her influence in every bar I composed. Years spent distancing myself from her memory, letting that empty hole fester and scab over. I had refused to treat the wound or find a way to fill it. Afraid to acknowledge the loss like it could become any more real if I allowed myself to think about her or look at a photograph.

But it was different now. Faced with the possibility of leaving this life, I saw all the work left undone. The wasted time spent squandering the gift she nurtured in me. If I didn't honor Carmen's memory, if I didn't do something with the experience of the short time we'd had together, what was the point? I was her only child, and I had all but abandoned her legacy.

Most of all, I didn't want my father to watch me suffer her loss anymore.

Sitting in his study, it was late in the afternoon when I finally worked up the nerve to call him.

"Hey, Dad."

"Josh, how are you?"

I sank into his leather couch. It smelled of the cigars Simon smoked in secret and the brandy spilled when Carmen found him out.

"Existentially? I'm experiencing a renaissance."

"Is that right?"

I heard the smile in his voice and hated to let it happen.

"I came close to demolishing her piano last night. Hadley and I had a fight."

I rubbed at my eye. The headache was unbearable. My vision in one eye had danced somewhere between blurry and useless for most of the morning.

"Instead I sat down and played Rachmaninoff."

"You're going to have to learn how to talk to that girl."

"I'm working on it. I've been at it all morning," I said. "The piano. It's coming faster than I can transcribe. Nothing like I've attempted before. I don't think I'm the same musician I used to be. You'll need to give me your opinion."

"Of course, son. I'm thrilled you're trying."

"I don't want the music to crawl too far up its own ass, you know?"

My heart raced. A praying man would have looked to the sky and begged for an asteroid.

"You'll have to tell me if I'm diluting myself. Deluding. Either."

"I doubt it, but I'd be happy to listen."

My throat convulsed in an attempt to swallow. "You'll need to come home, Dad. I...uh...I need you to come home."

"Josh, tell me what's happened."

It gutted me to say the words. No father should receive such a call, least of all Simon.

"I'm sick, Dad. I need your help."

A son witnessing his father cry is akin to nothing else. There is no comparison. Mothers and daughters can't possibly find a correlation in their relationship. It doesn't exist. Perhaps accepting that her mother masturbates. Maybe then. Short of that, no.

For a while, I sat on the smoke-infused leather couch and listened to my father cry. I had heard it before. He'd cried for days after Carmen died. No matter that it wasn't new, the sound still got to me. So foreign.

In some sense, I had always accepted that my life belonged to the people who loved me. My dad. Hadley. Experiencing the moment they pondered my mortality brought to light the truth that my life was a responsibility, a promise. It wasn't mine alone. It was an investment into which others had patiently, dutifully, selflessly paid. Whether or not the hands of a surgeon left me otherwise intact and functioning was beyond my control. What I did to pay out dividends after the fact would be within my realm of manipulation.

"I've envied you," Simon said. He sounded exhausted, both for the energy spent and the reserves he would tap in the coming days. "I'd give anything to have been with her at the end."

Revulsion to his sentiment was immediate and reflexive, though I did understand his perspective. My mother had died quickly and silently across my lap. His wife left this world while he was fifty fucking feet away doing fuck knows what. I stood and left the shadowy room, phone to my ear.

"Were there...signs?"

We'd never broached the subject. After the funeral and mourning and slogging through the grief, I had slammed the door on every attempt made to discuss her.

"Did I let your mother die?"

"Fuck. No. Dad, that's not what I meant."

"I asked myself that question every day for four years. Then it was every other day. Yes, there were signs. If a patient walked into a doctor's office complaining of headaches, irregular sleep patterns, memory loss, mood swings, and claimed she heard music when there was none, he'd order a CT scan and an MRI. But your mother—"

"She was always a little irregular," I answered.

"Yes. Eccentric at times. Alternately focused and dispersed. She carried on according to her own rhythm. The picture was not so clear until there was nothing to be done."

My mom liked to paint flowers. As in *Alice in Wonderland*, Red Queen taking a brush to roses and lilies. So of course Hadley was enamored. My mom taught her how to paint the smallest, most intricate scenes on the most unconventional of canvases, to build huge worlds in tiny places. Carmen didn't compose music, she told stories about little boys slaying dragons and fighting pirates while dancing her fingers across the keys. Every note was a syllable. I could play the tale of King Arthur before I learned to read.

"I'm going to find you the best possible surgeon," Simon said.

"I know."

"There are some specialists here I can consult with. I'll make the calls, then book the flight."

I found Punky on the back porch with the easel set up and splotches of paint running up her arms. Punky was the messiest damn artist outside of a preschool. The more material she got on her, the better the work turned out. Fascinating how that happened. I never saw her so uninhibited as when she worked. Or when we were fucking. That was pretty terrific, too.

"Thank you," I answered Simon.

Hadley set down her brush and turned around. She took my out-stretched hand and pressed her cheek to my chest.

"I'm not scared. Maybe I should be. Maybe anyone in his right mind would be. The most terrifying part is knowing how much this hurts you."

Both of them.

Chapter 33

"Tell them," Hadley whispered in my ear.

She sat on my lap, running her fingers through the hair at the nape of my neck. I'd fallen asleep twice during the movie. Near us, our friends covered the living room couch. It had been a week since my diagnosis, and Hadley was growing more insistent that I go public with this latest development. I was inclined to ignore it until it was time to go under the knife.

"What next?" Corey asked. He picked up the remote to scan through the Netflix queue while Asha and Trey bickered over the selections.

"Tell them," Hadley repeated.

"Why ruin a perfectly good afternoon?"

"Fine. I'll tell them."

I squeezed her ass. "No. My tumor, my news. Don't steal my thunder."

Punky rolled her eyes and flicked my nipple ring. Feisty little shit was going to make me bend her over this love seat with a room full of witnesses.

"Do it. Chickenshit."

"Chickenshit? Really?" I slid my fingers under her sweatshirt and over her ribs. "Careful how you proceed, sweetheart."

"Tickle me and I'll scream tumor. Try it, MacKay."

"I'm sorry." Trey leaned forward. "Are we interrupting your foreplay? Feel free to take it upstairs."

"Josh has something to say," Hadley announced.

"You're getting your sac pierced," Corey answered.

"You're getting warmer."

Hadley was not amused, glaring at me with violent intentions. I could end up with stitches in my scrotum if I tested her much further.

"I have a brain tumor," I stated as I reached for a handful of popcorn. "Let's watch *John Dies at the End*."

I crunched on popcorn as all else fell silent. Punky stared at me. Yep, there went my nuts. She was likely to go *Fight Club* on me with a rubber band and a machete.

"There," I said, picking bits of kernel from my teeth. "I told them."

"Oh, for fuck's sake."

"Are you for real?" Asha asked. "Is he serious?"

"As a craniopharyngioma," I said. Was that more or less serious than a heart attack?

"A what?" Trey asked.

"A benign pituitary brain tumor."

"Holy shit."

"What?"

I looked over the group, all staring at me like I'd just been handed a death sentence. I fully intended to live. The expectation to the contrary was starting to bum me the fuck out.

"Simon is flying in this weekend and he's going to help me narrow down my options."

"Which are?" Trey asked.

"Cherry, oak, pine—"

Hadley launched off my lap and stormed into the kitchen. Maybe that last bit was pushing it.

"I need to find a surgeon who can perform a supraorbital craniotomy. It's minimally invasive as far as drilling a hole in my skull goes. They cut through my eyebrow, push some muscle and brain matter aside, and then remove the tumor. Two weeks in the hospital, tops."

"That's it?" Trey propped his elbows on his knees, brow furrowed.

"I know, right? I thought I was looking at radiation and shit. Months feeling like death warmed over. But with some meds post-surgery, I'll be good as new."

"If the surgeon doesn't get twitchy hands and slice into your goddamn brain," Hadley shouted from the kitchen. "Or sever your optic nerve. Or you crash during surgery. Or—"

Glass shattered on the kitchen floor. Asha leapt up from the couch to help.

"Punky's taking it well," I told the guys.

"You're an asshat," she shouted. "It isn't funny."

But I didn't want to be sad. If I spent the next few days with the look of certain death in my eyes, Hadley and Simon would suffer more. The best I could do was dose the reality of my situation with irreverence. A pissed-off Punky was always better than a crying Punky.

"How did your dad take it?" Corey asked. "Shit. He must be a wreck."

"He agrees that my prognosis is good. Despite how it sounds."

"Wow." Trey sat back, slumping on the couch. "I don't know what to say."

"You don't have to. Just make a list of what you want and I'll put it in my will."

"I swear, Josh—"

Punky's tone had my testicles crawling inside my stomach.

"Okay, okay," Asha said. "Let's get you away from the sharp objects."

I'd make this up to Punky somehow.

"What are you going to do about school?" Corey asked.

"Keep going until I can't. I can go on medical leave for recovery, but I'm looking at a few weeks at most. Actually, I'm feeling creative again. Been working on my composition. It's sort of ballooning."

"Hadley said you were back at the piano."

I smiled. Couldn't help it. Playing made me happier than I thought possible without my mom there to enjoy it with me.

"Yeah, I'm choosing to believe the seizure knocked loose the blockage."

And weeks of therapy, but that wasn't as sexy.

"You had a seizure?" Asha yelled from the kitchen. "Damn it, Josh!"

I might have created an angry pair I was not prepared to fend off. But I did have an idea. "Let's play a show."

"Where?" Trey asked.

"Here. Tonight." I toyed with my tongue piercing between my lips, letting the idea simmer. "Yeah. Invite just a small group of friends. We can open up the garage and put out some tiki torches and shit. I'll get a keg."

"You're serious."

"Why not?" I looked to Corey, sensing that he'd be the more agreeable one of the two. "Let's just have fun and jam."

Hadley appeared with Asha beside her at the edge of the living room. I met her eyes, offering a silent apology.

"What do you say?" I asked her.

"I love that idea."

I nodded, gesturing for her come closer. Hadley curled up in my lap and I placed a kiss to her temple.

"All right," Trey answered. "The garage sessions at the MacKay house."

* * *

I had a moment of trepidation as the first cars pulled up to the front of the house. But the others went about stocking the makeshift bar and hanging strings of lights as if nothing was amiss. If anything, Hadley and our friends looked relieved for the distraction. Energetic, even.

So fuck it.

Vaughn watched as Kyle messed around with my Les Paul, Professor Monroe taking an interest in the next prodigy. Grace came with a small army of political science majors. Asha had invited a few people from the photography class she shared with Hadley. Likewise, classmates of Corey and Trey showed for the last-minute event. I really had been living in a hole, because I wasn't aware we knew so many people.

The garage felt tiny with two dozen others crowded inside and spilling out onto the torch-lined dirt drive. I tried to hold a conversation with my jazz ensemble from class, but my attention was across the room, where Hadley stood with Andre and his friends.

Asha was going in my will. Big, bold letters that read, "Give her whatever she wants." She had insisted the occasion called for a costume change, so she and Hadley had driven into the city while the guys and I went out for provisions. The result of the girls' excursion was my wet dream. Punky wore a black cropped sweatshirt with hand-painted lyrics to one of my songs. Below her bare stomach, which I wanted to either lick or cover up, she wore a pair of black leather pants that might as well have been sprayed on her legs. I wanted to fucking mount her, but the house was a bit overrun by spectators at the moment.

With the support of many of the people in this room, I hadn't become a complete catastrophe. There were flaws—some that were in remediation and others I held to, like proof of my battles—but mostly I was in working order. I had love, friendship, even mentors, and I was learning how to hand off some of the valuable lessons they had been patient enough to teach me.

Successful people always say that the trick to a happy life is never having regrets. That's a load of bullshit. If we regret nothing, then we've never truly failed, never truly hurt, and never really lost. Without regret, we have never acted with all our passion and anger and love and hope only to have our skull stomped on while we bite a street curb. Those soft, empty people don't know the satisfaction of rehabilitation. They have nothing but optimism, because optimism thrives where conflict is absent. Conflict makes us hearty. Hearty lives flourish in the blackest depths and the driest soil.

I wouldn't correct one single mistake.

I regretted not one regret.

Crossing the garage, I came up behind Punky and wrapped my arms around her stomach to slide my fingers across her bare skin. "I missed you, sweetheart," my lips whispered against her ear.

Hadley shivered and arched her back. "Josh, you remember the guys."

I nodded, tightening my hold on her body. "Thanks for coming."

My eyes met with Andre's. We'd graduated from challenging stares to flat indifference.

"Welcome."

There was no reason to be a dick. We didn't like each other, but we couldn't be enemies.

"Hey, brother." Corey came up and slapped a hand to my shoulder. "You about ready?"

"Yeah."

Hadley joined me as we congregated around the drums. Trey and I hooked into the amps while Corey tuned his kit. I got that nervous, excited jolt I always felt before a performance, but this was better. There were no assumptions waiting inside this garage, no expectations.

Hadley watched me like a cat prowling in the tall grass, hind legs poised to spring.

"You're having dirty thoughts about me," she accused.

"Do I have any other kind?"

"I've known you to be romantic once or twice."

"Sweetheart." I grabbed her around the waist. "Even when I

dream of singing under your window or penning sonnets to your beauty, you're still naked and touching yourself to the sound of my voice."

She bit her lip, rolling her eyes. "Why don't you put that sharp tongue to good use?"

I shrugged. "If you insist." I dipped my fingers into the top of her pants and dropped to my knees.

"Fucking Christ," Punky hissed. She grabbed my hair and yanked. "Get up. Everyone is watching."

Standing, I pressed my lips to hers. "We really need to work on our communication."

"Shut up and sing," she said with a laugh.

"Which is it? Shut up or sing?"

Punky pried herself from my hands, backing up. "I'm walking away now. You stay there. Stay. Good boy."

"Remember that when I take you over my knee tonight."

The room fell silent.

Hadley flipped me off, her face burning with embarrassment and anger. I'd let her smack me around a little, as long as we did it naked.

Trey came up beside me, an amused curve to his lips. "And to think you almost let her get away."

"Yeah. Why didn't you try to stop me?"

"Asshole."

Corey sat making eyes at the blonde in the front row. We would play the song he wrote for her first.

"You nervous?" I asked.

A huge dumb grin curved his freshly shaven mug. Turned out Grace wasn't a fan of beards, either. "Not even a little."

"Good. She's going to love it."

"I know."

I looked between him and Trey. I had lucked out somehow. "It's been an honor," I told them. "I'm grateful to have you in my life."

Trey glanced at Corey and back to me. "I didn't see an iceberg."

"This ship isn't sinking," Corey said. "No need to break out the violins."

"Fine, fuckers." I slid my guitar over my shoulder. "Count it off."

That night, to an intimate audience, we left it all on the cement floor covered with cheap Ikea rugs. We were the Ramones at CBGB, the Red Hot Chili Peppers at the Roxy in 1989. For a few hours, we were the Doors at Whisky a Go Go. Something significant happened among the screaming of my Les Paul, the dark rhythm of Trey's bass, and the thunder of Corey's drums. Maybe it was the liquor or the excited high of knowing that those were the last few hours of a closing chapter in my life, but the night felt fucking transcendent.

* * *

My second seizure came two weeks later while Hadley and I took a shower. Forty-eight hours after that, I lay in a hospital bed awaiting surgery.

"You understand why I set it up this way?" I asked my father.

It was easy to play unaffected while I carried on around the house like nothing could touch me. Here, in a hospital gown and all the metal removed from my body, the reality of my circumstances sat heavy on my chest. If I didn't make it, certain affairs had to be in order.

"Please." He held my hand between both of his. "Let's not have this conversation."

We'd talked of almost nothing else since he flew home to help make arrangements for my surgery.

"I need to know you understand," I said. "I need your word."

"You have it. Of course, son. It's your decision."

"Help her." I squeezed his hand, pleading. "She won't want this. She'll fight you. But you have to tell her it's okay."

"Josh." Simon leaned against the bed, dragging his chair closer. "Listen to me."

His blue eyes held my full attention. They were clear, focused. No sign of withheld tears.

"When we first brought you home, you were malnourished and covered in bedbug bites."

That foster home was a shithole, but my health problems went far beyond. My birth mother had been an addict, which meant I was born a weak, sickly child. When one foster family got sick of the doctors and medications and twenty-four-hour care, they shipped me off to a new home.

"Even then, as small as you were, you were so strong. Every day we saw improvement. Most children at that age wouldn't have survived."

I wouldn't have if not for Punky and my parents getting me out of there.

"You've been through worse than this and pulled through. My son is a survivor. You don't give up. Ever."

I wiped my eyes, choking on the lump in my throat. "Yes, sir."

My dad smiled, holding the side of my face. "I love you. You're all I have in this world. And you've made me so proud."

"I love you, too." I pulled him closer to wrap my arms around his shoulders. "Thank you," I whispered, "for everything you've given me."

Simon pulled away and placed a box in my hand. He gave me a last approving look before leaving the room. Hadley slid inside before the door closed.

"There she is," I said, holding my hand out while I stuffed the box under the blanket. "Thought you'd run off."

"What, now?" She took the seat vacated by Simon and brought my palm up to her cheek. "Not a chance. We're just getting to the good part."

"You want to go a couple rounds?" I skimmed my thumb over her bottom lip. "Blow a fuse in the heart monitor?"

She smiled and bit the pad of my thumb. "Scoundrel."

What was the procedure for entering surgery with a hard-on?

"Blow me for good luck, then?"

"Uh-uh." She kissed my palm and laid our entwined hands on my stomach. "I don't go down on guys in hospital gowns."

"Well, shit. Is that a strict rule?"

"Very."

I sighed, trailing the fingers of my broken hand up her arm. "Fine. Hop on my face and I'll eat you out instead."

Laughing, Hadley flicked my ear. Fucking hurt.

"Just think," she said with a smirk, "you have sponge baths to look forward to."

My dick twitched. Fucking hell.

"You're right. I'll pull through just for the privilege of dripping soapy water over every inch—"

"You, stupidhead. The *patient* gets the sponge baths."

"Is that how it works?"

She nodded, biting her lip.

"I like this plan. Wheel me in."

By gradual centimeters, Hadley's expression sobered as she combed her fingers through my hair. I wanted to leap off this bed and declare myself cured if only to get rid of that sad tilt to her lips.

"So...uh...there are a few things I want to cover before..." Under the sheet, my fingers found the box and traced the seam around the opening. "Hear me out. Bite your tongue until I'm done."

Hadley nodded. Those soft, loving eyes watched me with all the hope and fear warring inside her.

"I've named you the sole beneficiary in my will."

"Your what?" She jerked upright and released my hand. "Fuck you, Josh. Don't even."

"Too late. It's done."

"I don't want to hear this. Simon—"

"Sweetheart."

I took her hand and held it to my chest. She wouldn't get away without dragging me with her.

"My father is just fine. We've exhausted the topic. He doesn't need the money. And if he did, you'd be there for him."

"Of course, I would, but—"

"Stop interrupting."

Punky's lips snapped shut, though her defiant eyes glared at me.

"Second, and this is nonnegotiable—"

"Because that last part is?"

I kissed her knuckles. "No. The chances of something going wrong are slim, but just in case the surgeon gets a little scalpel-happy—"

"What are you saying?"

"In the event that a decision must be made whether or not to pull the plug, I want it to be you."

"No." She shook her head, her face turning red as tears gathered in her eyes. "Why would you do that to me? I don't want...no... please don't."

"I know." Every drop down her cheek landed against my heart like a lead weight. "I know. But it has to be you. Simon wouldn't ever stop fighting, hoping for a way to save me. He'd keep me alive on machines hoping for a miracle. I need you to be my voice. To tell him when it's time to let me go. I don't want to be a body in a bed, hooked up to machines for the rest of my life. Please, Hadley. Give that to me. The last thing I will ever ask of you."

"Damn it."

She draped her arms over my body and laid her head on my chest. I ran my fingers through her hair, listening to her cry.

"Why am I any different from him? Why would I be so eager to let you die?"

"Because you're my soul, Punky. You're my heart. No one knows or understands me better than you. And no matter what, you'll always protect me."

"I hate you," she muttered through broken sobs.

"I know. I love you, too." I pulled the box out from under the sheet and turned up her palm to place it inside. "I need you to be my wife."

Her fingers curled around the box as she raised her head. I opened it for her and revealed my mother's engagement ring.

"Marry me, Hadley."

She stared at the solitaire diamond on a platinum band. It wasn't big, but it held the purest love I have ever witnessed. Together, my parents had been as close to perfect as two people ever were. I hoped to live up to just a fraction of what they'd shared.

She stared, without a sound, for a goddamn fortnight.

"Say yes," I begged. Say anything.

"No."

"Try again."

"No, Josh." Hadley closed the box and set it on the table beside the bed. "I'm not taking that ring."

"You want a new one?" I reached for her hand but she stepped out of my reach. "Punky, get back here."

"I don't want a new ring. I'm not saying yes." All color drained from her face and she held her arms around her stomach.

"You don't want to marry me."

"More than anything I want to marry you," she replied. "I love you. You're it. End of story. But I'm not taking a deathbed proposal. Ask me again when you don't have a gun to your head."

"That's not what this is," I argued, sitting up and about to tackle her to the ground and drag a yes out of her. "Hadley—"

She pushed me back down and placed her lips to mine. "I'm right here," she whispered. "You have me. When you wake up, I'm going to be right here to hold your hand. One step at a time."

"You're really turning me down?" My fingers weaved into her hair, holding on, unable to give her up. This felt so…wrong.

"I'm giving you something to look forward to."

Two nurses walked in. After a few goodbyes, I was riding up an elevator to go under the knife.

Chapter 34

So much worry and to-do over cutting a hole in my head, but that was nothing. A dreamless sleep that came and went. Death was easy. Living, that was the challenge. And my struggle was an intensive course in genuine fucking agony with a humiliation enema thrown in for good measure.

I awoke from surgery far worse for the wear. The reminder that I would recover was no consolation for the wires that hung from my chest, the IV and arterial lines running into my arms, and the goddamn catheter shoved up my dick. My throat had played host to a drag race. One trip in with the breathing tube and one back out, stripping the soft, spongy lining of my trachea.

On the doctor's orders, I had starved myself to prepare for surgery. I'd spent hours with my attorney finalizing the details of all that I could leave behind. Again, I'd dragged Simon away from work, asking that he drop everything to cater to my latest emergency. I'd made Punky cry, and that shit was unacceptable. All of that, and I still had a goddamn headache. Hadley could have gone six innings with a bat across my skull and not done one tenth of the damage.

Beeping machines, bright lights, and constant voices passing in the hallway populated my corner of hell. Ticking, popping, swishing, dripping noises in my head, the result of air trapped inside my skull, left me questioning my sanity. The doctor had skipped that part during his cursory consultation before they put me under.

Hours passed without relief. It seemed the second I was able to glimpse the possibility of sleep, the nurse was back to poke and prod, and fuss over my vitals.

"How are you feeling?"

Give me more drugs and fuck off.

"Do you know what day it is?"

The hour of my discontent. Asshole.

"Can you tell me your name?"

I am become Death. Up my goddamn dosage.

Then they moved me to the neurological acute care unit. I wore fewer wires and tubes, but I was sporting a fancy new monster of a bruise where the arterial line had been stuck in my wrist.

"Hi, hon. My name is Sheryl. I'm going to take that catheter out now. It won't hurt a bit."

Lying cunt.

When the day came that I got my first bite of solid food, I promptly saw it again as I hugged the toilet. Later, they pumped me full of laxatives and stool softeners, for fear a rough shit would burst open the hole in my head, and insisted that I keep shoving food down my tender throat. So, one way or another, I spent a fucking eternity over that porcelain depository.

Simon was lucky enough to hear me throw a tantrum over the

exhaustively long process of building up the strength to reach back and wipe my own ass. Punky was awarded the unenviable duty of remembering how many times I shit, pissed, and threw up. Because the nurses were real fucking fascinated by everything that came out of me. These indignities did have one upside. I hardly gave a damn about the severe bruising over half my face and my eye that was swollen shut.

When they finally took me home after my two-week stay, I brought my Punky pillow to bed and checked out for eighteen straight hours.

"I love you," she whispered.

"Don't ever let me do that again."

Chapter 35

Session 11

"Most people consider *afterlife* to mean some plane of existence after death. Even the term is misleading. If we have consciousness after we fuck off this mortal coil, isn't that still life? *Afterdeath* sounds better."

I watched as the coin tumbled over my fingers. After four weeks, I had gotten pretty damn good at this. Gradually, I was regaining dexterity and control in my right hand. My knee bounced in time with each peak and trough the quarter traveled.

"Mortal coil," I repeated. "I think *Hamlet* gets the points for most recognizable use of the phrase. It's supposed to mean 'the bustle and turmoil of this mortal life.' Whatever. But here's something you didn't know."

I sat forward, captivated by George Washington's head somersaulting over my knuckles.

"In the second volume of *Parerga and Paralipomena*, Arthur Schopenhauer suggested that we've been using it wrong. *Mortal coil.* He thinks the word *shuffle* was a typesetter's mistake and that it should be 'shuttled off.' Like weaving, not space shuttles. Those didn't exist in 1851."

Shit. George botched the dismount and landed headfirst on the floor.

"So Schopenfucker says that the phrase should mean 'when we have unwound and worked off this coil of mortality.' He's referring to the Fates and the idea that life is a thread coiled on a weaver's spool. See?"

"Josh," Reid said.

"Right," I answered with a nod. "Sorry. Tangents."

George got his ass up to try again.

"So, what is life? The atoms that make up our bodies—the same that compose the stars and rocks and toilet seats—are repurposed, recycled, and reused. A tree falls in the forest and becomes bird shit and mushrooms and fur on a deer."

George was a little shaky, traveling the hurdles of my knuckles.

"*Afterlife* is a stupid word," I said. "However, if it must exist, I prefer the second usage: later life."

George took a nosedive to the floor. Fucking amateur.

"Did I miss the point or are you getting to it within the hour?" Reid tossed her chopsticks into the empty takeout container and threw it in the trash can beside the desk.

I sat back, pocketing the coin. "You've gotten mean."

"Only when you ramble to avoid my questions."

"Maybe if you asked better questions…"

"You'd find more creative ways to distract yourself?"

I rubbed at my eyebrow. Four weeks after surgery, I still had stitches through the incision, but the bruising and swelling had subsided.

"French and German scientists have created light bullets. Can't we just ponder that for a minute? Let's sit here and contemplate the astounding, terrifying implications of achieving the pew-pew effect."

"You died," she said.

"You make it sound so final."

"For most people—"

"I'm not most people."

"Your heart stopped for twelve seconds on the operating table."

"That's not a stop. A stutter, at best."

"You died."

"Impossible. I promised Punky I wouldn't."

"And yet…"

"Here I am. Spectacular, I know. But not a figment of your imagination."

"You died." Reid rolled forward in her chair, right up to the edge of the coffee table that held magazines and a candy dish and the untouched remnants of my lunch, but not coffee. "And you have nothing to say on the topic?"

"Of death? No."

"You've seen more of it than most people."

"The fuck do I know about dying?"

"What, then?"

"Later life," I said. "For me, the surgery happened and then it was over. What matters is what happens next."

Reid rolled away. With her poker face on, she appraised me, deciding how best to deal with my mood. I wasn't interested in looking backward. There was nothing there for me anymore. Everything I wanted, all that I needed, lay ahead.

I closed my notebook and set it aside. This was my last session with Reid. In the months she'd spent picking me apart, I'd done most of the talking. And while a confluence of events had transpired to insist that I face some of my deepest troubles, I could offer her the benefit of the doubt and say she helped a little. When she wasn't being argumentative and calling me names.

"How did it make you feel?" she asked.

"What are we talking about?"

Reid hated it when I did that, but my head was a cluttered place.

"Learning that your abuser had died. How did it make you feel?"

A few days before Hadley and I returned to school, my dad got a phone call. His lawyer informed us that the man sent to prison for molesting me had been found stiff and frozen under an overpass. Dead of a heart attack. He had been homeless since his release three years ago.

I stared at the ceiling and flicked my tongue piercing between my teeth. "I figured it out."

"Is that an answer or a segue?"

"The song," I said as I ignored her interruption.

It wasn't that I was avoiding the topic. There were few secrets I had left to hide from Reid. I couldn't respond to her question because I didn't have an answer. Truthfully, I didn't know what I felt.

"Right about the time the headaches started, there was this song I couldn't pin down. I couldn't get rid of it, no matter how long I spent trying to parse it out of the noise in my mind."

"I remember." She leaned back in her chair and crossed her legs, tilting her chin to rest on her folded fingers. Her "I'm listening" face.

"I mean I spent hours at a time scribbling clips and phrases on paper. Every time I picked up my guitar to work it out, the tune got farther away. Like trying to pick a speck of dirt out of a full bathtub. The closer you get, the more your hand displaces the water, and the harder it is to catch. The speck eludes you, twisting away in the current."

"What did you figure out?" she asked.

Reid had come to realize some time ago that asking leading questions, interrupting my tangents, tended to keep me on topic. My thought trains had a habit of skipping the tracks. I guess that was why we meshed well. She knew how to handle me. And I was the sort that needed a bit of handling or I'd steam halfway to Georgia before I realized I'd run out of rails.

"Help me out?" I had too much on my mind.

"You figured it out," Reid prompted. "How?"

"Right. I drained the tub. See, you don't know what you've forgotten until you remember. The images in my memory were always so vibrant, so present, that I didn't realize there were holes. So we get the call from the lawyer that the man is dead, and I get to wondering if it matters. The man is dead, but that doesn't change anything. A heart attack seems too elegant an end for such a disgusting monster."

I couldn't stop fidgeting. My knee bounced as I pictured his body cold and stiff. But my throat was clear and my pulse was steady.

"I took those thoughts to bed. Hadley fell asleep quickly, but I stared out the window with a song playing in my head. For a while there, I'd thought maybe it had been excised during surgery along with my headaches. Simon said Carmen sometimes heard music near the end. I could have bought into the same explanation. Only the melody came back."

Without any idea what I was looking for, I had taken my headphones to the piano room that night and went hunting for the E minor in the haystack.

"He had this old record player. The needle was so dull that everything beneath it came out among pops and crackles. Noise. He used to play the song to cover the sounds behind his bedroom door. To mask my cries. The same song. Every time. I don't know, it must have meant something to him. Or maybe it didn't. Maybe he was just a creature of habit or he was too fucking lazy to put on a new record. It doesn't matter, right? Because he's dead now, so why should I obsess over a fucking song I haven't heard in eighteen years?"

But I did. I did obsess, because I'd forgotten, and that was a goddamn revelation. Little details had slipped my recollection. Like I couldn't actually picture the tattoo on his back, only that I knew it was there. I didn't remember the color of his eyes, though I could still feel the texture of his hands. I smelled his foul breath, but I didn't remember the precise tone of his voice.

In a fit of rage, I had branded the memory to my chest. There was no ignoring the obvious. Truth be told, I didn't want to ignore it. If I let myself bury the memory, then it would be like it had never happened. Erased. That boy deserved better than to be swept under the rug.

"I sat at the piano and played for I don't know how long. Over and over, repeating chorus and verse. I recited the melody until it lost all meaning, until the notes were only sounds and the sounds were indecipherable from the hum of the air conditioner or the leaves rustling on the trees beyond the windows. White noise. Benign."

I had let the memory overtake me that night, overwhelm my senses and squeeze. I trembled at the piano. In a cold sweat, I felt my pulse race as my chest constricted. I had no idea how long I'd been at it until Punky walked in with a blanket and draped it over my shoulders. The first colors of the sunrise found their way inside the room as she sat beside me with her head on my shoulder.

"Are you still having panic attacks?" Reid asked.

"They're less frequent. A little less intense. I'm never going to get over it," I admitted. "I'm never moving past what he did, and I've accepted that fact. I'm not angry anymore. Really, what good does it do me to curse the dead? Maybe, in time, the memories will cease to rule me."

I had a goal, something to work toward. Reid had once made it a point to mention that I was lacking in that area.

"Forgiveness is something you've worked on lately," she said. "You forgave Scott."

"Mostly, yes. I'm trying to."

The ability to forgive had never come naturally to me. Like trust, it was something I tended to only dole out in small doses. But in Scott's case, I made the effort.

Chapter 36

On the Monday before final exams, I waited in a conference room with my attorney at the county courthouse. Scott was set to stand trial after the New Year, and the closer it got to the holidays, the more I thought about him sitting in jail and what it must have been like to detox in a prison cell. I didn't want to feel sorry for him, but a nagging sense of culpability had eaten at me since the break-in.

"You're certain this is what you want?" my attorney asked. He slid the stapled sheets of paper in front of me. "Look it over again. This is your last chance to change your mind."

Simon was right; I couldn't take responsibility for Scott's actions. But I would shoulder the blame for my part. Truth was, I should have helped him sooner. Looking back on all the petty bullshit between us—missing rehearsals and flaking on the band—that was a poor excuse for turning my back on a friend when he didn't have the will or wherewithal to help himself. Because if my circumstances had been different, I might have ended up like him somewhere along the way: angry, hopeless, and looking for anything to numb the pain of waking up and taking the next breath every day.

It didn't matter why Scott got hooked. Hell, maybe it was a fucking accident that spiraled out of his control. I didn't care about the why. Just that he be given a second chance to live a better life. I had gotten that when I needed it most, and it made all the difference.

"The prosecutor has already agreed to the terms," my attorney said, scrolling through e-mails on his phone. "And I'm confident the judge will sign off on it as long as Scott consents to be remanded into his parents' custody."

A pair of thick wooden double doors creaked and groaned. Escorted between a uniformed officer and a public defender in a cheap gray suit, Scott shuffled in wearing orange hospital scrubs and slip-on shoes. His hands cuffed at his stomach and chained to the shackles at his ankles. He jingled with every short step scuffed across the shiny floor. Those jingles, his little old-man steps, they laughed at him. Set deep inside his pale, gaunt face, his sallow eyes held profane humiliation. It hurt to look at him.

"Scott..."

I had come to tell him I was dropping the charges. To meet face-to-face and say that I could forgive him as long as he took this opportunity to start over. My attorney had worked it out with the court that Scott could avoid more jail time if he checked into rehab and stayed clean. I'd foot the bill. But seeing him hunched over the table, a broken shell of his former self, I knew that facing me in his condition only deepened his shame. Because it wasn't Scott who had threatened me or broken into my house. It wasn't the kid I'd known since high school who had pulled a gun on me at the bar. That person was a chemical creation that died of the DTs weeks ago. In front of me was the leftovers, and they didn't owe me anything.

So I left. My attorney stuck around to put the deal in writing and I got on with my life, leaving Scott in peace to do the same.

* * *

"Should we get you fit for a mouth guard?" I asked.

Punky gnawed on her bottom lip in agitation. She locked the back door and gave it a tug but released the handle without repeating the process.

"Or just have your mouth wired shut?"

"Fuck off," she snapped, huffing her way through the living room to the alarm keypad in the foyer. "You wouldn't last a week without a blow job."

I wouldn't last three days. Fucking sue me. After I'd made it past the pain and exhaustion post-surgery, I was a right cranky prick until Punky declared me well enough for a good lay.

Hadley had kept to her word and started seeing a therapist about her OCD. She wasn't two weeks in before she bit my head off after I made the terrible mistake of praising her for her progress. She hated the adulation. Gold stars for achievement were not the way to motivate Punky, as I discovered. Rather than being encouraging, she found "attagirl" condescending, as if we were placating her. If there was one thing she hated, it was being treated like a child. So, she got no pats on the back from me, just a swift kick in the ass to tell her she'd done well. It seemed to work out and kept heavy objects from flying at my head.

As she locked the front door, her hand lingered with the key in the dead bolt. I waited a moment to see if she'd let go on her own. Hadley appeared frozen in place, warring with her instincts.

"Go ahead, Punky. By all means, take your time. We've got all day."

She growled under her breath and kicked the front door, turning to flip me off. "Shithead."

"I know." I kissed her temple as she slid into my car. "Love you, too, sweetheart."

We were on our way to campus for the showcase that was the final exam for my Jazz Composition class. My fingers played over the steering wheel, revising bars of music in my head. It wasn't unheard of that I would rewrite an original work as I performed it for an audience.

"You look nervous," Hadley said.

My speed was excessive as we cruised toward the highway. The barbell in my tongue flicked between my teeth and I gripped the stick shift too tightly.

"I'm fine."

"Liar."

"I'm not nervous." So I was half a liar.

Truthfully, it wasn't the performance with my jazz ensemble that had me white-knuckling the steering wheel. Music was second nature. Getting the notes on paper had been the difficult part. Playing? I could do that in my sleep.

"The bulging vein in your head says otherwise."

"That's my Pestering Punky vein. It responds to how irritating you are."

"Whatever. You can't live without me."

"You got me there."

An hour later we were in the dressing room behind the stage of the campus music hall. My ensemble was up next, the musicians already waiting in the wings while I fucked with the bow tie on my tux and fingered the box hidden in my jacket pocket.

"I think you are nervous." Punky straightened my tie and smoothed her hands over the shoulders of my jacket, picking lint off the fabric. "You're stalling."

"I don't stall." Though I could barely breathe and my vision was going a bit sideways.

Punky had always set me on edge, off kilter. She had a way of tilting the ground under my feet to send me sliding, struggling to stay upright. But in this moment, I had never felt so sure in my footing.

"We could run away," she teased, sliding her hands down the front of my shirt. Hadley stared up at me, adventure and mischief in her eyes.

I pushed her hair behind her ear, running my fingertips along her neck. "Would you like that?"

"Hmm. Maybe. Screw our way across the country. Make love to me in every Springfield. Kick up trouble from one coast to the other. You could play guitar on street corners for tips and I would draw caricatures in the park. Happily-ever-after."

"There's no such thing. Endings are the saddest part."

"Okay, if you want to get all existential about it."

There was a knock at the door, followed by the stage manager's two-minute warning.

"Hadley." I wrapped my arms around her back, skimming my fingers along the skin above the top of her pants. "I know we said we were done apologizing, but I want to tell you I'm sorry."

"Josh—"

"I'm sorry for not trusting you. For not telling you the truth back then and trusting that you'd love me anyway. I should have had more faith in us, because every day, from the start, you've been there. You've always been kind, and loyal, and found the goodness in me when I didn't see it myself. You make me want to try harder. You make me a better man. Above all, you make me whole. I love you, and I'm forever grateful to know you. And as long as I live, I'll never stop trying to deserve you."

"Here." She reached into her pocket and pulled out a folded piece of paper that she placed in my hand.

"Not to be a dick, but I'm kind of in the middle of something."

"I've been saving this," she said. "Read it."

Hadley kissed me, a sweet, gentle touch of her lips to mine.

"Break a leg. I know you'll be brilliant." Then she darted off.

The letter, addressed to me, was dated on the morning I went into surgery.

Josh,

I hate this. It sucks. And I can't help but blame you for leaving me all alone. You've got it easy. Sure, there's some guy wiggling a knife around in your head, but at least you get to sleep through it. I can't seem to close my eyes. Every time I blink, it's like someone is going to be standing at the door to tell me you aren't coming back. So I won't blink.

There was a routine in our house. After dinner, I helped my mom clear the table while my dad caught the evening news. I was allowed to watch one episode of TV, and then dad would draw me a bath. He made sure I brushed my teeth, using a little sand timer to teach me how long to keep at it. Mom brushed and dried my hair before tucking me in with a bedtime story.

There was no dinnertime in the foster house. No routine. If we ate at all, it was something cold left for us on the kitchen counter. That, or we just got hungry enough to go looking for anything we could reach. There was no bath time. The tiles around the tub were rimmed with black mold and everything had a yellow layer of filth.

We slept because it was dark outside. We slept because there was nothing better to do or we just wanted the day to end sooner. My bed was a small, thin mattress on the stained carpet. It smelled like mold and sweat. I closed my eyes, my blanket pulled over my head to block out the headlights of passing cars outside the window and constant noise of dogs barking and sirens wailing.

I itched all over. It started on my arm, then my ankle, and spread until I was clawing at my skin so hard it left bruises and red splotches everywhere.

You cast a shadow through the doorway. A small, skinny shard of black that ran right over me. In only a pair of underwear, you stood shivering with your arms hugging your chest. So I pulled my blanket from around my shoulders and held it out, waiting.

You didn't talk. Do you remember that? It must have been days before I heard you say a word, and then you only spoke when we were alone and the others were asleep. The first sound I ever heard you make was the saddest, loneliest sob as you finally took the blanket and curled up on the floor next to my bed.

I think I loved you then.

You taught me how to survive in that house. You saved my life, and I've been trying to make up for it ever since.

—Punky

Chapter 37

I was eleven years old the first time I played for a paying audience. It had baffled me why anyone would spend money to watch one short, scrawny kid sit at a piano and recite someone else's work. Getting all dressed up to listen to me plunk at the keys. At home, dressed in my pajamas and strawberry jam still stuck in the corners of my lips, I had played for fun. To me, it had felt like paying to sit in a convention hall and watch someone else play video games. But then, that was a thing, too.

When I was old enough to start penning my own compositions, it began to make sense. As a child, I had never been good at making friends. Reading notations on a page and replicating the music was easy—the instructions were right there in black and white. Basic human interaction, though, wasn't a natural process for me. Until I learned to create music. Through that act of creativity, I could express the thoughts I was incapable of speaking aloud. And it didn't matter if the audience understood my meaning, because they were participating. It was an exchange of ideas. Upon the platform of music that I provided, they wrote their own stories. They interpreted their own emotions and imagined what untold narrative existed within the notes. In that way, we made a connection, and I didn't have to leave the relative safety of the pool of light that encircled the piano.

Since I started performing with the band at the Nest, I'd gotten better about my proximity to my audience. I had learned to feed off their energy rather than fear it. But for me, there was no comparison to the quiet anticipation and rapt attention that I could command when I broke the well-mannered silence as my fingers hit the keys. On an empty stage, above an audience hidden behind a black veil with bright while lights staring back at me, it was like drifting in space. Free.

The small audience of classmates, friends, and families offered polite applause as I crossed the stage to the piano. Professor Monroe announced my name while I took my seat on the bench and flexed my fingers, preparing my muscles. Upstage, my jazz ensemble filed in and took their places.

The song began like a nursery rhyme: simple, sweet. There was a melodic quality that felt familiar, like something from childhood. It reminded me of my mother and how she'd taught me to play. The hours spent learning the basic progression of notes that told stories of fairy tales and adventures.

As my fingers moved over the keys, the tune matured. The upright bass came in beneath the melody, then the saxophone and trumpet. A slow, gentle, gradual growth. The drums tumbled in, soft at first, becoming more excited as the rhythm sped. It was a tightly focused chaos. Sonic near-anarchy bellowed from the stage, filling the acoustically designed auditorium with frenetic energy.

Behind us, the curtain opened. Revealed was a ten-piece orchestra of horns and strings and woodwinds. The chaos coalesced into harnessed harmony. Full, rich, vigorous tones vibrated the floor beneath my feet. The hair on the back of my neck stood tall. My hands danced across the keys, pulling my body to sway, chasing the lower chords and charging after the high, exuberant sopranos.

I poured everything into that performance. My years of frustration and fear, elation and pleasure, and the hope that I might have once more found myself in the one passion that had transformed my life. The piece wasn't strictly jazz, not that I thought Professor Monroe would mind, but it was a reflection of me: a little off kilter and a bit too aggressive.

It only recently made sense to me that, despite my past, no one was stopping me from choosing the life I wanted to lead. For so long I had imagined all these tethers leashing me to an existence that was only about what I wouldn't do and couldn't have. Chains that bound me to destructive self-pity. That man had abused me, and though I had escaped his grasp more than a decade ago, I hadn't let myself free of his influence. Carmen had given me all she had for the brief time we shared, but I hadn't used any of it in any meaningful way.

Starting right away, I wanted my life to be about meaning, purpose. I promised myself that no matter my scars, no matter the work still left to accomplish, I wouldn't be a passive participant. The path before me wasn't entirely clear, but at least I had a direction, and I wouldn't have to walk it alone.

The symphony played on as I stood from the piano and left the stage, descending the stairs into the audience. Hadley sat beside my father in the front row. Her eyes met mine, wet with tears and growing more terrified with every deliberate step I took toward her.

This wasn't the plan. Hadley hated attention and would surely bludgeon me later for drawing her into the spotlight. I had intended to wait until after dinner to take her to the beach for a whole romantic scene under the moonlight. But fuck if I couldn't stop myself.

At her feet, I sank to one knee. The speech I had prepared evaporated. Every painstakingly revised line I'd spent weeks writing escaped me. Because when I saw the excited anticipation overwhelm her face, I couldn't think about anything else. This woman was the best part of me, and I didn't want to take another breath without her.

"I hate you so much right now," she whispered, her lips trembling.

I reached into my jacket pocket and pulled out my mother's engagement ring to slip onto Hadley's finger. "I can't promise you a happy ending," I said, leaning forward with her hand clasped in mine to speak at her ear, "but I can offer you a happy beginning. Marry me, Punky."

She grabbed me by the lapels and stood, dragging me to my feet. "Took you long enough."

About the Author

Tyler A. King was once an alternate contestant on the Emmy-winning game show *Secrets of the Cryptkeeper's Haunted House.* She would later grow up to earn an assistant director credit on the film *Fetus Fetish*, which isn't what it sounds like. She earned a bachelor's degree in Creative Writing from the University of Central Florida, and her work has previously appeared in *Orlando* magazine and *Orlando Business Journal.* Tyler is a proud army spouse moving around the country with her husband and a collection of guitars she can almost play.

Learn more at:

TylerKingAuthor.com

Twitter: @TylerAKing

Facebook: www.facebook.com/tyleraking/

CPSIA information can be obtained
at www.ICGtesting.com
Printed in the USA
FSOW01n1459090616
21347FS

9 781455 595235